Bell Bridge Book titles from Diana Pharaoh Francis

The Diamond City Magic Novels

Trace of Magic

Edge of Dreams

Whisper of Shadows

The Crosspointe Chronicles

The Cipher

The Black Ship

The Turning Tide
(coming soon)

The Hollow Crown
(coming soon)

Whisper of Shadows

Book 3 of the Diamond City Magic Novels

by

Diana Pharaoh Francis

Bell Bridge Books

This is a work of fiction. Names, characters, places and incidents are either the products of the author's imagination or are used fictitiously. Any resemblance to actual persons (living or dead), events or locations is entirely coincidental.

Bell Bridge Books
PO BOX 300921
Memphis, TN 38130
Print ISBN: 978-1-61194-702-1

Bell Bridge Books is an Imprint of BelleBooks, Inc.

Copyright © 2016 by Diana Pharaoh Francis

Published in the United States of America.

We at BelleBooks enjoy hearing from readers.
Visit our websites
BelleBooks.com
BellBridgeBooks.com
ImaJinnBooks.com

10 9 8 7 6 5 4 3 2 1

Cover design: Debra Dixon
Interior design: Hank Smith
Photo/Art credits:
Background (manipulated) © Unholyvault | Dreamstime.com
Woman (manipulated) © Julenochek | Dreamstime.com
Woman (manipulated) © Avgustino | Dreamstime.com

:Lsws:01:

Dedication

To my husband, the love of my life,
and the Boy of Size and Girlie.
I couldn't do this without you.

Chapter 1

I HAD A WHOLE lot of questions for the man standing in front of me. All of them starting with *why*.

Why did you leave, Dad?

Why didn't you tell me where you went, Dad?

Why did you abandon me and the rest of your family, Dad?

And probably most important of all: *Why did you put a psychic bomb in my brain to kill me if I breached your carefully constructed walls locking away my memories and my ability to trust, Daddy Dearest?*

That last question probably should have been the first. Having to ask the question at all says something about my life, as does the fact that the bomb in my brain wasn't even my most recent near-death experience of the last few days. I'd come close to dying at least twice since the brain bomb, plus had my thumb cut off.

I'll admit I wasn't in the most charitable frame of mind as I stared at my father. For ten years I'd had to wonder whether he was dead or rotting in prison somewhere or even living on Mars. Someone else might have gotten through all the emotional baggage and given him a big hug. Mostly I just wanted to kill him. Except killing him wouldn't get me the answers I needed.

While I tried to calm down from the shock of finding him in my step-mom's living room, standing there like he'd never ditched us, I rubbed a finger over my thumb knuckle just to make sure it was still there. Maya, a tinker friend who was quickly earning enough from me to build a vacation home in the Bahamas, had reattached it after a madman cut it off. The reattachment between my dad and me wasn't going to be so easy. Inwardly, I snorted. Impossible was more like it.

He'd been the last person, place, or thing I'd expected to see tonight. I don't see the future. I'm a tracer. I can see the magical trails people leave behind by merely existing. I can even see dead trace, which makes me unique and dangerous to all the wrong kind of people. My abilities are the modern-day equivalent of a chimera or a Sasquatch or a snipe. Only I actually exist.

My last couple of cases "outed" me. Now everybody wants a piece of me—whether to hire me, to enslave me, or to kill me. I'd formed an uneasy truce with Gregg Touray, the boss of one of the most powerful Tyet organizations in Diamond City. His half brother Clay Price is my . . . boyfriend of sorts, a former detective who'd traded his own freedom for mine, and quit the force to work for his brother as part of the bargain for Touray's leaving me alone.

Tonight was about finally introducing Price to the half of my family he hasn't met—namely, my stepmom Mel and my stepbrother Jamie. He's already met my sister, Taylor, and my other stepbrother, Leo. Since I've never in my life brought a date to dinner, it's a pretty big deal.

Actually, it was more like a gauntlet, where my metal-working stepbrothers would wrap him up in a cage and either threaten him if he hurts me or tickle him to death. They aren't exactly predictable, and even though they are older than me, they still have a healthy teenage practical-joker streak going on. That, or my stepmom Mel decides to get in on the action and interrogate him about, well, pretty much his entire life. As an FBI reader, she can read emotion. She's also an Einstein-level psychologist, so pretty much she's a walking lie detector who can get anybody to spill their guts about every last little thing. Another reason I'd been avoiding her since the whole thing with Price started. I couldn't keep secrets when she turned her detection skills on me.

On top of that, I had planned to announce that Price and I were moving in together. Silly me, I'd thought that last tidbit was going to be the shocker of the evening. Then my dad shows up. Now I had to wonder if he was planning to try to kill me or kidnap me. It wouldn't be the first time for either.

My stepmom felt the need to warn us. When she opened the door, Mel acted kind of cold, which is not her. When she shook Price's hand, I could tell she did something. As a reader, she can also transmit feelings when she wants to. Whatever she sent to Price morphed him into stone-cold-brutal mode.

"What's wrong?" I whispered.

Mel gave a brittle smile. "We have unexpected company for dinner tonight. It's quite a surprise."

"Who?"

"Come see."

From the way she and Price acted, the unexpected company was also unexpectedly *bad*. Price edged in front of me, lacing his fingers tightly through mine, using that connection to angle me behind him as we followed Mel into her expansive living room, which was nowhere near big enough to hold the tension.

My brothers, Jamie and Leo, stood on opposites sides of the room. Leo's expression was harsh, like he was made of rage. He had long dark hair that he combed back in waves. His face was chiseled. The only thing that kept him from looking pretty was that his nose was crooked and the bridge was flat.

Jamie had reddish-brown hair he kept clipped short enough to stay out of his face. Like Leo, he couldn't be bothered to shave more than every few days, if that, so he constantly had five o'clock shadow. He also usually had dimples, but right now, he looked like he'd never smiled in his life. He flicked a glance at me as I walked in. His jaw knotted.

Taylor sat on a stool at the mahogany bar. She looked shell-shocked. Not a look she wore often. She was a pilot and had worked in Iraq and Afghanistan for several years, flying for private security firms and other businesses. She usually had nerves of ice, but right now, she looked like she'd been stabbed in the chest a dozen times. Her hand held a glass, her knuckles white. I didn't think she even remembered she was holding it.

The focus of everyone's agitation sat in a hobnailed leather chair near the fireplace.

Dad.

"Look who's here, everyone. Riley and her beau," Mel announced, her tone carefully neutral.

My father stood as I walked in. The air went out of the world. A hurricane spun up inside me. I couldn't begin to tell what I felt. I wanted to hug him for a split second. I wanted to cry. I wanted to scream. I wanted to run. Then I wanted to hit him. Instead, I stood there, drinking him in.

As far back as I could remember, he'd had short red-blond hair. Now it was more silver than blond. His eyes were the same sleepy blue, but red-rimmed now, and he had crow's feet. He was tanned, like he'd been in the sun recently. He barely scraped six feet and looked fit—no paunch dewlapping his belt. It seemed that the last ten years had been kind to him—that is, as far as I could remember. But then again, I couldn't trust my memories about him, could I?

He'd made me forget things—I didn't know what, just that he'd done it. When his little brain bomb had gone off in my head, a dreamer friend, Cass, had gone into my head to put me back together. She'd saved my life, but she couldn't retrieve what my father had taken. All she knew was that real memories had been uprooted and fake memories had been planted. Maybe he'd done the same to the rest of the family. The thought was enough to loosen my tongue. Anger does that for me.

"Dad. You're back."

He smiled. "Riley. It's good to see you."

3

I wondered if he expected me to jump into his arms. I wondered if that was part of the programming Cass had yanked out of my brain. I tipped my head to the side, glaring. "Tell me, Dad, will the rest of us be remembering this little chat or are you going to fix that before you disappear again? That's what you do, right? Play with people's memories? Mess with their lives, and then go your merry way?" I asked.

Whatever he expected from me, that wasn't it. From the way his lips flattened, I could tell he didn't like the sarcasm. Or maybe it was the truth he hated. Probably it was the truth. Too fucking bad. Point for me.

That's when I noticed Dalton. He'd been my shadow for weeks. I'd thought that Price's brother, Gregg Touray, had hired him to keep me out of the "wrong hands." That meant any hands but Touray's. Unfortunately, he turned out to be my father's henchman. Point for Dad.

Dalton was handsome in a not-quite-finished sort of way. His face was long, his nose strong and blunt. He had high cheekbones like he might be part Native American. The weird thing about him was his eyes. They were discs of silver, and sometimes the edges would glow different colors. They were tinker mods, but I didn't really know what he could see. It gave him an eerie inhuman quality. If I hadn't already distrusted him, his eyes would have done the trick.

As I scanned him over, my brain kicked into high gear. A whole lot of dominoes started falling just then, and I could barely begin to grasp the meaning.

Dalton had come around with a security squad just after my secret talent as a tracer had been exposed. He'd said he'd been anonymously hired to protect me. At that point, I'd stupidly assumed that his boss was either Touray or Price, neither of whom I'd been talking to at that point. I'd been too stubborn and idiotic to pick up the phone and ask them. Instead, I did my own background checks, which didn't trigger any red flags, and when Dalton had known details about me only Price or Touray could have given him, I'd let him hang around.

Not my finest decision. He'd freed—or maybe just stolen—the megalomaniac nutjob who'd infected me and my sister with Sparkle Dust and then cut off my thumb. That would be Percy Caldwell, a sociopath and the maker of Sparkle Dust, a magical drug that had been sweeping through Diamond City, killing just about everyone who chanced taking it. The drug was literally made out of drug addicts. Their bodies were harvested to make more SD. That meant, if Dalton was working for my dad, then my dad had Percy Caldwell and the key to making SD. Was he setting up to manufacture it?

The idea made my stomach twist. Weeks ago I'd have been able to say no way—my dad would never be a part of anything so depraved and horrifying. Unfortunately, I now knew better. If he was capable of killing his own daughter, nothing else, no matter how awful, could be off the table.

"What do you want?" I asked finally, when he remained silent, refusing to rise to the bait I'd thrown out about erasing memories.

He smiled again, a quick quirk of his lips. My heart twisted. I remembered that smile. Despite myself, I clung to the memory. Maybe everything about my childhood wasn't a lie.

"Straight to the point," he murmured. "Just like your mother."

I flinched. Price's fingers tightened on mine. I held on to his hard strength. He had my back. He always had my back.

"Where did you go?"

Taylor. Her voice came out in a rasp.

She stared at Dad like somehow she could cut him open and see what he was really thinking. The wounded look had faded and been replaced with animal fury. There was a wild edge to her that hadn't been there a week or so ago. She'd seen her hangar invaded and then her friends and employees gunned down. A family in her waiting room had been slaughtered. Then she'd been exposed to Sparkle Dust. Cass—the same dreamer who'd mended my brain after Dad's bomb went off—had fixed Taylor as much as she could be fixed, but the drug had changed her. I wasn't sure what those changes were, but she didn't usually lose her cool. Right now, it was probably good she didn't make a habit of carrying weapons.

Dad's face softened. I caught myself. Did I still call him that? It didn't feel right. Calling him *Dad* implied love. Whatever I felt for him, love wasn't it. His old name had been Samuel Hollis, but I doubted he went by that anymore. Not that he went by *Dad* anymore either. He'd quit that a decade ago.

He faced Taylor. "I've mostly been out of the country and traveling."

"Why? Why did you leave?" Taylor swigged down the rest of her drink and set it down before standing up. She held herself still, her arms wrapped around her stomach, her gaze unblinking. "Why did you disappear and never call?"

Dad—Sam?—blew out a soft breath. "It was too dangerous to stay. For you. For all of you." His glance gathered all of us in. "I had—I have—enemies who wouldn't hesitate to hurt you to get to me." He looked at me. "One of them murdered your mother."

Sometimes my mouth gets going before I have a chance to really think. "So Mom gets murdered. Your reaction to your bloodthirsty enemies is to get remarried, have another kid, play house for years, and then out of the blue, you vanish off the face of the earth, but not before taking the time to set bombs in my head. It's like a Christmas movie. You're amazing. I mean, if it had been me, I probably would have just taken my daughter and—I don't know—gone into hiding with her instead of playing *Brady Bunch* for a decade. But clearly I don't have the vision you do."

"There are things you don't know."

"Yeah. There are. Things that some asshole scrubbed out of my head. Memories someone stole from me. The one thing I do know beyond a shadow of a doubt is that my dad raped my brain and then set booby traps to kill me if I broke through his walls. Thanks for that, by the way. Do you have any idea what it's like to watch yourself go insane, to have your brain so terrified that it tells your body to quit breathing? Worse, you made it Price's fault. You made the man who loves me so much he'd cut his heart out of his chest for me feel like I'd picked suicide over trusting him."

Price's hand clenched on mine so hard it hurt. Neither one of us were going to forgive my dad for putting us through that anytime soon. I tightened my grip reassuringly, never looking away from my dad.

"If it wasn't enough that half the world was out to kill me, I got to have you doing it, too. So back to the question. Why are you here? Oh! Maybe you want to explain to your wife why you abandoned her? Did you at least bring flowers? Fancy chocolates? Expensive jewelry? What *do* you get your wife when you disappear? Copper? Wood? Plastic? Is there an abandonment anniversary gift chart?"

I was shaking. I don't know if I was more mad or more in danger of falling to pieces. Price let go of my hand and put his arm around me. I leaned into him, grateful for his solid strength.

Mel, Jaime, and Leo still hadn't said anything. I wondered what they were thinking. Mel had loved my dad. My memories said they'd been gloriously happy. But my memories could be lies. So could hers. All the same, this was her husband. A man who'd abandoned her and left her to raise four children alone. A man who'd made her promises and then tossed her aside like used toilet paper.

"Perhaps we should hear Sam's explanation."

Mel sounded unfazed and totally in control. Her calmness gave me something to cling to. Right now I felt raw. I needed some sort of armor to protect me from him, from all of this. Mel wasn't armor, but she took his focus, settling on the emerald camelbacked couch, crossing her legs elegantly and lifting a brow at her husband.

"Provided you've come to explain?"

Dad tipped his head toward Mel. "As best I can."

His cagey answer made my stomach churn. Would we get any truth from him at all? Or would it be carefully cut and shaped, turning the ugly reality into a pretty snowflake lie?

That's when my rational brain caught up with my emotional-overload brain. My dad was a dreamer, which meant he could worm his way into any of our minds without touching us. He could cause us to see visions, change our thinking, give us false memories, all without any of us knowing. I had a knack for sensing magic, which meant I could usually sense when someone was actively attempting to use it around me. Plus I had a strong sensitivity to dreamer touch. I could feel it when one tried to wriggle into my head. I had to wonder if that had anything to do with him. Had he taught me that? Or had his tampering made me extra sensitive?

Didn't matter, and now was no time to consider. Dear old Dad hadn't attempted to come after any of us yet, as far as I could tell, but just in case . . . I slid my hand down to touch Price's belt. Inside the leather were a dozen silver disks, each one a null. I activated one.

A magical dead zone surrounded Price. No spell—good or bad—could affect him until the null was deactivated or its power was drained.

"I don't trust you," I said to my dad. "Everybody, activate your nulls."

I'd made each of my family powerful nulls in various shapes and forms. Sometimes jewelry, other times zippers on clothing—though nulls didn't hold up well to multiple washings. I felt each of theirs activate almost before I finished speaking. I took a little comfort in knowing I wasn't the only one so caught off guard I'd not thought about protecting myself.

Mel was the only one who hadn't triggered a null. I understood why. She wanted to be able to read Dad's emotions. She couldn't if her powers were nulled. Neither Dad nor Dalton had active nulls either, probably for the same reason.

I stiffened with another realization. Everybody leaves behind trace. It's a ribbon of light that only tracers can see. Some can only see it for a few minutes, others for an hour or two. I can see it always, even after a person dies. The only time I can't is when someone nulls out their trace, which means for as long as that null is active, their ribbon vanishes. Those were the rules. Except that when my father disappeared, his trace vanished with him. One day it's looped all around our house and my life, the next it's gone like he'd never existed. Every last scrap of it gone. Just like Dad. It should have been impossible.

For years, I'd tried to puzzle it out and just recently I thought I'd figured out the trick. He hadn't erased his trace, but rather he'd simply made it impossible for me to see it. He'd gone into my head and blinded me to him. Now I had the chance to test my theory. I dropped into trace sight. Nothing.

I don't know why it bothered me so much. I mean, he'd tried to kill me. By comparison, this was nothing. And yet—it went to the core of who I was. He'd made me doubt myself, made me feel like a failure when I couldn't find him. I bit my lips so that I wouldn't swear. My eyes burned with tears I refused to let fall. One of these days I was going to figure out how not to care. Thanks to my family, thanks to Price and my friends, I'd moved on. I'd broken through Dad's prison shackles. He didn't matter anymore.

I told myself that and tried to believe it.

Dad nodded to Mel. "That's why I came. I am here to explain what I can. Riley, I am glad to see you well after your recent interactions with Mr. Caldwell."

I glared. "Dalton told you about all that, did he? Did Dalton also tell you that he tried to kidnap me, too?"

"He merely wished to get you to safety."

Dad smiled. I sucked in a breath, my heart aching. I had so many memories of that smile. Good memories. Or they had been. Now they seemed fake, as if he'd been wearing a mask. Hell, for all I knew, they were fake and he'd planted them in my head.

"I doubt my safety was uppermost in Dalton's mind," I said, my lip curling.

Dad turned to glance at Mister Tall, Dark, and Broody, and then back at me. "You can trust him. He's a friend." He focused on Price. "Clayton Price, I presume?" He actually held out a hand like he expected a shake.

Price eyed it and then looked back up at my dad. "I am."

Dad let his arm fall, seemingly unfazed. "Your brother is Greggory Touray?"

"Aren't you the one who's supposed to be answering questions?" I demanded. "You aren't welcome here. So do us a favor, get to the point of this little visit and then get out. What do you want?"

He scanned us all, his gaze lingering on each of us, finally returning to me. "It's quite simple, really. My absence no longer protects you. There's no point in hiding anymore. It's time for us to be a family again."

Chapter 2

I THINK MY JAW might have actually fallen off my face. Mine wasn't the only one hitting the floor. Even Mel looked like she'd been hit with a baseball bat.

"If you're trying to make a joke, it's a bad one," Leo said. He went to put an arm around Taylor, who'd gone pale.

I wondered what she was thinking. Over the past couple months, Taylor's world had been turned inside out. Her boyfriend had been kidnapped and now refused to have anything to do with her, Percy Caldwell had murdered a half dozen of her employees before infecting her with Sparkle Dust, and now for the cherry on top, Dad—who it turns out wasn't anything like who we thought he was—walks back into our lives and announces he wants to be a family again. It had to be tearing her to pieces. I know I felt shredded.

"It's not a joke," Dad said.

"Then you are delusional," Jamie shot back. He'd gone to stand behind Mel, his hands resting on her shoulders. She'd recaptured her composure. The fruits of FBI training.

"Samuel, perhaps you should just tell us what you came to say," she suggested.

She simply ignored his pronouncement. It's not like there was any point in asking about what was never going to happen. Like Jamie said, the man was delusional.

Dad gave a little shrug and resumed his seat near the fire. "I can't tell you much. The less you know, the better."

"That's it," I said, anger shearing through me. "I'm leaving." I let go of Price and whipped around, striding for the door. I'd gone two steps before I spun back around. Price was right behind me. He always had my back, always supported me. He'd returned to me what my father had stolen—trust in another man, and unconditional love. More than that, I knew he would never abandon me.

I pushed past him to face my father, stabbing a finger at him. "You know what? I'm not leaving. You are. You have brass balls, you know that? You fuck with my head, you abandon us, and now you show up with some fantasy about being a family again. You've got some bullshit story about keeping us in the dark because of—I don't know—global warming? Radical vegetarianism? Maybe the Wicked Witch of the West is coming after us?

"Whatever you have to say, I don't want to hear it. It's all lies. That's what you do and I'm not falling for it again. I don't know why you really came here, but I'm done. You left once, leave again. Don't let the door hit you in the ass on the way out."

"Riley," Mel said quietly.

I shot a hot glare at her, wrapping my arms around my stomach. "You can't want to hear this."

"I think we must," she said.

I wanted to argue, but something in her voice asked me to trust her. I did. Completely. Especially since she'd taught me to stand on my own two feet. To make my own choices and believe in myself. After Dad's disappearance, I'd gone wild, but Mel hadn't given up on me, no matter what I did. I'd been a complete bitch. Even so, she'd managed to help me grow up and be independent. If not for her, hell, if not for my brothers and Taylor, I don't know where I'd be now. I wasn't alone in this. If Mel thought we should listen, then I would.

"You've got two minutes. Start talking," I told my dad coldly.

He gave me a measuring look, then nodded. "All right. None of you are safe anymore. My enemies have learned of your existence and they plan to use you against me. I did my best to erase all evidence of my life before I disappeared, but alas, some small clues remained, and some very motivated people followed up." He paused. "The people who killed your mother are after you now, too."

My mouth fell open. Again.

"When Elaine was murdered, I believed the crime was random. Certainly the police said so. Years later, I discovered Elaine had been killed because of her ties to some dangerous people. She'd always kept her past a secret from me."

"You're a dreamer," I said, fighting through the tightness in my throat. "You expect us to believe you never tiptoed into her skull to have a look around?"

He shook his head. "I should have looked, but I trusted her. I loved her. I regret it with all my heart, now. When I learned why she was killed, I promised myself I'd never make that mistake again. I'd do whatever I had to do to protect the people I loved, no matter the cost."

I bit the inside of my cheek til I tasted blood. If he thought that justified what he'd done to me, he had another thing coming.

"What exactly did you discover about Elaine's murder?" Mel asked.

Thank goodness for her. I wasn't sure I could stay logical. I just wanted to scream. He was blaming my mom for her death. At least that's what I was hearing. If only she didn't keep secrets, he could have protected her.

"Elaine had stolen things from people who don't tolerate that sort of thing. They wanted their goods back and they wanted her to pay." He sighed and looked at me. "I hate to say it, but your mom was a grifter. She knew how to run a con, and she was good at it. When she met me, she quit. I didn't learn about her previous profession until years later. I'm sorry, Peach, but I can't hide it from you anymore. Your mother wasn't the woman we thought she was."

My brain burst into flames. First, calling me Peach. He'd called me that as a kid, but he didn't have the right anymore. Second, my mom was a con artist? Did he really expect me to buy that line of bullshit?

I didn't want to believe him. Believe that Mom was responsible for her own death. But inside, I just didn't know. I couldn't know. I couldn't believe anything he said, and I couldn't not believe it. I had no facts, and none of my childhood memories were reliable. That's when I remembered I could actually ask my mom. She might be dead, but her ghost was hanging around in the spirit dimension, and she wanted to talk to me. Dad knew nothing about that. Doubt crept in again. What if she *was* a con artist? What if everything she said was a lie? God, what a complete cluster-fuck.

Taylor pushed away from Leo and went behind the bar. She poured herself a healthy drink, but left it untouched. I understood the need to do something, not to mention she'd put a massive piece of wood between her and Dad.

Abruptly, I strode over and picked up the drink that she hadn't touched and drank down half of it. It was pretty much straight-up vodka with a touch of lemon. It burned down my throat and made my eyes water.

Taylor met my gaze, her blue eyes sunken and bruised. Her lips ghosted in a smile as I raised the glass in a toast and swallowed the rest. She reached for a bottle and set up another one as I set the glass back down.

"Nothing like a dysfunctional family reunion to make you start drinking, is there?" she murmured. "Do you think he's telling the truth about your mom?"

My teeth bared. "I think we can't trust a word he says."

She lifted her glass. "Amen to that."

"You all right?"

"Sure. Why not?" Her smile was brittle.

I reached over and touched her hand. She gripped mine tightly, then let it go. I took a breath and let it out, then faced back around. Time to deal with this head-on.

I wasn't entirely sure what I was going to say, but I never got a chance.

A flash of brilliant light burst outside. At the same time, a rumble like thunder rolled underneath the floor. Wood groaned and strained.

"What the hell is going on?" Price demanded, glaring at my father.

Leo and Jamie had that preoccupied look they got when they were talking to metal.

Dalton had started talking into his hand. He eyed the walls and ceilings. Not for the first time, I wondered just what the hell he could see with those weird eyes. I didn't think they were X-ray vision à la Superman, but clearly they were specialized.

"We have to get going," he said, turning back to my dad. The outer rings of his eyes were green. I'd seen them orange, blue, and red.

"Report," my dad ordered.

Dalton gave that ever-familiar impatient snarl. "It appears the FBI has come calling. Time to go."

The FBI? I'll admit. I wasn't as surprised as I could have been. I'd had a run-in not too long ago with the super special agents of the FBI. The one in charge—Sandra Arnow—was a particularly nasty bit of business. She was ambitious, cold, and ruthless. She and I shared a mutual hate-hate relationship.

"What do you want to do?" Price asked, looking to me, but Mel answered.

"Open the door when they make it that far. Not much else we can do. Jamie, shut down the house."

Jamie jogged out of the room to turn off the house spells before our intruders launched binders, which they were sure to do any second now. Binders bound all the magic within their range so nothing worked. They also played havoc with active spells, sometimes twisting them so they didn't work again. I deactivated my trace null.

"What are they *doing* out there?" I asked as thunder rolled under the floor again. But then I felt their binders spring up and suck all the active magic down. "They've got the binders up," I said.

I hadn't been paying attention to my dad. He'd come across the room. Price stepped between us.

"That's far enough."

Dad stopped

"I have to go," he said. "You aren't safe. None of you." He turned to look at everyone else, then faced me again. "I can protect you if you come with me."

I didn't have to consider. "No thanks. So far your protections have been almost lethal," I said, tapping my forehead. "I don't trust you to get me a glass of water. I sure as hell won't trust you with my life."

He nodded, his expression unchanged. "Fair enough. I'll see you again. Soon."

With that, he and Dalton walked out of the room.

"Where are they going?" Price asked, watching them go.

"There are dozens of routes out of here. He built most of them," Mel said, edging aside a curtain to look out the window. "It is the FBI. They're coming in the gates."

"What do they want?" Leo asked.

"I guess we'll find out." I looked at Price. "You don't have to be here."

Connected as he was to his brother's Tyet organization, he was technically a criminal. For all I knew, the FBI had come to arrest him.

He narrowed his eyes at me, a line cutting deep between his brows. "I'm not leaving you."

I got the message. He wasn't going to betray me or abandon me to save his own hide. My heart swelled, and I grinned at him. My smile faded. "Our two weeks is going to get postponed, isn't it?"

I'd promised him that after the dinner tonight, we'd hole up alone for two weeks and spend it together, no distractions or interruptions. If my dad's arrival hadn't shattered that glorious plan, certainly a mass of super special agents showing up did.

He shrugged. "I'll still have you in my bed and sitting across from me at my breakfast table."

"Unless I'm going to jail."

"No one's taking you to jail," Mel inserted. She frowned at Price. "You're going home with this man?"

Not the way I wanted to break the news. I nodded. "We're moving in together."

Mel gave me a sharp look and then examined Price again. Finally, she nodded. "Good. Better you aren't alone right now."

She turned to Taylor. "You either. I want you to stay here."

Taylor laughed. "No thanks. Besides, Dad's not interested in me. He's all about Riley."

I could hear the pain stitching her voice. I could have pointed out that being the target of his interest had nearly killed me, but it wouldn't have helped. I understood. He'd always made me special by making sure everybody was watching out for me and protecting me. That put Taylor always on the outside. She didn't complain, and she and I had managed to be close for the most part, even though she lived with a constant wound. It amazed me sometimes that she didn't hate me.

"I agree with Mel. Dad might have been telling the truth about his enemies wanting to get at his family. I don't think you should go home. Your house doesn't have enough protections."

"Actually, it does," Price said. "Gregg and I had them installed this week. There's also a twenty-four/seven watch on the place, and Taylor's got bodyguards who travel with her now, too."

I eyed him in surprise. This was the first I'd heard about any of that. I looked at Taylor, lifting my brows in a silent question.

Her expression turned sour. "I told them no, but arguing with the two of them is like arguing with a couple of rocks. Or Jamie and Leo, for that matter."

Price smiled. "All part of the service. After all, we're family now."

"You are?" Jamie said, choosing that moment to return. "Since when did you adopt my sisters?"

Price snorted. "Adopt? Oh no. Riley is most definitely *not* my daughter. She's—"

I looked at him. Just what exactly was I to him? But just then someone pounded on the door. With a battering ram. Wood cracked. It was a very solid door.

We all jumped.

"What the hell?" Jamie exclaimed. "What the hell are they doing? Why didn't they just knock? Mom, you're one of them."

My stepmother's face had turned to alabaster, her lips pinching together in fury. She made herself relax, smoothing a hand over her hair. "I'm sure they'll have a good explanation," she said, but I couldn't imagine what explanation would be good enough. 'Course, her colleagues might be having a conniption fit about her inviting the brother of a major Tyet player to her house for dinner. Or maybe it had to do with my dad. It was awfully coincidental that this invasion happened now, right when he showed up for his first visit in a decade.

"Maybe it makes them feel like they've worked hard," Leo said with forced calmness, taking a seat at the bar. "Earned their money. How about another drink for me?" he asked Taylor. "I think I need it."

"Me, too," said Jamie, sliding into a seat. Red flags rode high in his cheeks. "Make it quick. They won't be long."

The battering ram slammed the door once again. Leo's jaw tightened, the muscles visibly knotting.

"Another one and they'll be inside," Jamie said, taking a strong pull on his drink.

Mel joined them at the bar.

"What do you suppose they want?" Taylor asked as she slid a neat glass of scotch over to Mel. "Think they came because of Dad?"

"Or Price," I said tightly. "Or me."

That caught their attention.

"You?" Jamie asked.

Just as I thought—they hadn't quite gotten around to putting that particular two and two together. "I've not exactly been Miss Clean lately," I said. "You know, interfering in an FBI investigation. A whole lot of breaking and entering. Trespassing. Theft. Consorting with a known Tyet kingpin. Not to mention generally having a magic talent that everybody seems eager to get their hands on, including the cops." I listed the highlights, but there were a lot more crimes the FBI could scrape up to throw at me, many of which I was actually guilty of.

Mel, Jamie, Leo, and Taylor exchanged looks.

"I don't like this," Mel said, the corners of her mouth deepening into a frown.

I hadn't liked the situation before she said that. But now that she had, my level of apprehension went zooming into the stratosphere.

I didn't get a chance to wallow in it. Just then the doorjamb finally splintered and the ornate double doors banged against the tables on either side of the entry. Incredibly expensive knickknacks shattered on the marble floor.

Agents dressed in full riot gear and carrying automatic weapons at eye height came thundering into the room and circled around us.

"FBI! Throw down your weapons! Down on the floor, legs crossed, hands behind your back!"

It was surreal. None of us moved.

"Get down on the floor!" a man bellowed again.

Someone grabbed me and jammed their knee behind mine, forcing me down. I landed on my stomach. My chin bounced off the floor. I'd have a bruise later. Price thudded down heavily beside me. In about two seconds, we were both handcuffed.

Pretty quick, the rest of my family joined us, even Mel.

"What the hell is going on?" Leo demanded. "Do you know whose house this is? Mel Hollis is one of your top readers. Your bosses are going to have your asses on a platter."

Nobody answered. I wasn't sure they were required to. Legally, I had no idea what our rights were, except to shut up, and I meant to do that.

Besides, my experience with cops of all stripes said that they didn't feel bound by the law. If it got in their way, they'd mow it down and stomp it into an early grave. Finding an uncorrupt cop in Diamond City was a lot like finding a four-leaf clover in the desert.

"Don't say anything," Price said to me. His face was scary. I'd seen him go all stone-cold dangerous before, but this face was a new level of stone. "If we're separated, go get Gregg. Promise."

Luckily, I was saved from an answer by someone kicking at our feet. "Shut the fuck up. No one talks. You've a right to remain silent, so do it."

Well, that was one way to handle suspects. The question was, what did they suspect us of?

Abruptly, someone grabbed Price's collar and yanked him up off the floor.

"Get him in the van," a man growled. I could smell the stench of stale cigarette smoke emanating off him.

"What about the rest of them?" A woman this time.

"Talk to Vilcott. Clayton Price is the one we were sent for. Now, move."

"I want to see your warrant," Mel declared.

Paper rustled. I heard the rev of an engine, and a vehicle drove away. A minute or two passed. They felt like years. Finally Mel spoke.

"The warrant's in order."

Panic twisted my gut. Even though I'd known he could be a target, I hadn't really thought they'd come for Price. Deep down, I thought they were after my dad. It seemed logical, given the timing. What did they want with Price? I forced myself to lie still even as adrenaline surged through me, demanding that I *do* something.

"You got what you wanted. Release us and get off my property. Now." Mel's voice was cutting. "If you don't move your asses in the next ten seconds, I'll have your badges. And trust me, I can do it."

Her threat was met with silence, then I heard the sound of someone moving and the clicking of her handcuffs coming off. She stood up, and a second later I heard her talk into her phone.

"Give me Director Erickson, please. Tell him Melanie Hollis is calling. It's urgent."

More sounds of movement and clicking. At the same time, I felt the binders go down. I guess we weren't a threat anymore. I was released last. A pair of boots settled on either side of me as a man bent down to unlock the handcuffs. The choking scent of stale cigarettes let me know just who he was. He twisted the cuffs and yanked, bruising me in the process. I made no sound, refusing to give him the satisfaction of knowing he'd hurt me.

"Director, are you aware that your agents just broke down my door? They didn't bother to knock."

I sprang to my feet, shoving against the asshole agent who'd freed me. He fell back a step. Swearing, he raised a hand to hit me. It never landed. His gun dissolved, along with every other bit of metal he was wearing or carrying. It flowed together into a thin cage around his hand that circled his waist so he couldn't move his arm.

"What the hell?" he said.

"You don't touch her," Jamie growled, his face gone feral.

"You've assaulted an agent. Your ass is going to jail," cigarette man snarled back.

"Not today," Jamie said. "You and your asshole crew are leaving. Without any of us."

"Fuck you."

"Director Erickson wants a word with you," Mel said, extending her phone so that the trussed agent could take it in his free hand.

For a moment he didn't move, then he took it, holding it to his ear. "Who is this?"

He listened as the director spoke. Yelled, really, though I couldn't make out the words. I glanced around. The other agents were equally trussed up. A really good use for their guns. They waited in hot silence for the phone call to end.

Finally, stinky cigarette man handed back Mel's cell phone. His lips curled back, his eyes hardening into chunks of ice. "I apologize for the damage we caused in executing our legal warrant," he said, spitting each word like it stung his tongue. "The FBI will compensate you for repairs. We will now be on our way." He glared at Jamie.

The metal cage around his hand dissolved, but the band wrapping his waist remained. It tightened so that the agent would have to cut it off. One by one, the other agents were released, each retaining part of their shackles. A spiteful reminder from my brothers not to fuck with our family.

They all went to the door. Cigarette man paused, turning as the others went down the steps and got into the vehicle. "This isn't over," he said.

"You're damned right it's not," Jamie retorted. "Don't forget it."

The agent gave a thin smile. "See you soon." With that, he trotted out the door, and a moment later, the squad of vehicles retreated off our property.

"Can you help Price?" I asked Mel.

"I'll try," she said, dialing her phone again.

"What about you two?" I asked Jamie and Leo.

They both shook their heads.

"Maybe if he was closer," Leo said.

"Maybe if he wasn't moving," Jamie said at the same time.

In close distances, they could work metal without having to touch it, or have some physical connection. Long distances, they at least had to be able to find a conduit to the metal they wanted to work. The rubber in the tires provided insulation from their touch. On top of that, moving targets were almost impossible to hit.

Everything inside me told me to go after him. He'd told me to call his brother and leave everything in Touray's hands, but I couldn't. I needed to go be with him. At least provide moral support. Maybe I could find out some detail that would help free him. Like the actual charges against him. I'd call Touray on the way.

"I'm going after him," I declared, heading for the door. I stopped short. Price had the keys to our car. I took a breath. That was okay. We had our bodyguards out there. Not that they'd been much use. But then again, going to war with the FBI was in no one's best interests. Likely they were already on the phone to Touray.

"I'll give you a ride," Taylor said, seeming to read my mind. "I'll grab my coat and keys."

"Wait, Riley," Mel said, then spoke into her phone, "get back to me as soon as you can. I need all the details you can find." She hung up the phone. "We all need to talk. Now."

She turned and walked away. Jamie, Taylor, and Leo looked at her and then at me, and went after her. I hesitated before following. Mel led us into a small sitting room, shutting the door after we filed in. It was deliciously warm inside. I hadn't realized how cold it had been out front with the door kicked in.

"Price has been arrested pursuant to the Magical Crimes Act," Mel announced abruptly.

We stared at her a moment, each of us trying to remember the details of the law and what exactly Price's crime could be.

"I don't get it," Leo said, shaking his head.

I was impatient. "Okay, so he's a part of his brother's Tyet organization. He's connected to some serious magic. This has to be their way of getting at Touray."

Mel gave me an unreadable look. "Sit down. All of you. This is important. It affects all of you. All of us. Well, Taylor only indirectly, of course."

"Of course," Taylor muttered and went to sit, crossing her legs and arms. "I'm all ears."

I perched on the arm of the couch, while Leo and Jamie settled on the couch.

Mel gave a little sigh. "I'm going to give you all the short and dirty version of the Rice Act. You probably know some of it, but bear with me. It matters.

"Senator Rice, from Tennessee, has strong religious values. Like a lot of people, that means that he thinks the magically talented are nothing more than demons, abominations made by Satan, and not quite human. So fifteen years ago, when he was fairly new to office, he made a stink over the talented having the ability to skirt and entirely evade the law through magic. Whether by changing a person's mind—literally—or perhaps destroying all the evidence through magical means, or any number of schemes. Anyhow, he argued that the talented had an unfair social advantage and that the law should offer equal protection to all citizens.

"The first Rice Act went through minus his major cornerstone, which would have stripped most legal protections from the talented. Undaunted, he's continued to press for tighter restrictions. Then about five years ago, when the Congress last leaned conservatively, he proposed an amendment to account for the difficulty in prosecuting magical crimes. It opened the door to give law enforcement wider leeway in their investigations. That amendment also incorporated elements of the RICO laws and Hobbs law. It was wide ranging and encroached on people's constitutional rights, so eventually the amendment was trimmed back before it passed.

"Again, Senator Rice counted it a victory, but was determined to keep chipping away at the resistance to his legislation in the name of homeland security. After the attack in Florida on the theme park there—a practical joke, according to the perpetrators, albeit a horrifying one resulting in four dead children—Rice succeeded in passing the cornerstone he'd failed to get through Congress before. The amendment took effect two months ago."

Mel looked at us expectantly. Two months ago was right about when my life had really hit the fan. I'd found myself in over my head with Price and rescuing Taylor's then-boyfriend, Josh. Since then, I'd barely had a moment to think, much less keep up with the news. I had no idea what Mel was getting at.

Taylor leaned forward, her head cocked, her eyes narrowed. "All right. But Price has no talent. So how does this apply to him?"

Mel grimaced. "*That* is the twenty-four-dollar question. I don't know."

"Unless he does have a talent," Jamie suggested.

"Never saw any of any hint of it when we went after that scumbag

Caldwell. What about you, Riley?" Leo asked. "Does Price have some sort of secret talent after all?"

"No!" I burst out, shoving to my feet. "Of course he doesn't. He's as mundane as Taylor." I drew a calming breath and let it out, making myself calm down. Slowly, I said, "I've been fairly busy the past couple months or so. Can you all tell me exactly what I'm missing with this Rice Act?"

"Rice changed the basic legal rights of someone charged with federal magical crime. Once someone is arrested—and the charges need only be approved by a special star-chamber sort of panel and don't have to meet the usual levels of proof for the mundanes—the suspect is brought in for interrogation. The feds have seven business days to question the suspect before they are required to continue into full due process. Meaning that for that seven days—plus the weekend—the suspect's rights are suspended. He can't have a lawyer. He can't make a phone call. Worse, the Rice Act says that the feds can use any means deemed 'reasonably safe and necessary' to get their answers."

Jamie chimed in. "That last bit means that so long as they don't do permanent damage, they can pretty much get away with any sort of torture they like. All in the name of protecting the public." His disgust was palpable. "Once they get a confession, the suspect goes on trial. You can bet they'll use every dirty trick they can, including magical methods."

I blinked stupidly, processing the information. It was almost too much to wrap my brain around. Or too fucking scary. "That's not fair," I said finally.

"Congress thinks it is and the president didn't veto. So it is what it is," Mel said.

I shook my head. "Okay, but that doesn't answer why Price was arrested and how the Rice Act applies."

"No, it doesn't," Mel said, frowning. "I don't understand. It's not a good idea for you to go to FBI headquarters. Not with the Rice Act in play. They could arrest you. You said yourself they have plenty of reasons."

I shook my head again. "If they'd wanted me, they could have taken me with Price."

"They may change their minds if you go waltzing in there," Leo pointed out. "I think Mom is right. Wait until her contacts come through."

"You won't be able to see him," Mel said. "There's nothing you'll be able to do."

The idea of not going made me sick. Like I was abandoning him. "I need to go," I said. "I need to be there. I can't just stay away."

Mel gave me a long look, then nodded slowly. "You're a big girl now. It's your decision."

Something in the way she said that gave me a shiver. I'd been living on my own a long time, and I didn't need permission to do anything. But Mel had raised me and guided me, even when I was a complete nightmare to deal with. Her words felt like a push out of the nest. Like she was saying I was ready to take on the world, dangerous as it was.

"Taylor should drive you. No—" she said when both Leo and Jamie blustered. "—you two are at risk under the Rice Act and there won't be anything you can do that Taylor can't." She looked at me. "Be careful. Hopefully I'll have more information by the time you get back."

I hugged her tight. "I will," I said, and then let go, turning to find Taylor waiting by the door.

I flicked a wave of my fingers at Leo and Jamie and left, grabbing my coat by the front door. I jerked it on before stepping carefully over the fallen wood and out onto the grand front porch. The cold slapped my face. I'd actually put on a dress for the night—a clingy sapphire-blue wool number that clung to all my curves. It came down below my knees. I'd put on silk stockings and black ankle boots with spike heels. All in all, not the best attire for taking on the FBI. Not that I had a choice. Which reminded me—

I typed a quick text to Touray. A Tyet boss was now in one of my speed-dial slots. That fact in itself was more than a little surreal. I told him that the FBI had arrested Price and we were on our way downtown. At least we knew where to go, thanks to Mel having worked in the main building.

"What was that?" Taylor asked.

"I let Price's brother know what was going on."

She nodded. I couldn't tell if she approved or not, but she didn't hesitate, just headed for her parking spot.

Taylor wasn't dressed any better than I was. She wore platform red spike pumps that made her legs look like a million dollars. Above that she had on a dark purple dress that came down to mid-thigh and fit her like a glove. Unlike me, she was slender. I'd have looked like a stuffed sausage in that dress. She looked like a runway model. Her coat was a sleek leather swing jacket. Her auburn hair was caught up in an elegant chignon. Between us, we looked a little bit like two-thirds of Charlie's Angels about to go off on a mission.

In winter, Taylor drove a daffodil-yellow Lexus SUV. We climbed in, and she gunned the motor, fishtailing slightly as we zoomed down the drive and onto the road.

We didn't speak. The silence pooled thick between us. I couldn't tell what she was thinking. She and I hadn't been talking a whole lot since I'd managed to rescue Josh, her ex-fiancé. Before his kidnapping, they'd been headed toward getting back together again, and now he wouldn't even talk to her. Then after I escaped from Percy Caldwell, the bastard had decided to force Taylor to fly him out of Diamond City. He'd killed a bunch of her employees and infected her with Sparkle Dust. Tonight was the first I'd seen her since then, and it didn't seem like she was all that happy with me. 'Course, I'd brought Price to the party tonight, and I knew she blamed his brother for what had happened to Josh—not that Touray had had much to do with the actual kidnapping. Plus, my moving in with a major Tyet player, as Price now was, made me something of an enemy. After all, Mel was FBI. No wonder they'd raided her house. Someone was making a point about her not being trustworthy anymore. Clearly Taylor was blaming that on me, too. Not that she was wrong.

I let out a frustrated sigh. "Why don't you just say what's on your mind already?"

She glanced at me. "What do you mean?"

"You've been pissed at me since Josh went AWOL after his rescue. Like it's my fault he won't talk to you. Why don't you just yell at me already and get it over with? The brooding thing is getting really old."

"I'm not brooding."

"Yeah? Then you're faking it really well. Come on, Taylor. I did my best to get Josh back for you, but the Sparkle Dust they gave him changed him. He's not the same guy he used to be." I remembered the way he'd attacked me, hitting me mercilessly. If Price and Touray hadn't pulled him off me, I'd be dead now. I wasn't the slightest bit sorry he'd stayed away from Taylor. Who knows what he might have done to her? "And I know you think it's my fault Percy came after you, but I had no idea he even knew you existed."

"He wouldn't have come after me if not for you," Taylor pointed out, then stopped. "Anyway, I'm not mad at you for what happened with Josh or Percy."

"So then it's my involvement with Price and Touray, especially now that Touray's decided you're family, which means he thinks he's got a license to poke in your business and look after your best interests, whether you like it or not."

"That's supremely irritating, but no, not that either."

I tossed up my hands. "All right, then why don't tell me what's got your panties in a twist?"

She pulled up at a stop light. Snow mounded a good fifteen to twenty feet high on either side of the road. She glanced sideways at me. "This isn't the time."

"When is? Please tell me, because I've no idea and I'm getting pretty sick and tired of all the silent accusations you're sending my way."

"You have no idea? That's just awesome."

"Just tell me." I probably shouldn't have cared at the moment. But for once I had her trapped and alone, which made it the perfect opportunity. Never mind that we were on our way to rescue Price. The distraction would keep me from banging my head on the dashboard.

She glared at the road, her knuckles whitening on the steering wheel. I waited. Not patiently, but I waited. Smacking her upside the head wasn't going to knock the words out of her, and it was the only thing I could think of to speed things along. Finally she spoke, which only served to confuse me more.

"Did you ever wonder why I took up flying? Or why I went over into the war zone to work?"

"You're a closet daredevil?"

That didn't win the expected laugh. Instead her mouth twisted, and she muttered something.

"All right," I said. "Why did you start flying?"

"Because of you. And Dad." The last word was bitter.

"Me? What did I have to do with it? And Dad hated you flying."

Taylor had earned her pilot's license by the time she was thirteen. Ironic, that. She had to be driven to the airport in order to fly a plane.

She nodded. "He said it was too dangerous."

I waited for more. Taylor hooked a corner, and another, heading for the Mariview Tunnel that led from Uptown into Midtown. When it was clear she wasn't going to say anything else, I prompted her. So far her explanation was more confusing than anything else. "If you think you made your point, I missed it. Maybe you should talk slower and use more words."

"All the time we were kids, we were taught the world was dangerous. That you needed special protection. We were all given basics—using guns, defensive combat training, plus we got drilled on escape routes and what to do when this bad thing happened or that one. You, Jamie, and Leo had more lessons. Stuff on magic and I don't know what else. I didn't get any of that."

Her voice had dropped, and she looked furious. I still didn't get it.

"You're—" I stopped. None of the words describing someone without any magic was very nice. *Neuter* had caught on lately, but the others—*mundane, ordinary, defective, broken*—each carried its own negative. I elected to be more politic. Score one for me. "You don't have magic talent. So what would you have done?"

"And that right there is the problem I have with you," Taylor said, shooting me an angry look. "Treating me like I'm breakable and incapable. All. The. Time. Yes, it's true: I'm ordinary. Neuter even. Not defective. Not broken. Not lacking. But none of you believe it. You always treat me like I'm about to shatter or I'm not capable of knowing the dangers that are out there. You treat me like I've got cotton for brains and all I know how to do is look pretty."

My mouth fell open, and I stared. "What the fuck are you talking about?"

She rolled her eyes again, punching the gas. The SUV fishtailed again. She straightened it easily. "All right. Let's try an example," she said. "Why didn't you tell me that Josh tried to kill you when you were rescuing him?"

"You were pretty shattered at the whole situation. I didn't want to make it worse."

She grimaced and nodded. "So lie to me. Protect me. Now compare that to Dad fucking with your brain in the name of protecting you. He didn't think you could handle yourself so he handled you for you. All for your own good. After all, what's losing a few memories and a little behavioral modification if it means you could be safe?

"And another example. Your boyfriend and his brother practically railroaded me on upping the security on my hangar. They didn't bother asking me what I wanted to do or how, they just assumed I wouldn't do enough. After all, I'm so fragile and, apparently, stupid as a box of hammers.

"You're always doing the same thing to me. Not just you. The whole family. None of you think I can handle trouble—or you think I don't have anything valuable to contribute because I'm not talented, and you wall me out. When you get into trouble, you never call me. You never tell me until after the fact, and then you sanitize the hell out of it, so I won't—what? Worry? Be terrified of what you've gone through? Too bad for you I was there for the last time when Percy chopped off your thumb. I'm surprised you didn't have your dreamer friend Cass do a little erasing of my memories. Just so I could be protected."

The words spilled out of her in an angry, acid torrent. About halfway through, I managed to close my mouth. Then I started to feel like a total and complete idiot. And a jerk. And a really shitty sister.

"Yes, I like nice hair and makeup and pretty clothes," she went on. "That doesn't make me some sort of idiot child without balls." She glared at me. "Don't say it. I know I don't have balls. It's a metaphor. Just because I like to look good, doesn't make me stupid, just like you dressing like a homeless person doesn't mean you are one. You clean up nice, by the way," she said, waving at my dress.

"Anyway, I'm sick of being treated like I can't handle myself, like I can't be useful. You know what's worse? Your new boyfriend has no more magical talent than I do, and yet you trust him. You don't act like he might break himself at any moment. You don't try to keep him in the dark all the time and you don't try to wrap him in Bubble Wrap."

"He was a cop and in the Tyet." I wanted to bite the words back as soon as I said them.

Taylor swerved into the bike lane and jammed on the brakes. Luckily, the roads here had been treated for ice and we didn't slide into a snow-bank. She twisted around, stabbing the air between us with her finger to punctuate her anger.

"I've piloted planes through war zones. I've been blown out of the sky and lived to tell about it. Twice. I've been shot at and I've done some killing of my own. I train five days a week in different forms of combat. I'm good with knives, staffs, and bare knuckles. I'm betting I can take you down nine out of ten times. There's not a gun I don't know how to shoot and hit dead center on a target. Price's being a cop and Tyet doesn't have a damned thing to do with the way you treat me or him. It's all about you not believing in me. Any of you. Leo, Jamie, Mom, and Dad. I'm so sick of it.

"Yeah, finding out about Josh broke my heart. But I'm a big girl and I'll get over it. I just needed a minute, one damned minute to deal with it. Just like I can survive Percy killing my employees and cutting your thumb off. Just like I can survive getting infected with Sparkle Dust." She knotted her hands into fists. "What's it going to take for the rest of you to start letting me be a full part of the family instead of the sickly idiot child you keep locked up in the attic?"

She had a point. I'd never looked at it from that particular angle, but now that I did, I realized she was right. We always figured her as kind of girlie, too delicate for danger, and too prissy for the grit and dirt of the life I'd come to lead. I'd convinced myself that flying planes in a war zone was more like playing a video game where she had been far away from the real action. Talk about prejudice and preconceived notions. If anyone had said I was too much of a girl to do anything at all, I'd have ripped them a new asshole. Here I was doing just that to my own sister.

"Okay," I said, gathering myself. "One"—I held up a finger to count. "I'm sorry. Two"—Another finger. "You're right. I need to think about it some more in order to fix myself, but I hear you. I will work on it. Three, and not to act like what you shared is unimportant or like I'm ignoring you, but can we drive now?"

She narrowed her gaze at me and then nodded. "Right. Driving."

She twisted the steering wheel and pulled back out into traffic. A horn blared as she cut someone off. My phone rang. I looked at the screen. Touray. It had taken him long enough to call back. I answered.

"Where are you?" he demanded before I could say anything.

"I'm heading to FBI headquarters now."

"Turn around and go back. Better yet, come here where I can keep an eye on you."

"No."

He swore and I held the phone slightly away from my ear. Not that he said anything I didn't want to say, but it was so loud, it actually hurt my ears. Finally he stopped. "I don't want you down there. I'll handle this. Stay the hell away." He hung up without waiting for an answer.

"He's very bossy," Taylor noted, having heard every word. "What do you want to do?"

"We're going to FBI headquarters," I said, sliding my phone back in my pocket. "I'm not his village idiot to order around."

"See what I mean? Makes you want to stab someone."

I held in my exasperation. Taylor had a right to her irritation. "I get it. Really."

She flashed me a wicked grin, the kind we'd shared as kids right before we broke all the rules. "Good. Then I'll stop beating the horse. But don't think I won't call you on it when you start in again."

"Better than the silent treatment."

"So you say now."

We didn't talk much more after that. Taylor concentrated on weaving in and out of traffic. She ran a few lights that took too long to change, passed in the center lane, and generally drove like a bat out of hell. She was absolutely brilliant.

We pulled into a parking garage down the street from FBI headquarters. Taylor found a spot near the exit. I had to admire that. She was thinking about how to get away. I wished that hadn't surprised me. She was right. I needed to adjust my thinking when it came to her.

We got out and met at the rear of the vehicle. I looked down at my boots. Spike heels on ice and snow.

"The clothes make the woman," Taylor said. "Use the way you're dressed to your advantage. Go in like you own the place. It works."

I gave her a doubtful look. "If you say so. I feel like a fraud."

"Just follow my lead. You can do this. And you might give some thought to the fact I may have a few skill sets you don't have and you need."

She strode away, head held high, her entire body regal. I followed, feeling like I was going to twist an ankle with every step. All the same, I kept my back straight and my chin lifted. Right up to the point where someone locked an arm around my neck and jammed a gun into the small of my back.

Chapter 3

"EASY NOW."

I recognized the woman's voice and went rigid with fury. Special Agent Sandra Arnow. I had to fight the urge to struggle. She'd shoot me. I had absolutely no doubt of it. Unfortunately, we'd outrun our bodyguards on the way here. More evidence of my sister's prowess. They'd catch up with us soon, I had no doubt, but that could be too late.

"Over there, into that door," Arnow said. "You, too, Miss Hollis," she said to Taylor, raising her voice only slightly.

Taylor's eyes widened, and she got a look of helpless fear on her face. For a second I believed it. Then I remembered our conversation in the car. If our family didn't even take her seriously, Arnow probably wouldn't. She'd been the agent tracking Josh after he was kidnapped, and had seen Taylor at her emotional worst. Taylor was banking on the fact that Arnow would assume she wasn't a threat. I hoped so, anyhow. And I hoped really hard that Taylor was about to show me how wrong I'd been about her.

Arnow pushed me toward a dinged-up orange door in the shadows beneath a small portico. It had no sign to say where it led. Taylor stumbled ahead and opened the door. We followed her through.

Light bloomed in the narrow stairwell. It smelled of cement, urine, and greasy French fries. I wrinkled my nose. To my surprise, Arnow released me, pushing me away. I twisted to face her. Taylor stood close behind me.

"What the hell do you want?" I demanded, then looked her over from head to toe. "What happened to you? Did you go to Kmart for a makeover?"

My experience with Sandra Arnow was that she was a fashion model in FBI clothing. Last time I'd met her, her ash-blond hair had been pulled up in a sleek chignon, and she'd worn a tailored designer suit. The stiletto pumps she'd been wearing might have been pulled right out of my sister's closet. Now, she looked more like me after I'd been crawling through the back alleys, under fences, and through bushes. Her hair hung behind her head in a ragged ponytail, with loose tendrils hanging in draggles around her face. She wore jeans holed at the knees to reveal a flannel lining, a green army pea coat, and battered boots too wet for me to judge what color they might have been. Without her usual heels, she was a couple inches shorter than me. She wasn't wearing any makeup, and grease smudged her cheek and chin.

"Keep it down," she ordered in her crisp, low voice. "This meeting is off the books."

"You think I'm not going to tell the world you shoved a gun in my back? Think again, sister. And I've got a witness."

Arnow grimaced and slid her gun into the holster beneath her coat. "There's no surveillance in the garage right now, and as far as anybody else is concerned, I'm miles away in Denver. So you can try to make accusations, but you won't get far. Especially as the girlfriend of a Tyet soldier."

"What do you want?" Taylor asked, still in that wide-eyed, breathless fashion. She set her hand on my lower back and tapped twice. Yep, it was totally an act.

"I need your help," Arnow said to me, totally ignoring Taylor. Did the rest of us do that to her all the time, too? No wonder she was pissed.

"Not on a bet." Helping Arnow was nothing I planned on doing, now or ever. She'd pulled Josh into the trouble that got him kidnapped and tortured, and her raid on Touray's warehouse nearly got me killed. Plus, I was fairly sure she'd set up the ambush with the other Tyet members once we'd escaped. I didn't have any evidence, but how else had they known to where to set their trap? The only way was if Arnow had tipped them off.

I couldn't interpret the flicker of emotion that swept her narrow face at my refusal to help. It came and went too fast.

Her expression flattened. "Maybe I should rephrase. You're going to help me. I'm not asking. I'm telling."

"Just how are you going to make me?"

She smiled. "Whatever it takes."

"So you'll what? Put Price in jail? Done. His lawyers will have him out by dawn. Threaten to kill me? Fine. Do it. I'd rather die than give you the time of day."

Taylor curled her fingers tightly into my coat, but didn't say a word, even though she knew me enough to know I'd probably follow through. Sometimes winning mattered more than living. At least, that's what my inner nine-year-old was saying. Fortunately for me, I didn't usually let the inner nine-year-old win.

"Maybe it's not you I'll kill," Arnow suggested.

My insides went cold even as the rest of me flared into a ball of flame. I lunged forward, grabbing her collar. "Listen, bitch. Even think about going after my friends or family, and I will make your life a living hell."

I don't generally hold grudges, and I'm not really that into revenge. But for Arnow, I could definitely make an exception. I had friends in very low places who'd relish the chance to have at her. I wasn't planning physical harm, either. I'd make sure to pull the rug out from under her so she lost everything—identity, security, job, money, sanity. Then I'd make sure she could enjoy her losses for a good long time.

Maybe I had more Tyet in me than I'd thought. I pushed her away from me, my heart pounding, lungs pumping like I'd been running uphill.

Arnow's face twisted. "Look, I don't have a lot of time. I've got people who are in trouble and you're my only hope of getting them back alive."

"And I should care about them because . . . ?"

"Because they have families," she said flatly. "Because they need help and that's what you do."

The worse part was that I *did* care. I didn't want to, but I'm a sucker for people in trouble, even obnoxious FBI agents. Not that I was going to tell her that.

"Gee, since you asked for the meeting so nicely, what with the gun in my kidneys, how could I possibly say no?"

"Get over it," she said. "I wasn't going to shoot you."

"Of course you weren't. I mean, that was so obvious."

"We don't have time for this. What will it take for you to help me?"

I folded my arms. "I don't know." My inner nine-year-old was feeling smug.

"What do you want?"

I was surprised when Taylor answered, her voice low and tight. "I want Josh back. The Josh he was before you came into his life."

Arnow ignored her. "The clock is ticking."

"Getting Price out of jail would be a start."

Before she could answer, a noise sounded outside in the garage. The door behind us started to pull open.

"I'll be in touch."

With that, she vaulted over the railing to the landing below and disappeared. I exchanged a look with Taylor, but didn't have time to say anything before our bodyguards showed up.

"Are you all right?" Mason asked. He was one of the guards assigned to me and Price. He was dressed in military pants and a black winter coat that covered a bulletproof vest and assorted weapons. He carried a Beretta combat rifle. The only reason I knew it was a Beretta as opposed to, say, Nerf, was because he talked about it more than any girlfriend he might have. I was about to ask how he'd found us, when I realized he had Taylor's scarf in his hand. She must have dropped it near the door, hoping they'd follow and find us. I took the scarf from him and handed it to Taylor, mouthing a silent "good job" at her. She smiled smugly.

My mouth lifted in a quick smile, and then I turned back to Mason. "We're fine. Let's get inside."

I hurried back into the garage, walking swiftly out onto the sidewalk. Taylor strode beside me, with Mason and three of his people bringing up the rear.

"What are you going to do?" she asked.

"Hell if I know. I doubt they'll let us see Price. We'll probably have to wait until Gregg's cavalry of lawyers gets here." I glanced at her. "What do you think?"

"I was talking about Special Agent Arnow."

I grimaced. "I know." I'd been dodging the question. I didn't know what the hell to do about her.

"I think you're going to help her."

"I can't trust her. She's a snake in the grass and she's bitten me before."

"I know. But it isn't exactly your style not to help people in trouble. Even the ones you don't like."

I couldn't argue. "But you think I shouldn't?"

"I think you should be careful. And I want in."

"Want in? What do you mean?"

"I want to come along and help."

I frowned. "Why?"

"So we can see each other in action. It's time, don't you think? Plus you need someone you can trust at your back."

"What about your flying business?"

That was met with silence. I sort of wanted to kick myself for bringing it up, but then again, Taylor wanted to keep it real between us from now on. Less than a week ago, eight of her employees had been killed, most of them pilots. Until she hired new ones, she was going to have to be taking most of the flights. I pointed that out in case she missed my point.

"Brent is handling the business up on the rim for me. I've got feelers out for pilots and should be hiring soon enough. In the meantime, I can lighten my schedule."

I considered, then shook my head. "Still doesn't make sense. You scratched and clawed to get the business going and make it a success. Stepping back now in the middle of a crisis doesn't make a whole lot of sense. What's really going on?"

Flanked now by a half dozen bodyguards, we crossed the street.

They'd tucked their weapons out of sight beneath their jackets. I picked my way across the hard crumbles of ice that had made little ridges and divots where snow had collected, melted, and refrozen. Halfway across, the light changed and traffic trapped us on the wide island in the middle.

"I don't know that flying is enough," she said finally. "I love it. Loved it a lot in the wars. The rush was incredible. But here? It's—" She broke off. "It's tame. Anyhow, I started flying to give me something of my own I could feel proud of, but it never made the other shit go away. It only pushed me farther to the outside of the family. I know I'm not a soldier or a spy or a cop, and I can't wrap people in metal cages at the blink of an eye, but I *can* be useful. I want to be. I want *in* for once."

"You know that means wading into the stink and rot of the Tyet swamp, right?"

She snorted. "With your boyfriend's brother breathing down my neck on my security, I'm already in the swamp."

"Maybe you've got a toe dipped in," I acknowledged. "This would be cannonballing into the deep end. Be sure you want to, because it doesn't wash off."

"I'm sure."

"Tell you what. I'll ask again after we get Price free. If you still want to, then the answer is yes."

We entered the foyer and passed through the first security scan. After that, chained aisles funneled us to the information counter. Our bodyguards remained outside, too loaded with firepower to pass through security.

The clerk behind the desk took our names, typed into his computer, then eventually gave us visitor badges and directed us up to the fourth-floor check-in. We passed through another set of metal detectors before entering the vast lobby. Apparently, they worried that in the fifty feet we'd covered between the last security check and the second, we might have acquired a bazooka in the gift shop.

By the time we got to the second-story landing, Mason had rejoined us, along with Taylor's security lead, Pia Cruz. Each dressed in black fatigue pants and black turtlenecks. The uniform of burglars everywhere. They'd apparently divested themselves of any weapons that might trigger alarms, and they quickly passed through security and overtook us on the stairs. I have issues with small spaces. I don't do elevators unless I'm bleeding. Literally. Even then I'd rather crawl down a dozen flights of stairs on my belly than get inside that little death box.

"Ladies," Pia said, her dark eyes scanning past us as she searched for escape routes and threats. She looked a lot like Cher in her pre-collagen, pre-plastic surgery years. Her straight black hair was woven in a fishtail braid down her back. Her bangs hung thick around her shoe-polish eyes. Her skin was a smooth, rich brown, and her entire presence was exotic, lush, and graceful. I envied her down to my toenails.

"Fourth floor," I told Mason.

He nodded and motioned for Pia to lead off. Taylor and I fell in behind while Mason brought up the rear. I wished their caution was overkill, but I knew better. Bad guys could be anywhere, even in the FBI. Or maybe especially here. Corruption was rampant in Diamond City law enforcement, and this was a nexus of criminals and corruption.

The center stairs spiraled up through the middle of the glassed-in lobby. Artistic chandeliers hung at varying levels, each lit with brilliant magic. None were the same. I'd have thought there'd have been echoes, with all the traffic below mixing with the reception areas on each floor, but the sound had been dampened so that it felt more like a library than an office building.

A massive U-shaped desk blocked the landing to the fourth floor. We stopped in front.

The receptionist finished typing something into her computer and glanced up at me. "May I help you?" Her pinched lips said she suspected I was a criminal.

"We're here for Clayton Price. He was arrested."

"Oh." There was a wealth of judgment in that sound. "And you are?"

"Friends," I said.

"I'll see who the case agent is." She tapped something on her computer and scanned down the screen. She gave a smile that probably was supposed to look friendly, but instead looked more like a crocodile about to have a snack. "If you'll follow me, I'll get you settled and let him know you're here."

She rose and walked down to the end of the desk. She paused beside a waist-high door and keyed in a code. A soft chime sounded, and the half door swung open. She motioned us through. "This way."

Interesting. I hadn't thought it would be so easy. We followed her down a corridor, past a number of matching closed doors. Finally, she pressed buttons on the exterior of one and opened the door. "Can I get you any coffee while you wait?" she asked as we walked in. "Special Agent Henry will be with you in just a few minutes."

This didn't feel right. I didn't know a thing about FBI investigations, but I was pretty sure that family members of arrested suspects didn't get special sitting rooms and offers of coffee. Already I felt trapped. The room felt more like an interrogation room than a waiting area, despite the comfortable chairs. One wall had a long mirror that I guessed was two-way. Otherwise, there were no windows. It felt clinical and cold. The receptionist started to retreat, swinging the door shut behind her.

I went to block her, but Pia arrived before me. She smiled at our irritated guide. "Is there a bathroom I could use?"

The receptionist nodded, and the two disappeared. The door shut firmly. Instantly Mason tried to open it, to no avail. We were locked in.

"Son of a bitch," I muttered. "What's going on?"

"We're no doubt being observed and recorded," Taylor said. "So if there's anything you want the FBI to know, now's the time."

I turned to look at the window. "When are you going to figure out who killed my mother?" I demanded, glaring at my own reflection. "The way I see it, you really suck at your jobs."

"Anything else?" Taylor asked, her lips twitching slightly.

"That about covers it. For now."

Pia returned, escorted by the receptionist. This time, though, Mason planted his foot in front of the door to keep it from shutting when the receptionist tried to leave.

"What are you doing?" she asked in annoyance.

"We prefer it open," I said. "You know, so we don't get that feeling like we've been falsely imprisoned. I think that's illegal, isn't it?"

"That's what I've heard," Taylor said.

"It's for security purposes," the flustered woman said. "You can't be wandering about unattended."

"We promise to stay put."

She gave me a withering look. "It's not a choice. If you don't wish to abide by the rules, then you'll have to leave."

"All right," Taylor said. "Let's go."

I totally agreed, but at the same time, I had no intention of leaving Price here without knowing just what the fuck was going on. Before I could say so, my phone rang. Touray.

"Hello?"

"I told you not to go to the FBI. Where the fuck are you?"

I was rattled enough to give him a straight answer. "Fourth floor in some kind of observation/interrogation room."

"Get your ass out of there right now. Don't say a word to anybody. I'm on my way up." With that, he hung up. He really needed to work on his phone manners.

I put my phone back in my pocket, even as both Pia and Mason got texts. Touray clearly didn't think I'd obey his orders and had sent the same message to the bodyguards. Not that I was going to disobey. I didn't really have a choice. I'd just had a lesson in how little I knew about dealing with the FBI. I expected he had a lot more experience. I hoped so, anyway. I looked at Taylor. "Lead the way."

"Agent Henry is on his way," the receptionist said, looking like she was going to throw her body in front of us to block our exit. "It shouldn't be long at all."

Probably as long as it took to get out from behind the observation window and around the corner.

"Tell him we waited as long as we could," I suggested before breezing past her.

"Oh but—!" She called out as Taylor, Pia, and Mason followed me.

We reached the exit gate. It had no knob, only a keypad. I was tempted to vault over, but Taylor motioned for our receptionist to come open it.

"Release us," she said, sounding imperial.

The other woman sputtered and tried to argue, but Taylor wasn't having any back talk. She pointed at the keypad. "Now." The other woman made an irritated noise, but she obeyed.

The door swung open, and we made our escape. At that point, Special Agent Henry arrived. He looked almost innocuous in a dark blue suit with a white shirt and a blue-striped tie, with polished black shoes and a high-and-tight haircut. His hair was dark blond and he wore horn-rimmed glasses—an affectation, given how cheap and easy it was to get tinkered to 20/20. Maybe he just wanted to look geeky-harmless so suspects wouldn't take him too seriously and would spill their guts. I wondered if it worked for him.

"My apologies," he said as he joined us. "I understand you are inquiring after the Clayton Price case? I'm the Special Agent in charge, Ezra Henry. And you are?" He held out his hand out to Taylor first.

"Taylor Hollis," she said, returning to that faintly stupid-but-sweet fashion-plate persona.

She smiled as she took his hand. He stared at her, mesmerized. And why not? My sister is beautiful. She's got lush auburn hair that tumbles down her shoulders to the middle of her back. Her eyes are ocean blue. Add in porcelain skin, full lips, elegance, and an athletic body swathed in high fashion—she *is* mesmerizing.

"You're so kind to meet with us, especially when you're so busy."

I kept quiet. I was willing to let Taylor play this game to see what she could find out. She'd wanted me to trust her more, and frankly, this particular investigation was in her wheelhouse.

Special Agent Henry stumbled over his words, saying something to the effect that it was his pleasure, then reluctantly let go of Taylor's hand

and turned to me. His eyes slowly focused, and he managed to reel in his hanging tongue. "And you are?" he asked, taking my hand.

Like he didn't know. I almost rolled my eyes, but decided to follow Taylor's lead and play dumb. "Riley Hollis." I pulled away.

"You're sisters?" He smiled, focusing back on Taylor. "I should have seen that right away."

He didn't seem inclined to get introduced to Pia or Mason, giving them a glance but clearly dismissing them as unimportant. I bristled at that, but let it pass. They preferred to stay in the background until needed on center stage.

"I'm happy to discuss the case with you," he said, mostly to Taylor. "Can I offer you some coffee or juice?" He pushed the gate open again and held it. The receptionist must have keyed in the code for him.

"Absolutely not." Touray launched himself onto the landing from the stairs. His glance slashed across us, then settled on Special Agent Henry. "They aren't going anywhere with you," he said, his mouth pulled into grim lines.

Price and Touray shared a father. They both had black hair and pale skin, but then the resemblance muddied. Touray's hair was cut short, almost military style. Price's was longer, down to his collar. Where Price was more lean, Touray was thickly slabbed with muscle. His face was square, and his black eyes held scary shadows. He radiated menace and ruthlessness. I expected Special Agent Henry to fold up under that scowling regard. He didn't. Instead, he sharpened into a hard blade. He turned to Touray, his brows arching above the nerdy glasses, his expression carefully deadpan.

"I'm sorry, who might you be?"

Again with the questions he already had to know the answers to. I had to admire his cool. Touray liked to call himself family now, and he still made me nervous most of the time. When he went into a rage, I mostly wanted to crawl under a rock and stay out of his way. Right now, wearing a tailored suit, he looked the part of a mob boss, which he was. That veneer of money and civilization didn't really hide the fact that he could easily tear someone's throat out. Just at this moment, that someone was Special Agent Henry. I was a close second.

"That might be none of your damned business." Touray glared at me. "You were supposed to come down to the lobby."

I could feel Taylor stiffen. On a good day, she didn't like Touray. This was not a good day. She tossed her hair. "We don't answer to you." She let her gaze run over him from head to toe, her lip curling, then turned to the agent. "I would love some coffee. It's so kind of you to offer."

He grinned and flashed a triumphant look at Touray before offering Taylor his arm. She slid her hand through the crook of his elbow with a feminine giggle. She glanced at me. "I'll catch up with you later."

I really hated letting her go off with the agent, but I'd decided to trust her, and my sister wasn't dumb. She could handle herself. I hoped. "Sure. Call me when you can."

I could practically hear Touray gritting his teeth. "Don't be stupid, Taylor. This isn't some game. He's a federal agent and he wants nothing more than to milk you for information. "

Taylor let her face go blank, and she blinked at him as though hurt. "Don't be silly. Special Agent Henry has been a gentleman and quite helpful. Besides, what information could he possible want from *me*?" She shook her head, then reached out to pat Touray on the shoulder. "Don't worry, Daddy Dear, I'm all grown up now. But if it makes you feel better, if it comes to it, we'll use protection." She laughed merrily and took hold of the agent's arm again. As they strode away, she bent and whispered in his ear. They both laughed.

I'd thought Touray was pissed before. That had been a shadow of the real thing. Now he was positively on fire. His fury was so thick, it made it tough to breathe. Pia started to follow after Taylor, but I caught her arm.

"Let her be."

Touray's head twisted, fast as a rattlesnake striking. "You're on board with this?"

"Taylor knows what she's doing." I hoped.

His lip curled into a sneer. "Like hell she does. You and your sister are damned fools. You realize you're playing with Clay's life?"

I bit back my response, more than a little aware of our audience. "Maybe *you* should offer *me* a cup of coffee," I suggested, my jaw jutting.

"Maybe I should offer you a gag and some duct tape," he muttered. "By all means, let us go have coffee," he said and grabbed my arm like he was afraid I might run off.

I let him drag me downstairs because I wasn't going to start a fight in the middle of FBI headquarters, and because I knew he was worried about Price. So was I. Only I was about to find out that I wasn't nearly as worried as I should have been.

Chapter 4

TOURAY MARCHED me outside. "Where's your car?"

"In the garage, but it isn't mine. Taylor's got the keys."

He nodded and gestured for Mason. "Get us a vehicle."

Mason punched a text into his phone, and in less than a minute, a black SUV turned around the corner. Touray maneuvered me into the passenger side, then went around to take over driving. He said something to Mason I couldn't hear and then floored it. The wheels spun on the frozen ground, then grabbed, and we jerked out onto the road, fishtailing before we straightened out.

"Where are we going?"

"Somewhere safe where you won't get into trouble."

"I'm not going to sit on the sidelines. I want to help Price."

He dragged his fingers through his hair and glanced at me. "You have no idea what's happened, do you?"

"Price got arrested by the FBI," I said. "I was there, remember?"

He shook his head, and then it shifted to a nod. "What do you think that entails, exactly?"

I frowned at him. "I don't know. I guess the usual. He gets interrogated, asks for a lawyer, gets one, sees a judge, gets bail—what?"

"He was arrested under the Rice Act—one of the provisions of the Magical Crimes Act."

"Which doesn't make any sense at all," I said. "That only applies to people with talent and Price is mundane. They made a mistake. So sic your lawyers on straightening it out."

Touray's jaw knotted. He didn't say anything, staring at the road ahead like it might suddenly disappear.

My stomach cramped with foreboding.

"What's going on? What aren't you telling me?" It was right there in front of me, but I couldn't believe it. Didn't want to believe it. If it was true, then Price had been lying to me all along. I reached out and grabbed the car's armrest, feeling like I was in freefall without a parachute.

"He doesn't know."

"Excuse me?"

"I said he doesn't know he has a talent."

I heard the words. I knew that they were a sentence—subject, verb, all that sort of thing. All the same, I couldn't make any sense out of them. Touray might as well have been speaking Chinese. My response, ever erudite and whip-crack smart, was "Huh?"

Touray sighed and dragged his fingers through his hair. I wondered if he worked with his barber to get a haircut that would look good when he was attacking it.

"It's a long story, but what it comes down to is that Clay has a talent. None of us know what exactly what it is, except—" He broke off and then shrugged. "It manifested once when he was very small, and never again after that. It was . . . traumatic . . . and he doesn't remember. We figured he'd suppressed both the memories and the ability. The doctors, tinkers, and dreamers we took him to all said that forcing him to remember could be disastrous to his psyche and to just let him be. One day he might remember on his own, or maybe he won't. In the meantime, he's not suffered any ill consequences."

"Until now," I said, reeling. I hardly knew what to think or feel. Price hadn't lied to me, knowing that steadied me. "How did the FBI find out?"

"Remember Madison's father?"

Madison was a young woman I'd helped rescue from Percy. He'd been holding her family prisoner, using them in his ugly schemes. Madison's father could sense not only that a person had a talent, but could tell exactly what it was. "He told you what Price's talent was?"

Touray shook his head. "No. He refused. Said if Clay wanted to know, he could ask, but he was done stealing people's secrets. But while the ability to read someone else's talent is almost unheard of, simply knowing that someone has a talent is less rare. Agencies like the FBI troll for those people. They have to be certified before they can be used in law enforcement, but then their word is enough to invoke the MCA."

I let that sink in and weave together with what Mel had told me. "Oh God," I muttered as the pieces settled into place. I swallowed so I didn't throw up. "They're going to torture him."

"Seven business days," Touray said grimly. "It's no accident they arrested him tonight. It gives them a free day tomorrow, plus next weekend, before they have to take the next steps. Ten days."

"Fuck."

"As you say."

"What do we do?"

"I'm working on it. It would help if I didn't have you distracting me."

I frowned. "Why did they grab him at all? Why not go after you?

You're the one they really want."

Touray sighed. "I can be a greater asset out of jail. Clay provides them with leverage. They can trade him for my help and information. Even once they release him, they can always take him again." He glanced at me. "They might be planning to use the same leverage against you. They may come knocking on your door for favors."

I thought of Special Bitch Arnow. Speaking of favors. I pushed the thought away. She didn't matter right now. "How do we get him back?"

"I'll get him out and you don't need to know. You just have to stay out of the way. Along with your blasted sister."

We drove into the Eisley Tunnel that would take us up to the Midtown level. On the other side, Touray eyed his mirrors, then turned sharply so that I jerked up against the door.

I glanced back through the tinted glass. Headlights followed us. Probably our bodyguards. "Is something wrong?"

He made a noncommittal sound that could have been a yes or no. I looked back again. He made another sharp turn and another. The SUV skidded and wiggled drunkenly as Touray straightened out. The lights followed us.

"That's not Mason?" I asked.

"It is."

"Then what's with the Indy 500 driving?"

He shook his head and didn't answer, instead doing another fast turn and speeding up. He ran a red light and two more, then turned again. The following car clung to our bumper throughout.

"Some people might worry about getting a ticket," I said, folding my arms to keep from grabbing the armrest. I kept my feet flat on the floor so I wouldn't stomp my invisible passenger brake, either. I was just hoping I wouldn't pee my pants. Also that he wouldn't turn us over. It felt like we went up on two wheels every time we hung a turn.

"I don't get tickets," he said, whipping into a grocery-store parking lot. He jounced across the speed bumps while our bodyguard's car slowed down, preventing anyone behind from catching up to us. Touray pulled back out on Valger Boulevard. It ran in a straight line across the length of the Midtown shelf. Because most of it was elevated, the only cross streets were when it touched down to the ground, a total of six times. Touray gunned the engine, and we sped along, weaving in and out of traffic.

"Are we really being followed or are you just releasing your inner suicide driver? If so, I know where we could get you a couple pounds of valium. Cheap." My stomach churned with fear for Price, fear for me, and general helplessness and rage at the mess that was currently my life.

"I'm always being followed," he said, almost absently.

"Do you always drive this way?"

He flicked me a glance. "No."

"So what's special about the here and now? You know, aside from the FBI arresting Price and all the rest?" I waved my hand dismissively, trying to obscure my mistake. He didn't know about my dad or Arnow's request for help. I didn't want to explain. Unfortunately, he wasn't stupid.

"The rest?"

"Long story," I muttered, looking down to avoiding his penetrating black gaze.

"Give me the highlights," he said. Ordered.

I bristled. I'd never been good at being bossed around. You'd have thought he'd have figured it out by now. "No," I said. "Maybe when I figure some stuff out. For now, none of your business."

"It is if it threatens you or Clay," he declared, getting that obnoxiously intractable look of his. Like a buffalo with a hernia. "And so far, for the couple of months I've known you, there's little in your life that doesn't get you into trouble. Explain. Now."

He might be helpful. I knew this, but I hadn't had a chance to think about my dad. I needed to process. I needed to talk to Price, my mom, and the rest of my family. Which, I supposed technically Touray was, since once I'd started dating Price, he'd declared that we were family. Of course, tonight had been my first actual date with Price. What a disaster that had been. I also wasn't sure I wanted to let Touray in on Agent Arnow's request. So I just stared out the window at the passing lights and said nothing.

He swore. I looked at him. "You have to trust me, Riley," he grated, clearly holding back some choice things he wanted to say.

I gave a little headshake. "No, I don't. I doubt I ever will. I believe you want to look out for me and Price, but I've learned the hard way that people will do things for 'your own good'"—I put air quotes around the phrase—"that end up being worse than whatever the bad guys have in mind. So whatever your intentions, I can't trust you. I won't."

"Even if it means Clay's life? Who are you to decide what might help him? I'm his damned brother! Tell me or—"

He broke off, and I couldn't help the shiver that ran down my back. He called me family, but the truth was that Price was Touray's flesh and blood, and if he had to choose, I wasn't the one who'd win.

"Or?"

"I'm going to do whatever it takes to save my brother," he said in a gravelly voice, and the look he turned on me was smoldering hot. As in, fire and brimstone and hellfire and damnation.

The threat was clear. He wasn't going to let me stand in his way.

"Message received," I said in a low voice. "Just so you know, I'm going to do the same." I grinned fiercely at him.

He growled.

"Down boy. Sit, stay, heel."

"You need to let me handle this. Clay would never forgive me if you got hurt."

"Actually, what I need to do is help Price, and then figure out my own damned life, thank you very much. I also need you to stop ordering me around like I'm your servant." It was good to have someone to snap at. Everyone else I was pissed at was off the radar. Touray was a convenient target, and itching for a fight himself.

"A servant? Hell no. You're not nearly competent enough to get paid for the trouble you cause. You're a child. A stupid, irresponsible, moronic, ungrateful child at that. You're going to get Clay killed, or yourself, and he'll blame me."

"Sucks to be you, doesn't it?" I said.

He didn't seem to hear me. He slowed the car. Ahead of us at the Bitner crossroad, sirens wailed and lights flashed. It was an ambulance. It veered around stopped cars and into the intersection. There must have been a patch of black ice. Instead of stopping to let the emergency vehicle through, two cars spun wildly and the ambulance T-boned one of them. The ambulance swirled sideways, then rolled over. Sparks sprayed as metal scraped across the pavement.

Other cars coming down the boulevard braked, and there were more spins and crashes as they hit the invisible ice and smashed into one another. Touray drove up on the sidewalk as he braked. A car bumped the left corner of our bumper and we jolted, but didn't lose traction.

He stopped, putting the SUV in park. He popped open the console. Inside was a stash of several handguns. He pulled two out and handed one to me.

"It's chambered," he said, leaning forward to slip his into his rear waistband. "I want you to get off the Boulevard and go somewhere safe. Call Mason and he'll pick you up."

"You think this is a trap for you," I said. It wasn't a question.

"I think it's a trap for one of us or maybe both."

"We could both run. We should be able to get away. And you can travel through dreamspace."

He grimaced. "It might not be a trap," he said. "People might need help."

"Help is probably on the way." He surprised me. I didn't see him as a guy who helped strangers.

"They might not have time, and I'm here now." The corner of his mouth quirked momentarily in grim humor at my astonishment. "I told you before—this is my city. My circus, my clowns, my problems. All of them."

I stared. As scary as he could be, as vicious and brutal and ruthless, he had a core of kindness and generosity that defied sense. He'd give his life for strangers because he'd adopted them as his own. For that, I could almost learn to like him. Didn't mean I wasn't going to roll over and play dead when he irritated me. The man needed someone in his life who didn't ask, "How high?" when he said, "Jump."

He pulled his door open and went around to the rear of the vehicle. I followed. From an emergency box in the back, he pulled out some flares. He handed me one. At my doubting look, he smiled. "Makes a hell of a weapon."

I nodded and put it in my pocket. I thrust the gun into the other pocket. I wished I had better shoes on and maybe pants. Teach me to get dressed up.

He drew out a shiny silver thermal blanket. It was wrapped in a pouch no bigger than the palm of my hand. "Just in case," he said.

In case of what? I wanted to signal space? I took it without arguing.

"Have you got money? For a cab or the subway?"

I nodded. Some things were old habit. My bra held more than my boobs. I also had an emergency pack strapped around my thigh. It contained a couple hundred bucks, a knife, and some ChapStick.

He handed me a pair of gloves. "Take these." With that, he shut the back of the SUV and pushed me toward the rail, out of sight of the road.

"Get going." He hesitated. "If this does go sideways, I'm counting on you to help my brother."

"I told you I wasn't backing off," I said. "For the record, if this goes sideways, I'll come for you, too." I flashed a slightly malevolent grin. "You'd better hope I'm not as incompetent as you think."

I didn't wait for his answer, since he'd probably have argued that he didn't need my help, and there was no time for that. More cars were stopping and already the traffic jam extended to the top of the rise in both directions. If this was a trap, the bad guys had planned it well, and they'd be moving in already. They'd be looking for us and expecting us to run. They'd be lying in wait. I needed to go carefully.

I did have one option they didn't know about, if they didn't stop me first with binders. Like Touray, I could travel. Different road, different mechanism, but I'd recently found out that I could pull myself from one place to another through the realm of the dead. It was dangerous. Possibly fatal. The spirit realm didn't exactly welcome live people. Staying too long was a sure ticket to the morgue, and you could count too long in seconds. I was still recovering from my recent injuries and adventures in the spirit realm. I wasn't sure I could actually pull myself through at the moment. I felt okay, but it had only been a few days since I'd been through hell fighting off Percy Caldwell and his goons. If I risked it and failed, I'd be too dead to help Price. On the other hand, trying it was better than getting captured.

I tucked the option in my back pocket and looked around. First I'd try for a good old-fashioned escape. Guilt twisted in my chest. I ignored it. Touray could take care of himself. Besides, someone needed to run away to return and fight another day.

Chapter 5

I DUCKED BACK behind the SUV, then jogged down the sidewalk. Maybe jog is too strong a word. I went as fast as I could without slipping and breaking my ass. I wasn't far above the berm where the elevated road met dirt. Unfortunately, mounded snow made it impossible to go that way. We'd had a thaw and then a freeze followed by some snow. The layer of ice beneath the new snow made for dangerous trekking. Traversing it wasn't a great option in snow boots and ski pants, much less in a dress and high heels.

I decided to stay on the sidewalk. I'd be too visible on the white expanse of snow to make a good getaway, and at least I had cars to hide behind.

Trying to keep an eye on Touray distracted me from my own escape. He'd strode up the road, pushing past the rubberneckers and into the thick of the accident, not making any attempt to hide. Probably he hoped our enemies would focus on him while I got away. He headed for the ambulance first. It still lay on its side, having done one and a half revolutions. He was first to get there and yank open the doors.

I skidded on some ice and remembered I was supposed to be fleeing the scene. I glanced back up into traffic. I knew Mason and the other guards were somewhere in the jam. I guessed they'd abandoned their vehicles and were coming on foot. I didn't have time to wait.

Beside me, a blue sedan sat idling, the people inside keeping warm. I moved past. The snick of doors opening sent chills up my spine. I didn't wait to see if they were enemies. I broke into a run, dodged in front of the next car, and then sprinted down toward the intersection. I slipped on ice. My arms windmilled, and I lurched sideways against the back end of a truck. The driver's door flung open.

"Hey! What the hell do you think you're doing?" A bulky gray-headed man launched out of the seat. He snatched at me.

I ducked sideways under his arm and kept moving. My near-fall gave me a chance to look behind and revealed several pursuers threading between the cars behind me. They didn't seem to be all that much in a hurry, which clearly meant that I was being herded and I was headed where they wanted me to go. Not good.

I cut through the traffic jam to the other side of the road. I was about halfway down to the intersection. I thought I saw Touray in the growing melee surrounding the accident, but I didn't pay a lot of attention. He could take care of himself. Or not. Not my problem at the moment.

I focused on remembering the details of my surroundings. I made a habit of walking the city, getting acquainted with every shelf that clung to the sides of the caldera. I'd covered every inch of the city on foot more than once. I never wanted to be lost, and driving it wasn't enough to teach me the nooks and crannies that were going to save my life tonight. I hoped.

Diamond City sits like a massive barnacle on the side of a prehistoric volcano—or really, the giant hole it left behind—which is about a hundred miles across. The city sits on three shelves sticking out on the east side, with the leftovers spilling down into the Bottoms at, appropriately enough, the bottom of the caldera. That's where most of the poor lived, and where you went to get lost when you didn't want to be found. Downtown, the lowest of the three shelves, was where most working people lived and where the business district was located. Midtown, the next level up, was where the just wealthy lived. Higher still was Uptown, where the dripping-in-money folks lived, and finally, there's the rim, where the more-money-than-God people built sprawling mansions made of gold bricks with platinum toilets. The shelves were connected by a number of tunnels.

A lot of money lived in Midtown. Most businesses here were the higher-end variety and included a lot of clothing stores, restaurants, and spas. On this side of the Valger and Bitner intersection was a broad, squat complex containing a couple swimming pools, waterslides, a gym, trampolines, and whatever other entertainment the Disney of workouts might include. The one thing it didn't offer was a good place to hide. Anyhow, the little valley between the building and road berm was filled to the flat with glistening snow. I wasn't getting across without being seen, that is, if I didn't just sink down over my head. Across Bitner was a golf course. I could slog across it, but I'd leave such an obvious trail that even a blind man could follow me.

I considered jumping into someone's car to hide, but I'd be trapped there when they started a car-to-car search, which I was certain they'd do.

A quarter mile away or so was a subway entrance. I might be able to disappear that way, but I was willing to bet it was guarded. This trap was too well planned. If I couldn't think of anything else, I'd risk trying to slip inside. Providing I could even get that far.

I was only a couple car lengths back from the intersection when I felt a powerful binding spell bubble up and spread outward, effectively shutting down any magic activity in the vicinity. That wasn't so great for the victims of the crash. Tinkers couldn't do anything for them. But it did keep Touray from travelling out to safety, which was no doubt the point. It would also kill the trace null I always wore. When I got out of the binder zone, it probably would go haywire. I deactivated it. I could always fix it. On the positive side, until the spell shut down, no tracer would be able to follow me.

Shit. I had a sudden bad feeling it would stop me from dropping into the spirit realm, too. I focused and tried to push my hand inside it. Nothing. I was cut off from that route unless I made it out beyond the binder's limits. That meant outrunning my pursuers.

I didn't let myself panic. I'd been in worse situations. I just had to think outside the box. I eyed the nearest car, but there was really no hope of hijacking a car to escape, not with the traffic jam spreading in every direction. Barriers prevented anyone from flipping a U-turn and zooming back along the other side, which was clear. The best thing I could do was get off the road and lose myself in the neighborhoods beyond. After that, I could find a hidey-hole until I could call for help, grab a bus, or catch the subway.

All of that zipped through my mind as I minced downward toward the intersection, ducking down to try to hide myself behind cars. I realized then I'd zigged away from where I needed to be, which was on the east side of the intersection. Over there was a collection of restaurants, clothing stores, a little cluster of antique shops, plus a bunch of eclectic businesses. Behind those rose some high-rise condos beside the popular Feltall Street. No motorized traffic was allowed down it, and the street contained dozens of music joints, eateries, art shops, and a few playhouses and movie theaters. If it weren't buried under snow, and everyone huddled inside for warmth, I might have had a shot of losing my pursuers in the crowds that frequented the area. As it was, Feltall was my best shot at ducking my pursuers long enough to get away. It appeared they were in no hurry. But then, they were herding me. Likely they had a vehicle waiting to carry me off and figured if they could get me close to it, their job would be easier.

I crossed back between the cars. In the distance, I heard more sirens. The arrival of emergency vehicles could be my ticket out. They might cause just enough distraction to let me slip away.

I hurried down to the front of the line of cars, where people gathered to gawk. Touray was helping to pull someone out of the rear window of a sedan. It had been smashed from the side and come to a stop against the back of a van. He knelt on the trunk and drew out the limp body of a teenaged boy. He passed the boy to the thicket of waiting hands and reached through to remove a child seat. Resting within was a baby who remained blissfully asleep.

I trotted over to the crowd surrounding the car, skirted around, and kept going past the van. I edged past the front of the ambulance, still lying on its side. The smell of spilled gas permeated the air, along with moans, screams, and crying. What sort of monsters caused this kind of damage, just to capture Touray and me? It was flat-out evil.

My phone rang. I fished it out of my pocket and glanced at the screen. Taylor. "You okay?" I asked by way of greeting, crossing the intersection to where more people gathered. I pushed between them. Two rock-jawed women started to move toward me. This was as far as they'd let me go. Now they would swoop in and pick me up.

"Yeah—I—"

"Good. Go to ground. I'll call you soon as I can." I hit *End* and dropped my phone back into my pocket, then broke into a trot again as I wove between the rubberneckers. I deliberately bumped into some to make them angry enough to get in the way of the women following me.

A gunshot ran out. People screamed and started running around like headless chickens. I kept moving, but my stomach churned at the thought that someone might have shot Touray. Three more shots popped off. I glanced behind me. I had four pursuers now—two men and two women. The woman in the lead caught my glance and pointed at me. She shouted something.

I reached the sidewalk and sprinted up it, dodging the people coming to see the carnage. I kept all my weight on the balls of my feet, giving me a better shot at staying upright, and prayed I wouldn't hit a patch of ice.

As soon as I could, I ducked off the roadway into a parking lot. It was revoltingly well lit. I zipped between cars and fled out the other side. I ducked inside a Mexican restaurant. The hostess stand blocked my way.

"I've got people after me," I declared, deciding that honesty was most likely to earn me some good will. "Back door? Please."

The hostess stared at me a moment. I guessed her to be about my age, with black hair caught up behind her head. Her eyes were outlined in black, with long lashes. She pursed red lipsticked lips, her gaze narrowing on my face. "You're that tracer," she said. "The one who's so good, who finds lost people and kids."

I don't know why I was surprised to be recognized. My face had been all over the papers when I got outted.

"That's me." I glanced over my shoulder and back at her. "Seriously, these people are a nasty bunch. Where's the back door?"

"You won't get far in those shoes," she said, and then her expression firmed as if she'd made up her mind to something. She pointed to a dark alcove full of tables. "Go in there. Sit." She passed me a menu.

I hesitated. I couldn't see how I had a choice, and scooted within, hoping to hell I could trust her. I found myself in a small bar area half full of diners. A few singles sat along the mahogany bar top. A fish tank on the wall provided most of the ambient lighting. I picked a corner booth, sliding over against the wall, as far out of sight of the door as I could get. At that point a waiter hurried in. He searched the room, saw me, and headed toward my seat. On the way, he grabbed a dirty plate off another table and plunked it in front of me, along with a half-drunk glass of wine. The other diners didn't pay any attention.

"Emily said people were looking for you," he said in a low voice, taking the menu that Emily had handed me. "I'm Luis. You should take off your coat so it looks like you've been here awhile." He was a handsome kid, with black hair slicked back into a stubby ponytail and cow eyes. He looked like he'd have dimples when he smiled.

I did as told. I heard the outer doors open and voices in the vestibule. He stiffened.

"Have you saved room for dessert? Our *flan de coco y queso* is *muy delicioso*." He kissed his fingers dramatically. "It has a hint of cayenne, and may I also recommend our Aztec coffee?"

My stomach growled despite everything. It had to be at least nine and I'd not eaten since breakfast. I'd been too nervous about taking Price to dinner at Mel's to even contemplate food.

Luis wrote something down as if I'd spoken, then collected the used plate. "Of course, Mrs. Delmire. It's too bad your husband couldn't join you this evening as usual. We always enjoy his company."

It appeared he was destined for a career in acting. I couldn't mind if it saved my ass. "I'll be right back."

I dug into my coat pocket for my phone. I stared at it a moment. Calling Mason risked having a war starting in the restaurant. Bad plan. Nor did I want to involve anybody else. I was better off finding someplace safe and lying low before I called for a ride.

Luis returned with a cup and a carafe. "Your friends left. Emily told them you ran out the back." He poured the coffee into the cup and set the carafe down. "I'll be back," he said and vanished before I could speak.

I picked up the cup and sipped, nearly moaning as bliss ran down my throat. Coffee, cream, cinnamon, nutmeg, cayenne, sugar, and a healthy dose of coffee liquor. Pure heaven. I took another sip, and warmth filled my belly and spread out to my limbs.

Soon Luis returned with a plate of enchiladas covered in cream sauce. I looked at him in surprise. "You're taking this whole scene awfully well. Why are you all so willing to help me?"

He shrugged. "We aren't doing so much. Anyway, you've done a lot of good for nobodies like us. Like that Alvarez kid who got taken. He was from my neighborhood."

I remembered him. Little Joe Alvarez, a six-year-old who'd been kidnapped off the school playground. Everybody had thought the culprit was the father who'd lost custody in the divorce. Turned out to be his grandfather's bookie. I'd found him alive. One of my happy endings.

"Anyway, you looked after him, we can look after you," Luis said and disappeared again. I stared after him. I'd done so much in secret over the years, and the Alvarez case had been one of my anonymous tips. After I became headline news, all that had come out, too. I'm pretty sure my best friend, Patti, had been the source. She'd wanted people to know I'd been using my talent for good. I hadn't thought it mattered, but tonight I was discovering how wrong I was.

I practically inhaled my meal. I couldn't remember ever eating anything so good. When I was done, I started considering how I was going to get at my money. I couldn't very well dig into my bra in the dining room or pull my skirt up to get at the thin pack strapped to my thigh.

Luis returned before I could throw discretion to the wind and hike up my skirt. "Your friends are watching the doors," he said, sliding into the chair opposite me.

"How do you know?"

"Carla took a smoke break out front to check and David went out back."

"I don't suppose you have any secret exits out of this place?"

He shook his head. "Just the back kitchen entrance, the front, and the side where we get our deliveries."

I hadn't expected a serious answer. He looked like a sad puppy, and I wanted to pat his head. "Don't worry. I'll figure it out."

"We'll help you."

I was already shaking my head. "You've done plenty for me and I'm hugely grateful. But these people won't mind collateral damage. I can't let you take the risk."

That raised the question of just how the hell I was going to escape. The binding magic still hadn't subsided. I doubted it would until they caught me, or until someone else got pissed and shut them down. That was unlikely. My guess was that the group that had organized this had made arrangements with the local Tyet bosses and cops. I had to figure this out without magic.

I mentally flipped through my list of options. I could try to disguise myself and leave with the staff. I was willing to bet none of them lived in Midtown. They'd either have vehicles or use the subway or bus to get home. I gave a little shake of my head. No good. The goons after me wouldn't hesitate to stop the group and check us all. But maybe while they were leaving, I could make a run for it out another door. I'd have fewer eyes on me at that point. Of course, the sentry watching would just summon back his friends. So, out of luck there.

Hiding out until the morning wasn't going to work, either. Once everyone left, my pursuers would break in to look for me. Right now, the only thing holding them back was the fact that this was Midtown and they probably hadn't gotten permission for a bloodbath in their negotiations with the local bosses.

So what did that leave me? I'd spent years honing my trade. Specifically, I'd sharpened my breaking-and-entering skills, my skulking skills, and my hiding skills. I should be able to figure my way out of this one. I just had to get creative.

"Is there any chance anybody here has some clothes and flat shoes that will fit me?" I asked Luis. "I've got some cash to pay for it."

He left to go check, and I refilled my coffee cup with the Aztec brew. I was going to have to learn to make this, or I'd be visiting the restaurant daily.

I still hadn't come up with a plan when Luis returned, followed by Emily—the hostess—and a couple of other women. One wore the white of the kitchen, and the other was dressed in the same black waitstaff uniform Luis wore. Emily carried a gym bag, and the others carried a collection of various other articles of clothing and shoes.

"Let's see if anything works for you," Emily said, plopping the gym bag down on the table and unzipping the top.

"You and I aren't exactly the same size," I said, eyeing her petite figure. She was probably size zero, and her feet looked like she shopped in the kids' section of the store.

She smiled. "These are Art's. He's on the line. He said to take whatever works."

The other two women set their burdens onto the table.

"I wear size ten shoes," announced the kitchen worker. "Size ten pants, too." She eyed my boots. "Those are slamming. I'd totally trade you."

"You've got it," I said, stripping off my pretty boots and handing them to her.

"Seriously? Those have to cost a couple hundred bucks." She turned them in her hands like they were made of glass.

"They'll look better on you," I said.

Emily pulled a pair of button-up Levi's out of the bag. I took them and slid them on under my dress. They fit a little loose and were slightly short, but good enough. Next she handed me a blue tee shirt that said, "I put the Pro in Procrastination" on the front.

The waitress—her name tag said *Salaleah*—held out a thick brown sweater. It had a red-and-white pattern woven around the yoke.

"My grandmother made it," she said in a quick voice. Her hazel eyes sparkled bright behind her fringe of bangs.

I pushed it back toward her. "I can't take it."

She smiled, and the weariness that clung to her lightened. "Don't worry. I've got a drawer full."

"Still—" I frowned at the garment as she shoved it back into my hands. "It's handmade."

"And warm. You might need it."

I sighed and decided to give in gracefully. She wasn't going to take no for an answer. "Thanks."

Emily handed me a clean pair of socks. I slipped them and the shoes on. They fit almost perfectly. After that, I went to the bathroom to take off my dress and exchange it for the tee shirt and sweater. I stuck my thigh pack into my front pocket, where I could get at the knife more easily, then returned to the dining room, where the others stood talking. They all looked at me as I came in.

"We're trying to figure out how to get you out of here," Luis said.

I started shaking my head before he finished. "No. It's too risky for you."

"What will you do?" Luis asked.

I had no idea. "When do you shut the place down?"

Emily checked her watch. "We should be done cleaning and getting everybody out in about an hour or so."

So I had an hour to figure out a plan.

"What about the kitchen garden on the roof?" Luis said, clearly not giving up on helping me.

"A garden on the roof?" I repeated.

Emily nodded. "There's a greenhouse for winter and a patio and beds for summer. The boss sometimes throws cocktail parties up there. There's a fire escape."

Hope sparked to life. "That could be my ticket out of here."

Luis frowned. "Won't they be watching for you to come off the roof?"

"Yep. And if I can convince them that's where I am going—"

"You can sneak out the front door," Luis finished.

I nodded. "Can one of you show me the door up to the roof?"

"I'll do it," Emily said. "Check on your tables," she told Luis.

The entrance to the roof was around the corner from the bathrooms, between the manager's office and a storeroom at the end of a stubbed hallway. Emily stepped into the manager's office and returned with a small brass key. A painted Cinco de Mayo skull hung off it. She turned the key in the lock and pushed the door open. On the other side, brightly tiled stairs led up into darkness. I flipped on the light and went up. Brilliant colors swirled beside me and overhead in a mural of some sort. I stopped on a broad landing. On the left wall were a dozen different switches, each carefully labeled, with a breaker box right beside them. The door out onto the roof was steel.

"Will the key open this one, too?"

Emily nodded and turned the lock. I swung the door open, and cold rushed in. I shivered. I hadn't put my coat on. I looked out. The entry let out onto an oblong patio surrounded by curved stone benches. A long bar area ran along the five foot wall surrounding the roof. On either side of the patio were two greenhouses with frosted glass walls. The snow had been cleared away so the lack of my tracks wouldn't be a problem. I smiled to myself. I might just get out of this, after all.

"I've got an idea," I said. "But I'm going to need a little more help to sell it."

Emily nodded readily. I was so going to owe her and Luis and the rest of the crew.

"What can we do?"

"I want the bad guys to think I'm hiding out in the stairwell. They'll come looking for me after you leave, and while they are trying to break down the doors, I'll be making my exit. All you have to do is drop loud hints that I'm still inside and waiting to escape off the roof once things quiet down."

"Where will you hide until you can escape?"

That I hadn't figured out yet. "Got any suggestions?"

She rubbed her chin, considering me. "Maybe. Come on."

I shut the upper door and rattled it to make sure it was closed. "I should brace this."

Emily frowned. "Why?"

"I don't want them to break down the door too quickly and find out I'm not hiding in here. They'll pick the lock pretty quick, I'm sure, so I need another way to keep them out. I just wish I could blockade both doors."

We went downstairs, and Emily opened the storage room for me. I grabbed a couple of brooms and took them back up and wedged them against the door. It was a heavy fire door, like the one closing off the stairwell below. I was just lucky they couldn't use magic any more than I could. They'd have to use good old-fashioned muscle to get through the door. I wished them luck.

The downstairs door was another story. Since there was no way to brace it, I just broke the key off in the lock. "I promise I'll pay to fix it."

"It won't be a problem," Emily said.

I hoped she was right. I hoped nobody would be losing their jobs for helping me.

She led me back through the main dining room to the kitchen. While most of the restaurant was decorated in brilliant colors and rustic tile, the kitchen was monochrome modern. The walls were white, and everything else was stainless steel. Rubber mats covered the floors.

My new friends collected around me again, along with the kitchen staff. I explained my plan.

"I thought we could put her out with the trash," Emily said.

Her plan was to put me inside a black plastic bag inside a rolling trash can. I eyed the one in question. It would be a squeeze, but I could fit. Getting out might take a minute, though. They'd pile some real garbage on top to deter anybody from looking. Then they'd leave, dropping a couple hints that I was hiding inside. The end result would hopefully be that my pursuers would immediately come inside to search for me, leaving me to escape unnoticed.

I could see only a few problems with the scenario. All my attackers might not come inside. I'd be blind in the trashcan and helpless. I'd also be in a tiny little space without air or light. The idea made my lovely dinner churn up into my throat. It could be said I had a touch of claustrophobia. It could also be said I turned into a basket case in small spaces. I swallowed. I could do this. I managed to ride the subway all the time. I just had to suck it up.

I nodded, already finding it hard to breathe. "Let's do it."

I waited until everybody was about ready to go. All that was left to do was take out the trash and the soiled laundry. They'd do that as they were all leaving for the night, as was their habit. They usually walked down to the subway in a group. Safety in numbers and all that.

They put a clean black bag into the plastic rolling trash bin. I climbed in, bracing on Luis's shoulder for balance. He grinned at me. The boy was going to break a lot of hearts. I'd put on my coat, but it was well below freezing outside. I pulled the little silver packet Touray had given me out of my pocket and shook out the thin blanket. I didn't know how long I'd be out in the trash, but it could help me from freezing to death. I wrapped it around myself and took a deep breath. It took me a moment to get my knees to unlock so that I could lower myself into the bin.

My helpers pulled the plastic back up over my head. Luis looked down at me.

"You going to be okay? You look like you're going to pass out."

"Not a fan of tight spaces," I managed to squeeze out, clamping my lips tight to keep from moaning. Cramps tightened in my calves and thighs from me clenching myself so tight. I couldn't make myself relax.

"You're kidding, right? You're not really claustrophobic, are you?"

"Only when I'm crammed into small spaces where I can't breathe." I tried to smile and failed. "Close me up."

"Wait a minute," Emily said and vanished.

I tipped my head back. I could do this. What's the worst that could happen? It's not like I couldn't tear through the plastic and escape. They weren't putting a lid on the can. Just a pile of rotting food.

Emily returned with the bottom of a turkey baster. "Poke it through the plastic so you can suck in air. Might help."

"It could," I said. "Thanks."

"All right then," Luis said. "Let's get the show on the road."

I bent my head forward and shut my eyes. *In 1 . . . 2 . . . 3 . . . 4 . . . Out 1 . . . 2 . . . 3 . . . 4 . . . In 1 . . . 2 . . . 3 . . . 4 . . .* I focused on my breathing, trying not to hear the plastic rattling around my ears. Someone patted my head, then squishy weight settled onto my hunched back.

"Are you okay?" Luis asked.

"Fine," I said, wrapping my hands around the basting tube and gripping it with all my strength.

I heard the shuffle of steps, and more things settled on top of me.

"Ew," Luis said. "That stinks. What *is* it?"

Somebody said something I couldn't hear. My heart thudded in my chest like I'd been running miles. Sweat trickled down my forehead and between my breasts. Trembles fluttered through my stomach and down my legs. Gooseflesh pimpled my skin, and I shuddered.

It's fine, I told myself. *You can easily get out of the bag. You aren't trapped. Just breathe. Breathe.* I started counting again.

I wasn't ready when they started rolling me. I jolted over the threshold and outside. More rumbling bumping, and then I came to a halt. Someone patted the side of the bin twice, and then there was a loud burst of voices and laughing. The voices faded as my new friends retreated. I was alone. But not for long.

Chapter 6

I WAITED, STRAINING to hear above my heart pounding in my ears and the harsh sound of my breathing. *If you don't get a grip, you're going to get caught*, I told myself. *If you get caught, no one is going to help Price. Or Touray*, I added as an afterthought. But it was the latter that spurred my control. Without Touray, without me, Price was alone. What were they doing to him? *Anything they wanted*, a nasty little voice whispered. The only limit to the interrogation was no permanent physical damage. That left a lot of open territory.

Price was counting on us to help him. I wasn't going to let him down.

I forced myself to relax. My breathing slowed and my heartbeat steadied.

I let sounds come to me, identifying the squeal of car tires, the grumble of engines, the distant rushing sound of cars speeding along Valger Boulevard. The accident must have been cleared.

I wasn't sure how long it was before I heard anything else. At first I thought the rasping scuff was my imagination. I tensed, concentrating. Footsteps followed by a mutter of voices. I couldn't make any words out.

They grew louder.

"—come in," a man said, his voice high-pitched and young.

"If she is hiding inside, we'll let you know. In the meantime, stay put and keep a sharp watch," another man said. He was older. "The boss won't like it much if we let her slip through our fingers. And what the boss don't like, you will hate for the rest of your miserable, short life."

"You think they were lying? Faking it?" The younger one sounded both defiant and scared at the same time. "They're stupid food grunts."

"And you are a stupid muscle grunt," replied the second man. "It pays to be careful and cover all our bases. Now shut the fuck up so Ally can concentrate. It's blue-ball cold out here and I want to finish this job so I can get a drink and a hot meal."

I heard breathing after that and not much else for several minutes.

Finally a woman spoke. "Got it."

I heard sound of the door opening and the scuffle of feet. I remained still, certain that the younger watcher still remained. The minutes ticked by.

I could stay here all night, I told myself. I might freeze to death, but I could stay here.

"She's playing possum in the stairwell," the older man said. "Get the others and bring them inside where it's warm."

"About fucking time," the younger man groused. His steps retreated away from the back door. I waited. A few minutes later, he returned with several others.

"Wonder if there's anything to eat?" a man asked.

"Christ, Jerry. Do you ever stop eating?" a woman asked.

"Gotta maintain my girlish figure," the first man said.

"Your girlish figure is nine months pregnant." Several voices laughed at that.

Their banter continued, but I couldn't make out the words. Abruptly, the sounds of their voices ceased as the door shut. I didn't wait for another chance. I took my knife and cut around the side of the bag just above my knees. I pressed the point hard enough to dig a groove into the plastic of the can. I traced the slit with my fingers. When I'd managed to cut three-quarters of a circle around myself, I figured it was enough.

I lifted my arms, pushing away the top of the bag and, with it, all the trash that had been piled on top of me. The employees had used another bag to help contain it, so rotten food didn't slide down over my face and down my back. Thank goodness for small favors. The stuff *smelled*. Almost enough to make me want to throw up. The stench of fish gone bad combined with who knows what else filled the air. My eyes watered.

I used the edges of the can to hoist myself upright, grimacing as I encountered something sticky. I waited as circulation returned to my legs. My flesh prickled, and then little stabbing aches thrust down through my thighs and calves. With absolutely no grace or coordination, I dragged myself out of the can. Lucky for me, the wall was close by. I grabbed an electrical conduit and used it for balance.

Once I was steady enough, I made a beeline down to the end of the row of buildings. I stuck close to the darker shadows against the back wall and ducked behind every bit of cover that presented itself. The back of my neck prickled. How long before the goon squad broke through into the stairwell and realized I was long gone?

I reached the street and turned toward the subway-station entrance. Even as I did, I changed my mind. At this hour, the trains only ran every twenty-five minutes. If I went down to the platform, I'd be a sitting duck until I could catch a train, and if my pursuers caught the same train, I'd be up a creek with no paddle, no hip waders, and no rubber ducky.

I turned right up a dark street. My coordination had returned, and I broke into a slow jog. I wanted to run faster, but there was a lot of ice and spraining my ass was not going to help me escape. I thought about breaking the flare I still carried so I'd have more light, but that would be a beacon for anyone looking for me. I was freezing. I'd pulled on the gloves Touray had given me, but I still wasn't sure I could manage to hold my gun, much less shoot it. Not that it would do me a lot of good against multiple assailants.

I zigzagged through an apartment complex and crossed the next street. I swore as I realized I was at the back side of Livingston Manor. An iron fence fortified with a variety of powerful spells prevented trespassers. I'd left the range of the binder spells behind about a block ago, so the security was in full force. Given time, I could have ripped through those spells, but I didn't have any. Plus I needed to save my strength. For Price.

With little choice, I ran up the sidewalk. It made a long white streak between the roadway and the fence. I decided to cross back to the other side of the street and look for a place where I could hole up for a while. Maybe an all-night coffee shop. Maybe I'd just break into someone's car and wait until morning and the streets grew crowded again. I'd get lost in the shuffle.

I'd just turned into the parking lot of an urgent-care center when a car pulled in behind me. I stiffened, but moved to the side, keeping my head down. The car rolled up next to me. The passenger window rolled down.

"Glad to see you didn't get yourself dead. Get in."

At the sound of Special Agent Bitch Arnow's voice, I went from freezing cold to searing hot. I turned to face the car, my fingers wrapping the grip of my gun in my coat pocket.

"How did you know where to find me?"

She flung herself across the seat to thrust open the door. "Just get in the damned car before you get yourself killed."

"So you can what—kidnap me? Sell me to the highest bidder? I don't think so." I started walking.

"They called in backup. You won't get far if you don't let me help you."

I stopped. "How do you know?"

"Because I know. Get in."

I glanced around. I didn't see any of the goon squad, but that didn't mean they weren't hunting for me. I got in. I had a gun and a knife. Having her hands on the wheel meant Arnow couldn't do much to me. Plus she wanted me to help her. That meant she wasn't going to turn me over to Morrell. Not right away, anyhow. I had to risk it.

I sighed as warmth hit me. The heater was blowing full blast. Arnow hooked a U-turn and pulled back out onto the road.

"How did you find me?" Would she lie? Tell me she was just in the neighborhood?

"I followed you from FBI headquarters."

"So you you're saying you didn't have anything to do with those goons hunting me."

"Would you believe me if I said no?" She shot me a sideways glance.

"Probably not."

She shrugged. "It was Savannah Morrell."

"You're on her payroll."

Another shrug. I took that as confirmation. I'd already thought she was. When I'd been trapped in Touray's warehouse, the FBI had attacked at Arnow's instigation. We'd escaped, but ended up ambushed by Savannah Morrell and her Tyet cronies. I'd always thought Arnow had a hand in it. This just made me more sure.

"You told her Touray and I were at FBI headquarters."

"What makes you think so?"

It wasn't a denial. I glared. "Am I wrong?"

"I didn't tell her."

"I don't believe you."

"Why would I? I need you free and alive." Arnow dragged her fingers through her hair, pulling strands out of her already-messy ponytail. When she gripped the steering wheel again, I noticed that her hands shook. Both gestures were totally unlike the cool and collected control-freak agent I'd come to know and hate.

"If not you, then who?" I asked, still not believing.

"Another agent, maybe. Maybe one of your bodyguards. Maybe she's having you followed."

The last one was more than a little likely. Even so, I wasn't sure I believed Arnow. Still, it was true that if she really needed me, then she didn't want Morrell to get her claws into me.

"You could have stepped in to help me sooner," I pointed out.

"I figured Touray would travel you out." She shook her head. "He had a window of opportunity. He should have taken it. What was he thinking by running into that mess?"

What she didn't know was that the one and only time Touray had taken me through dreamspace, I'd nearly died. Even if he hadn't gone on the rescue mission to help the injured in the accident, he wasn't in a hurry to try again. He needed me for his plans. Not to mention he claimed me as family now, though I wasn't sure that was nearly as important to him as my trace talent was.

"And yet you followed us anyhow," I said derisively.

"You don't always do what's expected," she said. "Plus I didn't have anywhere else to be. I figured I'd hang around just in case. Lucky for you I did."

"And Touray?"

"They got him."

"Dammit." What would Savannah Morrell do to him? She wasn't exactly known to be Glinda, the good witch. She was more the psychotic witch from the land of We Are So Fucked. She'd probably enjoy torturing him. At least she'd keep him alive. He had some of the Kensington artifacts, and she wanted them. Until he gave them up, she wouldn't kill him.

Zachary Kensington had formulated a magical weapon in the early days of Diamond City, when the place had been an Old West-style Tyet war zone. Though no one now knew what the weapon could actually do, supposedly it had allowed him to establish order in the city and bring the other Tyet factions to heel.

At some point after that, Kensington had broken up the weapon into different pieces and hidden them. He'd thought the weapon too powerful for anybody else to use. Or maybe he thought someone else would use it to become the next Hitler or Caligula.

I'd stumbled across three of the pieces while trying to find my almost-brother-in-law, Josh, when he got kidnapped. Touray had ended up in possession of those pieces. He was determined to find the rest and repeat Kensington's feat. In the last ten years or so, the violence and killing had increased exponentially in the city. Just last year, the *New York Times* or *Time Magazine* or some other news outlet had declared our fair city the murder capital of America, and well on its way to becoming deadliest in the world. Touray's mission was to stop the eruptions of violence. I'm not saying he was Martin Luther King Jr. or Gandhi—peace and joy weren't exactly his hallmarks. Touray just wanted to bring the death toll down to a tolerable level. Whatever the fuck that was. I wasn't so sure that having the Kensington weapon was the best plan. Let's face it—that kind of power, if it was true, would seriously tempt a saint. Touray was anything but.

He also wasn't the only one after Kensington's weapon. All the bad guys were, too. I groaned inwardly. Since when was Touray *not* on my bad-guy list? I gritted my teeth, disliking my train of thought. Maybe since he ran into an ambush to help people trapped in an ambulance.

I sighed and turned my attention back to Arnow. It annoyed me that she had been just as surprised as I was that Touray had jumped into the Good Samaritan role without thinking about his own safety. No, that wasn't true. It was worse. He had thought about his safety and totally disregarded it. I didn't like that she and I shared anything, even a little bit of surprise. It made me want to reconsider my opinion of him, which irritated the hell out of me. Because if he was a good guy, if his default reaction was to run toward the fire, he was actually going to do good things with the weapon, which meant I was going to have to help him.

I decided to jump off that cliff when I came to it.

"I could have used a hand in the restaurant. They almost had me."

"Couldn't risk it. I'm supposed to be in Denver. Anyhow, you're not stupid. I figured you'd worm your way out. You're good at that."

"And if I didn't? What about these people you want me to find? What happens to them if I don't help you?" I wanted to yank the question back. I didn't want to know, because then I'd feel guilty, and then I'd have to help.

Arnow's chin jutted, and she punched the gas. The car skidded, and she took her foot off the accelerator and steered into the slide until she had control again.

"Looks like I hit a nerve," I observed.

"With or without you, I'm going to find them," she said.

"That's good, because I wouldn't spit on you if you were dying of thirst."

One corner of her mouth lifted. "And yet you *are* going to help me."

"Like hell."

"Where do you want to go? Back to your stepmother's?" she asked.

I flinched. I hated that she knew where Mel lived. Not that it was a secret. Not that the FBI hadn't broken down the front door. Arnow was FBI—finding Mel's address would have taken a couple of keystrokes.

"Yes," I said.

"You aren't going to ask why you're going to help me?"

I shook my head. "Not interested in fairy tales."

"Sure you are. Here's a good one. Once upon a time, a princess fell in love with a dark prince. One night, bad men took the dark prince and locked him away. The princess was heartbroken. She had no idea where to find him. Then a mysterious stranger shows up promising not only to guide the princess to her lover, but help her rescue him. In return, the princess helps the stranger locate her missing friends."

She flashed me a sharp grin. "You don't know where your boy toy is. The agents nulled him the moment they put him in the car. Standard operating procedure. But I know. I can take you there."

"Fuck you," I said. "I can find him myself." I wished I sounded more certain. I could do things no other tracer could do, and my ghost mom had told me that no trace could ever really disappear for me—if I was as strong as she thought I was. If. But I didn't know for sure. So while there was a possibility I could find Price without help, there was a decent chance I couldn't. I also couldn't afford to waste time looking.

Arnow snorted. "Right. How are you going to do that exactly?"

"I've got my ways. Anyhow, I wouldn't trust you to take out my trash."

"No? Think about this, then. These are the stats the public never gets to hear about. Nine out of every ten people interrogated under the Rice Act have ended up in jail, dead, or in a loony bin. Are you going to find your precious boyfriend before he's toast? How long after you find him is it going to take you to break him out? I know where he's being held and I've got clearance inside the facility. So make up your mind. Even trade. My services for yours, or you jump out and take your chances. Just remember, if you're not going to help me, there's no reason for me not to turn you over to Savannah Morrell and earn my brownie points. So either way, Price has close to a 100 percent chance of never seeing the light of day again."

She flexed her fingers on the steering wheel before shooting me a dogged look. "So what's it going to be?"

I didn't have to think. I couldn't risk Price's life or sanity. "I'm in." I paused. "But we free Price first and then Touray. Only then will I help you. If you betray me in the slightest, you'll be on your own."

Her jaw knotted. "That's fair." She hesitated. "I hope it's not too late."

I knew she was talking about the people she wanted me to find, but my mind flew to Price and the ugly statistics Arnow had quoted at me. I prayed we wouldn't be too late for him.

Chapter 7

"WHERE IS HE?"

"Facility up in the mountains. Maybe an hour away, depending on roads and snow."

So not far away. Relief made me slump in my seat. Here I had some resources. If Price had been taken far away, I would have had far less to work with. Then I remembered Gregg had said they might move him.

"Will they keep him there? Or take him somewhere else?"

"The local agents want a crack at him. It would be worth a commendation, if not a promotion. So they'll work on him here, at least for a few days, or until the sharks up the food chain hear about the arrest. Then the bigwigs will move in and take over. Whether they decide to question Price locally or not is anybody's guess."

"So we should hurry."

"Faster the better. Could be only hours before the news gets out."

I sat and stewed about that for a few minutes. Anxiety made me want to fidget. Finally, I pulled out my phone and sent a text to Taylor to meet me at Mel's, then sent a message to Mel to tell her we were coming. I didn't mention Arnow. That would be better explained in person. I tabbed my phone off and stuck it back in my pocket.

The silence in the car ate at me. It was late enough that traffic wasn't that heavy, but Arnow drove like a granny on her way to Sunday church. I mentioned this.

"Don't want to call attention to ourselves," she said, glancing in the rearview. I looked over my shoulder. Lights turned off in another direction. I faced back around.

Before the silence could settle again, I spoke. "Who are these people you want me to find, anyhow? What's the story?"

"It's going to take longer than a short car ride to explain."

"Give me the nuts and bolts."

She blew out a breath. "All right. The nutshell is this: I've discovered that there are two levels of Tyet organizations. Hell, there's probably hundreds. But you know how there's the internet and the dark web underneath that's tons bigger and a lot more powerful? The Tyets are like that.

There's all the stuff we see day to day, the players in the papers and on the news, and then there's a deeper, bigger, stronger, more dangerous level where the heavyweights play in secret."

I frowned. I didn't know what to think of what she was telling me. I hadn't been expecting anything like it. Not that I knew what I'd been expecting, really, but this surprised me.

Seeing my frown and taking it for confusion, Arnow continued. "Think of the Tyets here in Diamond City and everywhere else as local clubs. Small fry, bush leagues, mom-and-pop organizations. That sort of thing. The deeper level is muscular with tentacles everywhere. They are far more organized and run everything. Not just one group, but hundreds. Maybe thousands. They have factions, too, but they run countries. They have the real power. I've been trying to tap into them for a few years now."

The idea that there were deeper and bigger Tyet groups made sense. It also made my blood run cold. Weren't the ordinary Tyet factions bad enough? Arnow had called them mom-and-pop organizations. Next thing you'd know, they'd be sponsoring Little Leagues and bowling teams. The Savannah Morrell Killers against the Gregg Touray Kneebreakers. I swallowed a giggle. I was losing it. I needed sleep. Unfortunately, I wasn't going to get it.

"You're doing this on your own?" It made sense, I supposed. The FBI was as corrupt as any organization in Diamond City. She wouldn't know who she could trust, and worse, who she couldn't. The Lone Ranger thing would be safer. Plus she might not be able to get official permission. "Being in bed with Savannah Morrell gives you credibility for getting in, I take it."

She nodded. "Something like that. But yeah, I'm off the reservation. The FBI doesn't know I'm working on this, which is why I can't call in backup. Savannah would slit my throat if she knew. She doesn't mess with the deepwater Tyets."

I had a hard time picturing anything that would scare Savannah Morrell. I wonder if Price and Touray knew about these so-called deepwater Tyets. Of course they did. How could they not, in their line of work? Arnow kept speaking, and I turned my attention back to her.

"I put together a team for a mission. Five of us. It was supposed to be recon at an industrial complex. The next thing I knew, three of them disappeared. I've got to find them, without letting anybody know my fingerprints are on this."

I smiled without any humor. That gave me a lot of power over Arnow. It also showed how committed she was to her team. I had to respect her for that. A little.

"Who took them?"

She shook her head. "I wish I knew."

"I hope you've got more details than that."

Her hand tightened on the steering wheel. "There'd been a string of ritual murders. The local LEOs focused on nailing the killer, but I was sure it was bigger than one person. I thought it had something to do with the Consortium."

"Consortium? What's that?"

"One of the deepwater Tyet groups. It does a lot of business in the US, Canada, and has interests in a lot of other places."

"I take it you decided to investigate these murders?" I asked.

"Unofficially. My team is civilian, so it's been totally off the books."

"Civilian? That's not cheap."

"They have their reasons for working for me," she said.

"Everybody has to eat," I pointed out.

On the other hand, if you'd lived in Diamond City for at least two years, you qualified for the diamond dole. It was enough to cover most of your basic living costs, with emphasis on *basic*. That and a job made sure you could afford to live in the city and work, which was the whole point. The wealthy needed employees. Of course, wages were higher in Diamond City than anywhere else, so the diamond dole often served as a bonus.

"They get paid."

Something in the way Arnow said it caught me up short. Then I put two and two together. "Bounty. They get some kind of a bounty on what they do for you."

She shrugged. "It works out. Bad guys get stopped and the team stays happy. Since we're off the books, we can't report what we confiscate anyhow."

"I expect there's a lot of money to be made."

She nodded. "It's good incentive."

"So what happened?"

"I did a little digging in our systems about the murders. Next thing I know, there's nothing there anymore. Everything gets wiped clean. Big-time cover up, like the murders never happened. Even the other investigators weren't saying anything." She waved a hand dismissively. "Anyway, I decided to check out the crime scenes. See what we could find. Ran into trouble at the third one.

"The place was an old machine shop. Big. Several buildings. Since we came to the investigation secondhand, we didn't know exactly where the murder site was. We split up to search. Me and Kelsey found the killing room. The walls were covered with arcane symbols painted in blood.

Other than that, the room was empty—except for a ping-pong table."

That startled me. "A what?"

Arnow snorted. "Not what I was expecting either. On the table were two paddles and three balls. Each of those sat in a pool of fresh blood. The names of my other three team members were written on each. There was also a note. It said, 'Welcome to the game. Take up your paddle and play.' Kelsey and I searched the rest of the place and it was empty, no trace of foul play. I had the three blood pools checked. They came from my people." Her voice dropped into a rasp. "I have to find them."

"You think they are still alive?"

Arnow hesitated. "I'm hoping you can tell me for sure."

I didn't like her. In fact, I hated her. But I was feeling a little sorry for her, or at least for her team members who'd gotten captured. I knew more than I wanted about being a prisoner of the Tyet. I sighed and put out my hand. "Give them to me."

"Give you what?"

"The ping-pong balls, or whatever else you're carrying around that has their trace on it."

She eyed me sideways, then reached into the inside pocket of her coat and pulled out a plastic baggie containing three rust-colored plastic balls. She handed them to me.

I didn't read the names. Instead, I opened myself to the trace. Nothing. Not even the gray of dead trace. I handed her back the bag. "They were nulled when they touched these. I need something else." If necessary, I'd try to dig harder to see past the nulling. See if my mother was right that I could, but not here, not with Arnow watching me.

"I've got more in the trunk." She tucked the balls back inside her coat.

"You think they are still alive, don't you?"

"If they were going to be killed, I wouldn't have gotten balls on the table. I'd have gotten their heads." She shook her head. "I'm supposed to play the game. Whatever it is." The vulnerability in the way she said it floored me. Arnow was made of steel wrapped in Teflon with a core of liquid nitrogen. She plowed forward with all the confidence of a runaway train. Only now she'd gotten in over her head, and she knew it.

I didn't say anything more. A headache throbbed in my forehead, like someone swinging a pickax against the inside of my skull.

We were only a couple miles from Mel's house. Something had been niggling at me all night. Several somethings, actually.

"Why did the FBI come after Price? They must have known he had a talent for a while now. Why go after him now? Why him and not his brother?"

Arnow made a face. "I'm not sure. Dante's running the op—Dante Wolfe. He's senior agent in charge of the Diamond City territory. A couple months back, when I reported I'd had a couple run-ins with you and your boy, he asked a lot of questions, wanted updates on Price as the case progressed, wanted to know if I'd seen any evidence of his talent."

"But Price doesn't even know he has a talent or what it is." Touray had said Price didn't know, and I believed him. I needed to believe him, otherwise Price had lied to me, and that possibility hurt too much to contemplate. "Why did Wolfe think he'd be using a talent?"

She shot me another of those sidelong glances, her eyes narrowed like she was debating something. Then she hitched one shoulder in a shrug.

"Stop me if you've heard this. When your boyfriend was three years old, he was kidnapped."

She glanced at me, and I nodded for her to continue. "At least, that was the assumption at the time. His parents never reported it. Word got to the streets, however, and the city boiled. People feared an all-out Tyet war. At that time, his father served as a senior lieutenant of the Clavage syndicate. They were at the height of their considerable power. Taking Easton Touray's kid occurred at a crucial time. A deal was going down between Clavage and Sandoval Corp. Together, the two would have dominated Diamond City. Maybe all of Colorado. Easton Touray was the architect. With his son missing, he wasn't going to be there to hold it together. The Bureau figured at the time that the kidnappers were maybe using the boy as leverage to queer the deal. They'd string Touray along, get him out of the way, and then Price would turn up dead."

"But he didn't," I said, my stomach clenching with pointless fear. This had happened before I was born. Maybe even before Arnow was born.

"No, he didn't. The deal did fall apart and pretty quick, Clavage and Sandoval went head-to-head. Nobody could figure out who took the boy—was it someone on the inside trying to block the merger? Or was it someone on the outside? Was it someone who hated Easton Touray? There was no end to suspects.

"The FBI figured Touray knew, though he didn't say anything. He left Clavage and within a year put together his own business. It was a turning point. He was out for blood and his methods were brutal and merciless. Within five years, he'd wiped out both the Sandoval Corp. and the Clavage syndicate."

"What about Price? How did they find him? What does all this have to do with his talent?"

"The FBI put every team they had into the field, hoping to prevent all-out war. It would have been Armageddon. Then word comes that your boy was home. No explanations how. At that point, since everything calmed down, none of the FBI big shots cared much what had happened to him. They were just relieved to get out relatively unscathed. A couple stubborn agents disagreed. They figured that just because Easton Touray got his kid back, that didn't mean he wasn't going to get revenge in a big way. They wanted to know who'd taken Price and how, and how he'd been retrieved. They believed the future of Diamond City depended on figuring it out.

"It took them over a year to piece together what must have happened. At the time of the kidnapping, Easton Touray and your boyfriend's mother, Oriana Price, had been divorced a number of years. It was Easton's second marriage. His first wife, Gregg Touray's mother, died of trauma after a ski acccident.

"After the divorce, Oriana Price continued living under her former husband's protection with a generous allowance. Up until her son disappeared. It turns out she vanished at the same time."

I remained silent and tense. The story was riveting. There was so much about Price I didn't know. He never talked about his parents. I knew that Easton Touray had died a few years back. That had been all over the news. But Price's mother? I'd never heard anything about her.

"The agents on the case figured that someone inside the Clavage organization helped to kidnap the two, most likely Irvin Borender, Kyung Kim, or Aldo DeLacerda. They each had access and motive. Possibly they worked together. The agents believed that mother and son were spirited out of the country into Belize."

I frowned. "Why Belize?"

"When Agents Davy and Ellison couldn't find any evidence in the US, they started looking around the world. The searched for just about anything, especially anything referencing magic and/or a three-year-old boy. They had a couple techs doing nothing but running down leads. Finally they hit paydirt in Belize. It seems that locals found an unconscious white boy beneath a tree on the edge of the worst disaster in Belize's history. Half the mountain had been scoured down to bedrock. Several villages simply got scraped off. All the debris washed down into the river below and created a new dam. It's so big they didn't take it down. No one saw how the disaster happened because of a massive storm that moved in at the same time.

"After, they couldn't wake the boy—the only survivor. He was bloody and bruised all to hell. The local LEOs took pictures of the scene and the kid and sent them out over the wires, hoping to get a name. The next thing you know, the boy vanishes and the locals can't seem to remember a damned thing about what happened."

"The boy was Price? And you think he was responsible?" My mouth was dry. What kind of power erupted in a three-year-old that allowed him to create such deadly destruction?

"It's impossible to tell from the pictures we have. But word of his return came just after that, and Oriana Price turned up in Wisconsin with a Belize passport stamp. She claimed amnesia. She's never changed her story, though some suspect that she had a hand in the kidnapping. Anyhow, if Price was responsible for the devastation, you see why Agent Wolfe might be interested in his talent, and why we tend to be cautious around him. If he could do that at three years old, what could he do now that he's a grown man?"

"But why arrest him now and not years ago if they thought he was a threat?"

"Maybe to put pressure on his brother. Maybe to lure you into working for them. Maybe they thought his power was manifesting. I don't know."

At that point, Arnow pulled up to Mel's gates. Or rather, what used to be gates. Since I'd left, they'd turned into a solid wall of plate steel with razor-sharp barbs all along the top. Jamie and Leo had been at work on them. I couldn't see a seam where they might open, no rollers or tracks.

Arnow looked at me. "What now?"

I got out of the car and went up to the gray steel wall. I pressed one hand flat against the frigid metal, and knocked loudly with the other. Not that the sound made a difference. Jamie or Leo would be monitoring the wall for invasion or visitors. They'd be able to read through the metal that it was me.

After a moment, a split crept up the middle of the wall, with hinges on the sides and room on the bottom to allow the new gates to swing open. I pushed them wide enough to let Arnow drive through. Before I could shut them, the steel drew back and reformed into the solid wall. I got back in the car.

"Handy," Arnow said.

We drove around to the main house. Since I'd left, a new door had taken the place of the one the FBI had broken down. This one was made of steel. Price's SUV was still parked outside. Taylor's bright yellow Lexus slotted in beside him. Arnow parked next to Taylor, and we both got out. We'd gone about two steps when the door opened and Jamie, Leo, Mel, Taylor, and silver-eyed Dalton came out.

I eyed Dalton warily. He gazed back without any expression. What was he doing here?

Taylor pulled me into a hug, then stepped back, wrinkling her nose. "You smell," she declared.

"You try hiding out in a trashcan with spoiled food loaded up on your head, and let's see how fragrant you get," I returned, squeezing her tight.

"A trash can?" Jamie repeated, next in line for a hug. He held me at arm's length, looking me over. "Those aren't the clothes you left in. What happened?"

"I'll tell you inside."

"Who's your guest?" Mel asked, taking her turn at hugging me. My throat knotted as I pressed my cheek against her hair. She was my rock. I always knew I could depend on her. She was smart and calm and didn't let her emotions get the best of her. I needed her to figure out what to do next.

"This is Special Agent Sandra Arnow of the FBI," I said as I reluctantly let go of my stepmom.

Taylor scowled at Arnow. "What's she doing *here?* With you?" Venom dripped from her words. I couldn't blame her. Not after all that had happened.

"She says she'll help me with Price in exchange for me helping her to find some missing people." I glanced at Jamie, Leo, and Mel. "You all might remember her from when she got Josh involved in Tyet affairs and attacked Touray's stronghold with me in it, and set me, Price, and Touray up to get captured by a cohort of Tyet sociopaths."

I didn't mention her holding me at gunpoint in the parking garage. I caught Taylor's questioning look and gave a little shake of my head. At the moment, that detail wasn't important.

"Amazing. She doesn't appear to be insane," Leo said, eyeing the grungy-looking agent.

"Obviously appearances are deceiving," Jamie replied, his eyes slivers of blue glacial ice. "Otherwise she'd not show her face here."

Both of them knew full well all she'd done during Josh's kidnapping.

"She's a psychopath," Taylor said.

"Likely," I agreed. I glanced at Dalton. "She's not the only one."

His mouth twisted downward. I turned away.

"Can we discuss this inside where it's warm?"

I wasn't worried we were being observed or that the FBI was listening in. I could feel the house's security magic tracing through the air and knitting through the ground. For the first time since I could remember, all the systems were fully engaged. The equivalent of DEFCON We-Aren't-Coming-Out-Alive. The density of the security web made every hair on my body prickle. Inside the house would be more insulated against the effects.

"By all means," Mel said, leading the way. She now wore wool pants and low boots, with an indigo sweater.

Instead of taking everybody into the sitting room of the earlier debacle, Mel led us into a salon with white French-style furniture and a variety of purple accents. She called it the Lilac Room. Glass doors led out onto a red brick courtyard with a fire pit and intricately wrought benches, courtesy of Jamie. A Mother's Day gift when he was in college.

Mel stood in the doorway as everyone trouped inside. I halted on the threshold, eyeing the white sofas and chairs. "I know you don't want me in here. I'm covered with dirt and who knows what else."

"Take a shower," Mel said. "I'll arrange some something to eat and coffee."

I hated to delay, but I needed a few minutes. I wanted to clear my head, and I wanted to see if I could reach out to Price through the spirit realm. For that, I needed privacy. I nodded. "I won't be long."

I started to leave, but my gaze hooked on Dalton, who stood broodingly in a corner, arms crossed, and scowling. "What's *he* doing here?"

Mel's forehead crimped and then smoothed. "Sam sent him. He thought Dalton could be useful."

"And you just let him in?"

"They say you should keep your enemies close."

"Is he the enemy?" I wondered. Was my father? He'd tampered with my head, supposedly for my own good. Like Arnow, he thought any means justified the ends. Maybe Dad wasn't *the* enemy right now, but as far as I could tell, he wasn't a friend. I didn't know what he wanted from me, but I knew he wasn't going to let me have any choice about it. Not if the past was anything to go by. Of course, my dad was Mel's husband. I had no idea how she felt about him turning up after all these years. If I were her, I'd be ready to cut his balls off.

Mel's brows rose. "You think we can trust him?"

"Absolutely," I said. "We can trust him not to be trustworthy. He's Dad's minion through and through. On the other hand, Dalton has skills. I can't afford to turn down any help at the moment. Not if I'm going to rescue Price." I paused. "And Touray."

The corners of Mel's mouth turned down in a slight frown. "Gregg Touray? Clay's brother? What happened?" She shook her head as if the question wasn't important. "Whatever has happened, he isn't your responsibility. He's got plenty of soldiers and staff."

Except he was. Embracing Price meant embracing the people he loved. Once free, he'd be off to rescue Gregg with or without me. On top of that, Touray had made himself a decoy tonight so I could escape. I owed him.

I grimaced. "Yeah, Touray is my responsibility."

When had my life turned into a soap opera? Pretty soon I'd find out that an international billionaire-spy-sheikh uncle I never knew about had fathered Price and that Taylor was pregnant with Touray's illegitimate baby, and Dalton was the reincarnation of Jack the Ripper.

Suddenly I wanted a very strong drink. A shower was going to have to do. That, and coffee. Lots and lots of coffee.

Mel's eyes narrowed. "Are you sure? You've spent your whole adult life avoiding the Tyet and the law, living under the radar. Now you're bogging deeper into the Tyet world every day. Is that really what you want?"

I lifted my shoulder. "I love Price. Price loves his brother. I don't really have a choice, do I?"

"You do, but the fact that you can't see it means that you've already chosen. So that's that. Hurry and shower." She put her hands on my shoulders, meeting my gaze. "Understand one thing. You will *not* be doing anything alone. Whatever it takes, we are going to help." It was both a promise and an order.

I almost cried as I pulled her into a tight hug. "Thank you," I whispered. It's not that I had believed she wouldn't help, but I'd expected that she'd put up limits for how far she was willing to go. After all, she worked for the FBI. She was a white hat and I, at best, was gray. Rescuing Price meant breaking laws. I'd expected she'd have lines she wouldn't cross, not for me, and especially not for Price or Touray. But she'd deliberately given me a blank check. No conditions. It was almost more than I could handle without bursting into grateful tears.

She squeezed me, then gently pushed me away. "Go. Time is nobody's friend right now."

I nodded and went to clean up. Whatever my father had done to me, he'd given me an enormous gift in Mel, Taylor, Leo, and Jamie. He might be as reliable as a wet paper bag, but I could depend on them. They'd never let me down.

Chapter 8

MEL KEPT A ROOM for me complete with a variety of clothing and shoes, plus my favorite toiletries. I decided I'd shower before trying to find Price. I held out hope the water would refresh me. I needed all my brain matter to be as awake and energetic as possible. I downed a couple of aspirin before stepping under the hot water. I like it just on this side of blistering. Jets from all sides warmed my muscles and got the blood flowing. I soaped up and washed my hair. I was back out and dressed in under fifteen minutes.

My headache had subsided a little bit, for which I was thankful. I sat on my queen-sized bed and folded my legs. I took several breaths to steady my scrambling pulse and dropped into trace sight.

Everybody has trace. It's a little streamer of colored light that follows you everywhere. You can null it out and it will disappear, but otherwise, any tracer can see where you've been. For most tracers, by the time a few hours have passed, they can no longer see the streamers. Very few can see dead trace—the gray ribbons of the dead. As far as I know, I'm the only one.

I was wrapped in a tangle of ribbons. Mel's dark pink rippling with pearl, Jamie's dark brown spun around with egg yellow, Taylor's scarlet and gold, Leo's emerald, my own silver green. There were more—many more—but I focused on the most important: Price's. A streamer of burgundy streaked with blue.

I reached into the chill of the trace dimension and gripped it, wrapping it around my hand and drawing it back out. The cold went up to my elbow and shoulder, making them ache. That was fast. It had only been a couple of days since I'd been rescued from Percy and been healed. At least my body had been fixed up. I'd stretched my magic to its limits, and I still hadn't fully recovered. Inwardly I shrugged. Bodybuilders stretched themselves all the time. The process built muscle. Runners pushed harder and longer and faster. Their pain was a sign of growth. Well then, I was growing.

I smiled to myself. Always better to look at the bright side. At least it was less depressing than the what-could-go-wrong side.

My smile faded to a frown. Normally I can sense things through a person's trace, especially strong emotions. I could feel nothing from Price. Life energy still flowed through it, but it was like he was on the other side of a wall I couldn't reach through.

I licked my suddenly dry lips, fear for him thrilling through me with new urgency. 'Til now, I hadn't had a chance to really think about what he was going through, what the FBI might be doing to him. I'd been distracted. I couldn't dodge the terror anymore. The helplessness. Only maybe I wasn't helpless. Maybe this would work. Please God, let it work.

When I'd previously travelled along my own trace, I'd sent my power out along its length, following it to Taylor's hangar, where she was being held prisoner by Percy. This time, I wanted to go wherever Price was, which theoretically should be easier, since I didn't have to figure out a spot to stop and get off. I was powerful enough that nulling out his trace couldn't keep me from following it. Which meant if I could get to him, I could pull him out of prison. Providing he could survive crossing through the spirit realm.

Given what he was likely facing from his interrogators, I figured it was worth the risk. To both of us.

Taking a breath, I collected my power. It readily welled up. Maybe I'd been more right than optimistic with the notion that stretching my limits had strengthened me. I kept pulling until I practically vibrated. Holding his trace in both my hands, I sent a massive pulse along its length. This time I couldn't really follow. Not the way I could along my own trace. I was aware that my body stayed on the bed, while my mind fled after the magic I'd launched. I'd had to wait until I was somewhere safe to try this. Otherwise someone could come along and kill me or kidnap me before I could return to my body to fight.

Price had been nulled the moment he left the house. Though his trace faded, I could feel it, an organized thickening, a fluttering of sparks spinning away in a cable of life. I told myself not to be reckless, but urgency made me rush. In the end, I doubted it would have made a difference how fast I went.

One second I was sizzling along his trace, the next I crashed into something solid. My spirit seemed to explode. Or that's what it felt like. Searing pain flared along my shattered self. On the bed, my body snapped backward so hard I launched onto the carpet. I convulsed. I went completely rigid as I arched off the floor. My spirit self fluttered and buzzed like a flock of drunk moths. Electric, razor-winged, venomous moths. I pulled on them, willing them to return to me, but I felt like someone had shaken my head before banging it on concrete. I hung on the edge of unconsciousness, my mind a shredded tangle of yarn bits. I couldn't put two thoughts together.

Instinct saved me. That and sheer bullheaded determination. I *wasn't* going to die or go insane. I *wasn't* going to fail Price. I *wasn't* going to give up. I *wasn't* going to lose this fight.

Gradually I reeled all the bits of myself back, following Price's trace like a lifeline. It was a lifeline. When I could think, I made my body relax, collapsing flat onto the floor. Instantly cramps snatched up clumps of muscle and twisted them viciously all along my back, legs, and shoulders. My knee and ankle joints locked under the onslaught. I must've held them so rigid that relaxing triggered the cramps.

I rolled over onto my stomach and made myself get up. I staggered back into the bathroom and grabbed a cup from the cupboard and drank down several glasses of water. Then I forced myself to stagger in a circle around the room, lifting my arms and stretching as best I could until the cramps eased.

When I was done, I peeled off my sweat-soaked clothing and took another shower. I wanted to cry. I wanted to scream and kick, and if it would have helped, I would have. But I needed to hold my shit together. I hadn't really thought I'd be able to pull him out through his trace, I reminded myself. Still, I had to squeeze my eyes hard to keep the tears from falling.

Mechanically I washed, then left the shower and dried off. I avoided looking at myself in the mirror. If I looked anything like as bad as I felt, I didn't want to know. I also swallowed four ibuprofen for my sore . . . everything. The aspirin from before my shower wasn't going to cut it. Hopefully a few gallons of coffee would take care of my exhaustion.

After I got dressed again, I returned downstairs. Even I could tell I was smelling a whole lot better than earlier. I wore my usual uniform of jeans, tee shirt, hiking boots, and a light jacket. I hadn't taken the time to dry my hair, instead letting it hang loose around my shoulders. In my pocket was a ponytail elastic for later. When I returned to the Lilac Room, Taylor, Jamie, Mel, and Leo clustered at the far end. Dalton listened in from a few feet away. Arnow stood looking out through the French doors, though I didn't doubt she was absorbing every word.

"What's going on?" I asked.

Everyone faced me. I had an urge to run, just like a kid caught shoplifting. I forced myself to stand still. Like it or not, I was in charge of this mess. I'd come up with the outlines of a plan in the shower, but it was risky at best, suicidal at worst. Just another day at the office lately.

"You look like crap," Taylor said. "What did you do?"

That she knew I'd done something was testament to how well she knew me. "I tried to reach Price through his trace. It didn't work."

"You can't go doing that kind of shit on your own," Jamie said, looking pissed.

I wasn't in the mood for brotherly love, at least not the kind that tried to wrap me up in cotton and Bubble Wrap. Before Leo could gang on, I went on the offensive.

"What exactly were you going to do to help me?" I asked. "Not much anybody could do. I decided the reward outweighed the risks and took a shot." I shrugged. "Didn't work. Time to move along to plan B."

"We've been discussing what to do," Mel said, interrupting Jamie's heated response. She motioned me inside and gestured at everyone to sit. She brought me a cup of coffee from a pot on the sideboard, liberally adding sugar and cream.

Manna from heaven. I sipped and about melted.

Mel returned to her seat. "Agent Arnow has kindly filled us in on your activities. Taylor and I have a few things to add. Taylor?"

She pushed her hair behind her ears. "I spent awhile talking to Agent Henry."

I frowned at the reminder and glanced at Arnow. "You said that Agent Dante Wolfe was behind the arrest, but we met Ezra Henry. He said he was in charge of the case."

Arnow nodded. "There's always two agents in charge on a Rice arrest. One takes lead on the interrogation, the other runs the other side of the case—gathering intel, interviewing witness, and pursuing the investigation. Throughout the interrogation period, the two maintain constant communication. There's not a lot of time and it's critical that they work all the angles simultaneously. Often what one learns will enable the other to make inroads and vice versa. Wolfe runs the Diamond City office and wanted to question Price personally, so he assigned Henry to the other side."

The fingers of my empty hand curled into talons. It was all I could do not to rip her face off. She made it sound so civilized—question Price. As if they weren't doing unspeakable things to him. Less than a week ago I'd been in the clutches of Percy Caldwell. He'd burned my arms with cigarettes and later cut off my thumb. It had been one of the most painful and horrifying experiences of my life. I knew to the bottoms of my feet that Price's suffering would be ten thousand times worse.

I felt myself starting to shake with my fury and fear for him. I tamped it down. I needed to be as cold as Arnow if I was going be of any use to Price.

"Okay," I said, looking at Taylor. "What did Agent Henry tell you?"

"Nothing," she said. "He wanted to milk me for information. He kept asking about Price's talent and what I knew about it. He also asked about you and your relationship with Price and Touray."

"So what's—" I started.

"Let me finish," Taylor snapped.

I bit my lips. "Sorry," I said. Sitting on the couch didn't feel the least bit like helping Price, and I itched to *do* something. But first we needed a plan, which meant talking and listening.

Taylor's expression softened. "We'll get him back. He'll be all right."

She met my gaze, her blue eyes determined. That I wouldn't have to suffer what she'd suffered in losing Josh. She knew my fear and love and helplessness. She'd been there. I nodded, and she abruptly came to sit beside me, lacing her fingers in mine and squeezing. I held on to her tightly as she continued.

"As I was saying, he didn't tell me anything, but just before I left, he got called out. That gave me a chance to poke around. We were in an interview room with an adjoining door. I peeked inside the other door and found his real office.

"One whole wall was devoted to Price and Touray, with all kinds of notes and photos and strings connecting them. A picture of Dad was in the middle, with you and me on the side. Above were Mel, Leo, Jamie. Below was your mom. It was a crime-scene picture from when she was murdered. There were more pictures on the side of people I didn't recognize. The weird part was that Dad was in the middle of everything, like he was the one under investigation."

I shot a look at Dalton. "Why is the FBI interested in Dad?"

His shoulders lifted. "I don't know what drew the FBI's attention to your father."

"You're lying." I let go of Taylor and stood up.

His expression hardened. Dalton was a warrior and a soldier. He had his marching orders from my dad, and I could tell he wasn't going to give up information or abandon his duties just because I didn't like him. Not that I planned to give him a choice.

Dalton was wearing a trace null, but no others. Good for me, bad for him. He stared at me as if daring me to make him move. All right, then. Time to throw the dice.

"Leo? Jamie? A bit of help, please?"

Every bit of metal that Dalton carried on him melted away. More flowed over the ground and dripped down from the ceiling. In moments he was encased in a filigree cage made of razor wire. My brothers didn't like him either.

"If you can't be honest with us, then I don't want you part of this." I looked at Mel. "Should we continue this conversation somewhere else?"

She rose. "Absolutely."

She started out of the room, and I followed without another glance at Dalton. Leo put a hand on my shoulder. Jamie slid an arm around my waist and hugged me to his side. He was all solid muscle, which was comforting.

"It's going to be all right," he said against my ear. "We won't let you down."

I nodded, my throat knotting. I wanted to believe we could do this, that we could rescue Price and then Touray. But we were going up against both the FBI and a powerful Tyet syndicate. Did we have even a snowball's chance in hell?

"Stop," Dalton growled from his prison.

I did, but didn't turn around, barely daring to hope. "Why?"

"You need my help."

I turned halfway. "You're a liability. The smartest thing for me to do is leave you here so I don't have to worry about when you'll stab me in the back."

His mouth pulled flat, and his jaw knotted. His eyes seemed to flash with internal light. "Your father sent me to help you. He doesn't want you falling into the wrong hands."

He must have realized that was the wrong thing to say as soon as he said it. Fall into the wrong hands? Like I was some sort of *thing*? I felt heat steaming up from my belly and suffusing my face.

"Your father loves you," Dalton said, changing strategies. "He doesn't want you ending up hurt."

I wanted to believe him. Deep down, I desperately I wanted to think my father loved me and was fighting to keep me from harm. But I didn't. I felt like a piece on a chessboard. If that's all I was, I wasn't going to be a pawn; I was going to be the queen or a knight or a rook. Somebody with power. Somebody who could run the board. Maybe my father loved me in his own peculiar, twisted way. Maybe he thought scrambling my brain and stealing my memories was a sign of that love. Not me.

"My dad," I began, and stopped as emotion boiled up in me. I felt so much and none of it good. "My dad wouldn't know love if it drove over him in a tank."

I was in the doorway when Dalton spoke again.

"He left because it was the only way to protect you back then."

I turned slowly, my whole body flickering with electricity. "What do you know about it?"

"Your father held them off for a long time," he said. "Long enough to build his power base so he could protect you when they decided to come at him again. Now they're back. You're in deep now and you don't even know how far. All of you. You need him, Riley. He needs you, too. More than you know."

"Who? Who's coming after me?"

"The bastard who murdered your mother."

"You aren't going to tell me who that is, are you?"

"I don't know."

"You know how I know you're lying?" I asked. "Your lips are moving. I'm done."

"No, you're not. You need me." With that pronouncement, Dalton's body blurred, and he stepped outside of his cage. He solidified again and gave himself a little shake.

I stared.

"Nice trick," Leo said, but he sounded as shocked as I felt.

"Useful," Jamie added.

Useful was right. I hated to even think it, but we *could* use him. As if he sensed my softening, he faced me, his silver gaze boring into mine. "I know it means little to you, but I swear on all that I hold holy, I will not betray you on this mission to rescue Clayton Price."

I wondered what Dalton might hold holy. My lips twisted. "That's it? After that you'll go back to screwing me over?"

"Would you believe me if I said you could trust me beyond?"

"Not on a bet."

"Then just so far and no more. I give you my word."

Not that his word was worth anything. Still, we could use his skills. "If you try to hurt any of my family, and that includes Price, I will personally kill you. On that, you have *my* word."

"Are you certain you want to trust him?" Jamie said beside me.

"I don't trust him," I said, my gaze pinned to Dalton's. "But this is David versus Godzilla, and if we're going to win this battle, we need all the help we can get. Walking through walls might be what we need to tip the scales in our direction. Plus Dalton is good at what he does."

"So were Adolph Hitler and Joseph Stalin."

"All the same," I said, "he'll be useful."

I turned and walked away, wondering if I'd just pulled the pin from a grenade and stuck it in my pocket. Dalton would betray me, sooner or later. I just hoped I could save Price before the bomb went off.

Chapter 9

MEL RAISED AN eyebrow when Dalton followed us into the dining room.

"He can walk through walls," Leo said in answer to her unspoken question.

I had to smile. I was willing to bet that Dalton hadn't wanted that secret broadcast. Too bad for him.

"A useful talent," Mel said, settling in at the head of the table.

The maids had set up a sideboard with platters of eggs, sausage, bacon, waffles, fruits and cheeses, plus coffee, tea, juice, and milk. Sometimes money was nice. Food magically appeared when you wanted it. My stomach growled. I filled a plate and grabbed a carafe of coffee to set by me on the table. I filled my cup three-quarters full, then poured in cream and stirred in a healthy dose of sugar. I drank the cupful and filled another before diving into my breakfast.

Mel had pointed Arnow and Dalton to the chairs beside her. No doubt she was planning on reading them. Jamie and Leo had bookended each of them, and I sat beside Leo while Taylor sat across from me. For a few minutes, all we did was eat.

"I spoke to several of my contacts," Mel said suddenly.

I glanced up at her. "At the FBI?"

She nodded. "And other places."

"Did they say what the hell they were doing breaking down your door?" Taylor asked.

"Just business," Mel said, her expression shuttered. "I shouldn't be consorting with known criminals. But they thanked me for bringing him out where they could get to him."

That turned me to ice. Because of me, because of dinner with my family, Price had been less protected.

Mel leaned forward, her hands pressed flat against the table. "*None* of this is your fault," she said.

"Touray wouldn't have let this happen," I said, guilt pressing hard on my lungs.

"But he did. He knew where you were going, did he not?" Before I could answer, she continued, driving her point home. "Unless Price stayed entirely out of sight and under the radar, he was going to be taken. It was only a matter of time. Everything I've learned about him convinces me he would not be content to hide, even if he knew the FBI was hunting him. Am I correct?"

I had to nod. That was true. Price was determined to live his life, not just exist. That meant doing dangerous things like going out in public. Meeting his girlfriend's family. Mel wasn't quite done.

"Do you blame yourself for Touray's abduction?" she asked, sitting straight and lifting an auburn brow.

"No, of course not. I couldn't keep him from running into the middle of that wreck, or Morrell from chasing us down."

"But you were in the car. If not for you, he wouldn't have been on that road at that time."

I snorted. "Morrell's people herded us where they wanted us to go. They probably had several other traps laid in case we didn't go the right way. Anyhow, whether I was there or not, he'd have gone to help the accident victims and been taken."

"How is that different from Price?"

Because he'd been here for me and I should have protected him somehow. I wanted to say it, but Mel's expression wouldn't let me. She required honesty, and the truth was I was being ridiculous. Because whether he was driving across town or going to the hardware store, Price was going to be arrested. Now that we'd learned the FBI had been watching him since childhood, it clearly had only been a matter of time. I finally nodded when Mel's gaze continued to skewer me and it dawned on me that we weren't moving on with a rescue plan until I acknowledged the truth.

"Good," she said. "Now that that is settled, we have one more thing to get out into the open." Her gaze gathered in everybody at the table. "Be aware that aside from the possibility of death, the other likely consequences from this mission are that each of you will become fugitives. Your businesses may be forfeited, or at the very least, you won't be able to return to them without getting arrested. Nor will you be able to freely associate with friends as they may become targets, or they may turn you in. Your lives, in a nutshell, will be turned inside out. If you are unwilling to accept that, you should go now. None of us will think less of you." She looked at Taylor, Leo, Jamie, and me. Arnow was already committed on account of needing me, and Dalton's life wouldn't hardly change, unless he got killed. Something I would be willing to take care of for him.

"I'm in," Leo said, not skipping a beat.

Jamie nodded. "Me, too."

"Are you sure?" I asked, guilt pecking at me again. "You could lose everything for a man—"

"Shut up," Taylor said. "We're all helping. Get used to it."

I shook my head. "The Rice Act—"

"Didn't she tell you to shut up?" Jamie asked.

"But they could—"

"That's enough," Mel said with a quenching look at Leo as he threw his balled-up napkin at me. "We've all decided, then. Now, there's a lot to do and little time. We need a plan and to get started implementing it. How are we going to rescue Price from the interrogation center?"

I basked in the warm and fuzzies for a moment, promising my eyes I would poke them out of my head if they let one tear fall. We all started tossing out questions and ideas. The discussion went this way and that as we came up with ideas and discarded them, hashing out the details of what we actually could do.

It was decided that Arnow and Mel would use their FBI credentials to get inside the building before the rest of us broke in.

"Can you get all the way in to where they're holding Price?" I asked.

"I think so. My clearance should be enough." She glanced at Arnow, who shrugged.

"Wolfe will be over the moon to have you—not only as a potential witness, but you're the da Vinci of readers. He'll be kissing my feet for bringing you in."

"Once you're inside, Jamie and I should be able to pinpoint your location. We'll insert some metal into your shoes to make sure. That will help us find Price quickly," Leo said. "That is, once you null out the building's magic-dampening security," he said to me.

"I'll need to fetch some nulls from home," I said, thinking of what I wanted to use.

Taylor scratched out notes on a pad of paper, creating a time line and a list of supplies.

"How do you plan to get inside the building?" Dalton asked. He'd mostly kept quiet up to this point, only offering opinions on the efficacy of various plans. "I can obtain explosives."

Jamie nodded. "We might need them if we can't open a hole in the wall. Depends on what it's made of. Too much concrete and stone and Leo and I won't be able to do much."

I'd seen them do pretty miraculous things using their metal talents, not the least of which was helping me build my house out in the abandoned Karnickey Burrows. But I knew from past experiments that creating a hole in a wall was no easy task. Walls didn't like holes, and they didn't like alterations. There was a whole lot of physics and science about that that I didn't bother to try to understand, but the upshot was that having backup explosives was smart.

"We'll need a way to get up close without being seen," I said. "A tunnel maybe. Think you two can find one?" I was proud of the way my voice didn't shake, nor did I vomit up what I'd managed to eat. I had claustrophobia. Being underground was almost a fate worse than death. Yet it always seemed necessary, whether because I had to ride the subway, or because I needed a secret way into an FBI installation. Maybe I should get therapy to get over it. Repeated exposure sure wasn't helping.

"Shouldn't be too hard," Jamie said. "We've both done a lot of exploring in the area."

Mel had produced a map and pinpointed the installation on it. I'd been startled.

"I thought that was a research facility for that big seed company—the one in the news last year for developing rice that needs a third of the water."

"Marchont. That's the cover. The FBI certainly doesn't want to advertise itself. For certain considerations, Marchont allows the use of its name and record. Rest assured, however, it is an FBI compound."

"There are some good possibilities in the area," Jamie said and pointed out where he thought tunnels were.

"The entrance has to be somewhere that our vehicles won't get discovered, and that will leave us escape routes off the mountain," I said.

"I want to be able to land a 'copter up there," Taylor added. At my glance, she explained. "It's a faster escape and we can get a lot farther away without anyone tracking us."

I shook my head. "They'll hear and see us up there and get suspicious."

"I've got this covered," Taylor said. "Don't worry."

I hesitated and glanced at Mel. She was watching me, waiting for me to decide what I wanted. She'd been doing that since we started planning, I realized. For better or worse, they'd all let me take charge. I thought of Touray. *My monkeys, my circus.* Dear God, I wasn't ready. I wasn't good enough for them to count on me. Was I? I took a slow breath and let it out, a heavy weight settling on me. Until recently—until Price had come into my life—I'd mostly worked alone, responsible only for myself. I'd liked it that way because the only one I ever could hurt was myself. Everybody's got to grow up. Like it or not, Price and Touray had no one else but me to help them. Me and my family and Arnow and Dalton. Together we could do this. We were talented, strong, and smart.

I nodded at Taylor. "We'll need to camouflage all the vehicles," I said, my voice turning slightly gruff with emotion.

"We'll handle that for the wheels," Leo said. "Have you got the helicopter covered?" he asked Taylor.

"Five by five," she said, military-speak for *perfection*.

We kept talking, hashing out as many variables as we could. Jamie and Leo would take the morning to locate a passage for us. Luckily, the entire mountain was riddled with old mine shafts and caves, and they had the ability to increase the size of passages, and even sometimes make new ones, using their metal work. It all depended on the flaws in the rock they were working with, the amount of metal permeating the area, and how much time they had.

In the meantime, Dalton would gather his supplies. Taylor and I would fetch nulls from my place and go to her hangar for a helicopter. Once Jamie and Leo had a location, they'd send us the coordinates. Mel and Arnow would arrange to see Price.

"You're sure they'll let you?" I asked.

"Your mom is a rock star," Arnow said. "No one would turn down her services. Not even with her connection to Price," she added, correctly reading my doubt.

"What about our bodyguard teams?" Taylor said in the lull that followed. "Could we use them?"

Dammit. I'd forgotten to call Mason and tell him I was okay.

"More of us won't be useful," Dalton said. "Not for a stealth incursion."

"We're hardly going to be stealthy," Taylor argued. "Once Riley sucks the magic out of the place and Leo and Jamie start doing their thing, the FBI will be coming after us. They're going to have a lot of security personnel."

"He's right," I said, hating to agree with Dalton. "Too many of us driving up into the area might put them on alert. If all goes well, Jamie and Leo will be able to lock the place down and trap everybody where they are. That will limit how many people we'll run into. Since they ought to be able to disable FBI weaponry, we'll have the advantage there."

After a moment, Taylor nodded. "Maybe we can have the bodyguards set up some kind of diversion."

"How?"

"If the agents at the facility call for reinforcements from Diamond City, we want to delay them as much as possible. Maybe Mason and Pia can come up with a plan."

"Good idea. Call them," I said.

Taylor stepped out of the room, while the rest of us continued our discussion. She returned about ten minutes later.

"They'll take care of it," she reported.

"What will they do?" asked Jamie.

She shrugged. "They're working on a plan. They said to tell us all good luck."

"Did they know anything about Touray?" I asked.

"Nothing more than that Savannah Morrell has him. They've been trying to figure out a way to get him back, but it sounds like things are in chaos with both Touray and Price gone. They said—" She broke off.

"What?"

"They said if you want to take the wheel of the organization, they'd back you."

I goggled. "Me?"

Taylor shrugged. "I guess Touray's generals are having a pissing match. Pia and Mason figure Morrell or another organization might take a run at Touray's business at any moment." She hesitated. "People would die."

I rubbed a hand over my head. Me? Run a fucking Tyet? The idea would have been belly-busting funny if it hadn't been about to come true. I'd have said it was my worst nightmare, but even I hadn't dreamed up something that insane. "Christ."

"One thing at a time," Mel said crisply. "First we go after Price. Once we retrieve him, he can step up into his brother's place."

She didn't say what would happen if we didn't get him back, or if he was in no shape to take on the job. I didn't let myself wander down that horrific road either. He was going to be fine. Period. Over and out.

IT WAS FOUR IN the morning before Mel chased us all off to sleep. She held me back as the others departed—Jamie, Leo, Arnow, and Dalton out the front door, Taylor up the stairs.

"One more thing," Mel said, shutting the door for privacy. "First, I want to say how proud of you I am."

"Me?" I almost squeaked.

She smiled. "You. In the past couple of months you've really grown. Matured. You've never backed down from trouble, but this time you're facing it in a way you never have before. Carefully and thoughtfully."

"I think you just said that I have had a habit of going off half-cocked," I said, scrunching my nose.

She smiled, giving me a little shrug. "You are smart and have a good heart, but too often you don't think through your decisions. You also have a habit of doing things on your own. I'm pleased you finally understand you're not alone, and that this family stands together."

I swallowed, confessing my fear. "What if something happens to one of you? Because I dragged you into—"

"Stop." She put a finger over my lips. "Did you put your life on the line for Josh?"

I nodded.

"How would you have felt if you didn't try and Josh ended up a Sparkle-Dust wraith or dead?"

She didn't let me answer.

"Nothing could have stopped you. You had to try. All of us do. Because we love one another and we wouldn't be able to bear letting each other down. If anything happens to one of us, remember that and don't blame yourself. Each of us are doing this because we want to."

Emotion knotted in my throat, and I hugged her. I wanted to tell her how much I loved her, how much she meant to me, how grateful I was to her for always being there, like a rock under my feet. I couldn't find the words.

She hugged me back. "I know," she said against my ear. "I love you, too."

That's the nice thing about Mel being a reader. She always knew how I felt.

Chapter 10

I DIDN'T THINK I'd sleep, but I must've have passed out almost immediately. For a while I slept heavily. Once the worst of my exhaustion was gone, I started having nightmares of Price reaching out to me, begging for help. I tried to grab hold of him, but I couldn't. He kept calling my name, and his face broke into pieces like a bad Picasso painting. Then the nightmare started all over.

Taylor woke me. The overhead light made me blink as it came on, and she shook my shoulder.

"Up and at 'em," she said.

I groaned and sat up. The blankets were knotted around my legs, and I'd knocked the pillows to the floor. My eyelids felt sticky and dry when I tried to blink. My entire body ached.

"Here. This will help," Taylor said, offering me a cup of coffee. She'd mixed in a healthy dose of cream and sugar.

I sipped, closing my eyes as the nectar of the gods warmed my insides. "I needed that." I glanced at my curtained windows as the coffee got the blood circulating to my brain. "What time is it?"

Taylor returned, handing me a glass of water and aspirin. "It's just about three. Just got the coordinates from Jamie. Get dressed, we'll eat, and then be on our way."

Urgency zinged through me like an electric charge. My nightmare spun through my head. What had happened to Price in those hours? I must have looked as scared as I felt. Taylor sat down and put her arm around me, saying nothing. Stillness wrapped her in quiet folds. It wasn't calmness. Everything about her radiated coiled readiness, but overlaid with a shell of steady patience. This is what made her a good pilot, I realized. She kept a cool head. Not always. Not when the love of her life had been brutally kidnapped. Now she was steady as a rock.

I leaned into her, gathering myself, pushing away my fear. The best thing to do was to get moving. I pulled away and got up, heading for the bathroom to pee and wash my face. When I returned, I pulled on my clothes laced on a pair of boots.

On top of the dresser was the gun Touray had given me. I pushed it into my rear waistband. I stashed my phone in my front pocket and turned back to Taylor. She was wearing tactical gear—black pants and a long-sleeved shirt, both with pockets and fittings for optimal movement, storage, and protection. She'd braided her hair tight to her head. Leather boots completed her outfit. All of her clothing looked creased and well-used. Familiar.

I could hardly believe this woman was the same sister who kept a house that could grace the pages of *House Beautiful*. Ordinarily she dressed in designer clothes and shuddered when a nail broke. How could both sides of her coexist in the same body? I'd have thought she'd explode, like mixing vinegar and baking soda. Or maybe marrying a Hatfield to a McCoy.

"What?" she asked when she caught me staring at her.

"I just haven't seen this side of you," I said. "We never saw any pictures from your war years, and you don't talk about it. When you do, you don't say much."

She rolled her eyes. "I like nice stuff. And a good mani-pedi. Sue me. Besides, it helps with cultivating the Diamond City upper crust. They don't want a foul-mouthed, ex-private-military pilot with all the manners of a goat stinking up their excursions. They want class. I give it to them. They don't care that I can dig around in an engine and fix it; they don't care that I can do a strafing run at a hundred feet. They want Grace Kelly touring them around in the sky. For that, they pay through the nose. As for the war stories—" She shrugged, a haunted look flickering over her face. "Not much to tell."

That was a lie, and we both knew it. But if she didn't want to talk about it, I wasn't going to push.

"I hate that you're going to lose your business."

"I was getting bored, anyway."

"Right."

"You're more important to me than any business. End of discussion."

Emotion welled up in me. For all that my dad had fucked with my mind, for all that I didn't know if anything about my childhood was true, one thing was certain: my sister and my adopted family loved me. Far more than was reasonable, even.

I reached out and gripped her hand and let it go. It wasn't much of a thank-you, but for the moment, it was the best I could do.

We stopped in the dining room to have an early dinner of roast beef, baked potatoes, roasted vegetables, Waldorf salad, and cherry pie. And coffee. I ate like a starving coyote. I didn't know how long it would be before I got my next meal, and the food was delicious. Mel didn't join us.

When I asked, Taylor explained she'd been taking care of some personal business. I translated that to mean Mel was preparing not to be able to return home. Suddenly the food in my stomach hardened into rock. I pushed back, downing the rest of my cooled coffee and standing.

"Ready?"

"I've just been waiting on you to stop shoveling food," Taylor said. "You eat like a horse."

"You weren't exactly picking at your meal," I pointed out.

"Still finished faster than you."

"Didn't know it was a race," I muttered as we made our way into Mel's basement. One of them, anyhow. From there we went into the wine cellar and through a hidden door in the back. It was keyed to members of the family. My dad, too, I thought, since he'd had to have used one of the doors in his escape. The idea that he could come and go at will irritated me.

"Has he been in the house before? Since he left ten years ago? Has he been spying on us?" I wondered aloud.

"I doubt he cared enough for that," Taylor said, not having to ask who *he* was.

"He sure as hell seems to care now."

"About you, maybe. The rest of us can suck eggs."

I could hear the brittleness beneath the scorn in her voice. "You're better off."

"I know."

"I'm sorry."

"Not your fault. He's fucked up. Never should have been allowed to have kids."

Since I had nothing to add to that, I let the subject drop.

On the other side of the wine cellar, we went through a long straight tunnel. Lights flickered alive as we opened the door. The walls were rough, but it was dry. The mineral smell of being underground made me cringe. I'd managed to get through going down into the basement without hyperventilating. The wine cellar was still big enough that I didn't break out in hives. But now the walls closed in. My skin went cold, and tremors ran through my muscles. I clamped my teeth tight together to keep them from chattering and wrapped my arms around my stomach. My shoulder scraped against stone, and I flinched away, only to stumble into the opposite wall. I clenched all of my muscles and then forced them to relax, breathing deeply.

"Stupid, stupid fear," I muttered as I managed to start walking again.

"Haven't gotten over that yet?" Taylor asked cheerfully, striding along ahead of me. "Have you tried counseling? I wonder where it comes from, anyhow," she said.

"If, by counseling, you mean stupidly going into small places with great regularity, then yes, I'm counseling the hell out of myself. It doesn't come from anywhere. It's a phobia. It just is."

She gave a little shrug. "Sure."

"What? You think something caused it?"

"Maybe."

I frowned. "Like Dad?"

"Who knows?"

It sounded ridiculous, but my father had deliberately made me paranoid about trusting people. He'd gone so far that his little tinkerings in my head had sent me rocketing into a sort of fugue state when I tried to reveal that I'd discovered I could touch the trace realm. I'd gone so deep inside myself I might never have come out if not for my dreamer friend Cass fishing me back up. So it was entirely possible my claustrophobia *was* a special gift from him.

"God, I'm so tired of wondering where I leave off and Dad begins," I said. "How am I supposed to know what's real and what's not anymore?"

Taylor didn't answer. There was something about the quality of her silence that sent little prickles of worry through me. I grabbed her arm and turned her to face me. "What's up?"

She licked her lower lip and her eyelids dropped to hood her expression. "Reality is overrated."

My frown deepened. "What does that mean?"

She grimaced and pulled away. "It means that you aren't the only one having trouble figuring out where reality stops and everything else begins."

That's when I realized what she was talking about. My stomach dropped. "Sparkle Dust? But Cass fixed what it did to you. You're clear of it, aren't you?"

"She did what she could."

"You haven't started using, have you?" The claustrophobia panic was nothing compared to the sudden terror of Taylor using Sparkle Dust, of thinking her fading into a wraith. Relief made my knees sag when she shook her head.

"I'm not using. I want to, but I'm not." She made a little face. "I'm fine, really. I've had some weird dreams and nightmares, that's all. Stuff that feels really real, you know? When you talked about trouble separating what's real from what's imagined, it hit me. But I'm good. Now, let's go. Your boyfriend's waiting."

The mention of Price got me moving again. I wanted to ask more, but

Taylor just waved away my questions.

We reached the end of the corridor. It simply stopped. While I made myself stand still and wait for her, Taylor crouched next to the left wall and ran her fingers upward until she found the spot she was looking for. It looked like an outcropping, but her hand passed through easily. Another bit of magic keyed to family blood. She tapped out a sequence with her fingers, then drew back. We waited a few seconds, and then the wall melted away. We stepped across into the small chamber beyond. I shuddered as the wall reformed solidly behind us.

"Only way out is through," Taylor said, but sounded more sympathetic. "Can I help you?"

I shook my head, my teeth clamped together.

Before us sat a small car on rails that ribboned away into darkness. It was cigar shaped with single padded bucket seats. Both ends had levers, though the rear set controlled the speed and braking, depending on which direction the cart was running. All in all, it resembled a Disney ride. If Leo and Jamie built Disney rides.

Taylor climbed into the rear seat. I took the one in the front. There were five seats in total. I buckled the seat belt and gripped the arms tightly as I pushed myself back as hard as I could. The tunnel ahead was black. Taylor turned on the bright headlights. There were five. A string of small lights sprang to life along the top edge of the car, with more underneath the canopy to light the interior.

"Ready?" Taylor called. She didn't wait for an answer. Instead, she released the brake. We shot forward like a bullet.

I gasped, my stomach twisting. We sped up a slight grade, and then the tracks plunged downward along a corkscrew pathway, taking us from the Uptown level all the way to the Downtown level in a matter of a few seconds. The rails and wheels were spelled, so there was no danger of jumping the tracks. Taylor would have done a precheck of the alert system that would have warned of any debris on the tracks or any other obstacles.

Just below the Midtown shelf, we flattened into a long wide curve without slowing down. I knew we were nearing my house when the car abruptly hooked and turned back, then dropped down a steep slide before rising up an even higher hill. Luckily, magic made sure we made it to the top, just as magic would guarantee an equally swift return back to Mel's. Not that we were going back there.

My heart pounded as we came to a rest in a chamber nearly identical to that we'd just left. Taylor set the brake and shut down the lights. I unbuckled and hopped out, then leaned against the side of the car as the ground shifted and rolled beneath me. I breathed deeply, trying to calm my pounding heart. I'd sweated enough to soak my tee shirt beneath my hoodie. Thank goodness for deodorant. I never used the cigar car unless I had to, which was more often than not, since traveling the subway up to Mel's would have been just as bad. Worse, really, since I was underground longer.

"Come on. We're wasting time."

Taylor hooked me under my right arm and pushed me to the wall. She opened the passage and closed it again. On the other side was a set of steep rock stairs leading straight up. I grabbed the rail and went ahead. The passage was tight. I kept my eyes on the steps and tried not to notice how low the ceiling was or how the walls leaned inward.

At the top, I fumbled with the lock and opened it. The wall pivoted with part of the floor. The other side was my basement. Taylor swung the door back around, securing it behind us.

"Nice," she said, glancing around. Mostly the place was dusty. I kept a collection of potential null-making material on the racks down the opposite wall. Other than that, it was bare. "Love the decorations."

"It's a basement," I said.

"I'm sure the upstairs is much better."

By her standards, it wasn't. I didn't say so. No point in stating the obvious.

The basement wasn't much more than a ten-by-ten space, and given how little I liked being underground and in tight spaces, Taylor ought to have been surprised that I used it for anything at all. I hurried up the steps and escaped into my kitchen, heaving a huge sigh as I did.

My house, if you could call it that, had been custom built for me by Leo and Jamie and some good old-fashioned muscle.

A couple hundred years ago, a fellow by the name of Frank Karnickey had located an incredibly lucrative diamond mine in a narrow snaking canyon on the north side of the Downtown shelf. He'd built a compound to protect it. The area rapidly expanded into a warren of ramshackle buildings for his miners and their families, which came to be known as the Karnickey Burrows. With the towering trees on the heights and the steep walls of the canyon, it had been a gloomy place, but inside the buildings it was comfortable and cozy enough, especially since Karnickey provided the housing for free.

Then Karnickey had fallen in love. The woman had been remarkable in her own right. Lily Enwright James had been cut off by her family in the East and had come to Diamond City with a hundred dollars and a lot of chutzpah. She'd managed to open a general store and rapidly parlayed that into half a dozen stores. She bought a hotel, and then two, and fairly quickly she had her own little empire. She'd been beautiful, with glossy dark hair, a round face, and a lot of swagger. It's no wonder Karnickey had fallen in love with her. He was famous for writing poetry to her and publicly begging her to marry him. But he had competition.

His main rival for Lily's affections was Alan Madstrom. Like Karnickey, he'd found a rich diamond mine. Where Karnickey was all rough edges and bullheaded charm, Madstrom was snake-smooth elegance. He liked that Lily came from wealthy breeding, with polished manners and cultured style. She was his ticket into a level of society he couldn't achieve by himself, and he liked showing her off. Except Lily refused to marry either man. She wasn't going to give up her independence. Instead, she let Madstrom and Karnickey vie for her affections, promising she'd become the winner's exclusive mistress.

It became quite a spectacle, with each man trying to outmaneuver the other. It was all the papers had talked about. Eventually, Karnickey started looking like the likely winner. That's when Madstrom decided to play dirty. He waited until a January storm had snowed Diamond City in. Then he released a tinkered virus into the Burrows. Just about everybody died within a week. After the bodies were cleared out, the place was abandoned. Supposedly it was cursed. That made it a perfect location for my home.

Using all the scrap metal left in the Burrows, plus a whole lot more we'd hauled in, Leo and Jamie had built the house. It was a marvel. The outer walls were made of all sizes of stone mortared together with steel. It had an open plan, largely because I lived alone and didn't like being closed in. A massive circular fireplace, enclosed by a grill and surrounded by a knee-high stone hearth, rose up through the middle of the house. The grill was five feet tall, and above that the chimney was made of more metal-bound stone.

On one side of it was a living area. The furniture consisted mostly of giant cushions, with a couple of mosaic-topped tables. The kitchen was on the other side. It was much bigger than I'd ever need. I barely had enough dishes and pots to fill a couple of the cupboards, and as far as food went, I had some jelly in the fridge along with some sodas and water, and some peanut butter, ramen, and microwave popcorn on a shelf. I ate most of my meals at the Diamond City Diner, owned by my best friend, Patti, and her business partner, Ben.

Off to the side, between the kitchen and living area and under the spiraling staircase, was a sliding wood door. The wide steps beyond led into a sunken bathroom with a toilet, a natural hot tub, and a massive shower. The pool was filled by an underground spring my brothers had managed to divert and then I'd heated with a spell I'd bought. A round roof with two skylights capped the space. I'd set candles into just about every rocky niche. Broad doors of mullioned glass slid apart onto a little courtyard, maybe ten or fifteen feet wide. Tumbled boulders made a wall around the little space. It was neck deep in snow at the moment, but in the summer, I put out birdfeed next to the little trickling waterfall and shallow pool. It was filled by the same spring that fed my hot tub. I'd leave the doors open and sit in my tub to watch the birds or at night I'd look at the stars.

Upstairs was my bedroom. Like downstairs, it was sparsely furnished, with a dresser, a nightstand, and a low-sitting platform bed piled with a bunch of brightly colored pillows and a down coverlet. Thick wool rugs covered the smooth stone floor. On the other side of the chimney was my work area. Tables and shelves lined the walls. They contained bins full of all sorts of things I could use to make nulls. Most of those appeared innocuous. They were easier to hide in plain sight. On the end were two enormous cabinets, each five feet wide and two feet deep. One contained finished nulls, and the other was packed with other magic spells I'd collected over the years. My kitchen pantry was empty, but I tried to keep my magic pantry well stocked.

Up against the chimney were three wood half barrels I'd picked up at a garden store. I'd attached wheels to the bottoms to make it easier to maneuver the heavy contents within. The first held a giant hunk of silver sheen obsidian. It weighed at least two hundred pounds. The second half barrel contained a green cement toad statue, about four feet tall. It had a silly grin on its face and oversized bug eyes. A solid glass ball about four feet in diameter perched on top of the last half barrel. It was lilac colored and not entirely round. I didn't care. It suited my purpose well.

All three were nulls. I'd spent years adding to their power. Each pulsed with captured magic. They weren't particularly useful. It wasn't like I could haul them out of here very easily. On the other hand, activating them would wreak havoc with the magic in Diamond City. Once I'd learned the knack of creating a spell sink that would absorb nulled magic and recycle it to reinforce the nulling spell, I'd made sure each of these nulls would do the same. Where binders suppressed all magic in a vicinity, nulls absorbed the active magic like big sponges. When the binders lifted, the magic would return, though it often got shorted out. Binders tended to have that effect. Nulls simply killed the spells until they got recharged.

Activating my three big ones could possibly suck the magic out of the entire city. At least, in theory. They could also overload and burn out, in which case my house and the Karnickey Burrows would be leveled. Not that I planned to set them off. I've never had any intention of using them. They're more vanity spells than anything else. I'd wanted to see just how powerful I could make them. Plus I could siphon power off if I needed it. If I'd had had time, I would have recharged my tattoo nulls, but I didn't.

The house was comfortably warm, heated as it was by magic. I liked a good fire, but I also liked to come home to warmth, and most of the time I wasn't around to stoke the fire. I ran up the stairs, leaving Taylor to trail behind. By the time she joined me, I was digging in my closet for an empty backpack. I had several, since I used them with frequency and I didn't like having to unpack every time I wanted to shift jobs.

I went to my workroom and opened my null cupboard. I grabbed what I needed before moving to the other cupboard. These were spells that I'd purchased. Some unlocked doors, others created faraway sounds to distract guards, some deflected bullets, and so on. All the sorts of things that might be useful for a tracer on the job. I grabbed a few things that might prove useful and stuffed them in with the nulls. I handed Taylor the heavy pack and returned to my closet. I pulled off my boots and peeled off my socks. I put on light wicking socks followed by a pair of thick wool ones. I donned a different, more comfortable pair of boots, and changed my sweaty shirt. Not that there was much point. We'd be traveling underground again. Next, I grabbed a jacket. It was thin and light, but would keep me warm down to fifty below zero. Finally, I grabbed gloves, a fleece balaclava, and pulled a couple of hand warmers off the shelf and stuck them in my pocket. They might come in handy.

Price didn't have anything to wear. He'd been taken without a coat. I turned helplessly in a circle as I examined my closet. I didn't have anything big enough for him to wear. Besides, we needed to travel light and move quickly. An extra coat might get in the way. Hopefully we'd find something on the premises.

"Are you ready?" Taylor called.

I stepped out into the bedroom. "I feel like I'm forgetting something."

"You've got the nulls?"

I nodded.

"That's what we came for. Let's go. We're burning daylight."

We went back downstairs, but instead of going into the basement, we went out through my front door. It opened under a massive slab of basalt that leaned up against the wall of my house, adding to the ruined look. From the outside, my place looked like a pile of rocks. The original buildings had been several stories tall and linked with burrowing hallways and underground tunnels. Leo and Jamie had used the old ruins to disguise my place. I could have all the lights on inside, and nobody down on the road would see. The entire Burrows was shielded with turn-away spells and briar magic that guaranteed no one could just wander in—if its status as a cursed place didn't keep them away.

Since our next destination was Taylor's hangar, the number four exit was the quickest. I led the way. We wove through what appeared to be piles of rubble. They were strategically placed and shored up with steel. After about seventy feet, we came to a set of narrow steps leading downward. I sucked in a deep breath and forced myself to go down, fingers gripping tight on my backpack. As I reached the bottom, lights flickered to life.

Another set of tracks and another cigar car waited for us. As I lowered myself into my seat and settled my backpack between my feet, I accidentally let myself notice how low the ceiling was. Instant panic. I gripped the bars on the inside of the car and bent my head down. Taylor put us into gear. As I'd predicted, by the time we stopped, I'd sweated through my shirt yet again.

Escape tunnel four let out underneath the Albert Street subway stop in Downtown. A ladder led up to the platform level through a pipe. We climbed up and into our bolt-hole, with me leading the way. I'm pretty sure that was so Taylor could prod me from behind if I froze up. I climbed on autopilot, my cramped fingers hooking over the rails.

At the top, I released the trapdoor and flipped it back. Dim lights glowed inside the cramped space, barely bigger than the size of a bathroom. One wall had shelves with a variety of emergency supplies. Taylor climbed out behind me and lowered the trapdoor back into place. It locked automatically.

I grabbed a bottle of water and drank from it, feeling parched. Panic did that to me.

"Ready?"

I nodded. Taylor opened the door a crack and looked out. A second later she swung it wide and stepped outside. I followed, shutting the door behind me. We stood inside a niche in the subway tunnel. The air was cool and smelled of minerals with a hint oil. From the outside, the door we'd come through looked like solid rock.

We went right, guided by the light from the Albert Street platform. Gravel crunched under our feet. Nobody noticed us emerge from the tunnel. I opened the maintenance door under the platform. We stooped and stepped inside a narrow hallway. The walls and ceiling were thick with conduits. We went down to the end and up the stairs, coming out at a nondescript door leading out onto the platform. We slipped out and joined the small crowd waiting for the next train. They ran every thirteen minutes.

Five minutes later the train arrived, and we boarded, taking seats near the back of the car. Taylor and I hadn't spoken. I kept my head down, my eyes closed, and concentrated on breathing. When the speaker announced the Porter Creek station, I opened my eyes and stood. Just a few more minutes, and we'd be clear of the underground.

Our stop was only ten blocks from the hangar. The wind was blowing, and the cold slapped my face. I pulled my balaclava over my head and stuck my hands into my pockets. The Kensington Bank said it was five below zero. The windchill dropped the temperature another five or ten degrees. The weatherman had promised a storm sometime in the next couple of days.

The sidewalks had been cleared, but patches of thick ice made the going slower than I liked. Taylor looped her arm through mine so that we could balance each other, and our speed increased.

We'd gone two blocks when a limo slid across the intersection in front of us, blocking our path. Dad rolled down the rear window. "I'd like to speak with you. Let me drive you to the hangar. It will be faster."

I tossed him a glance but didn't stop. Neither did Taylor. "No, thanks. We're more likely to get there walking," I said.

He winced, and the expression was achingly familiar. So many times he'd made that face. It was self-deprecating and apologetic. And probably fake as hell.

"Whatever you want can wait," I said. Forever, if it was up to me, but I didn't think it was.

"Feel free to go to hell in the meantime," Taylor added.

He frowned, the limo coasting along beside us.

"Very well. I will walk with you."

He opened the door and climbed out, buttoning his knee-length cashmere coat before setting a fedora on his head. He looked like a 1940s detective. A woman came after, and from the other side of the limo stepped a bald-headed giant. Bodyguards. I guess they were worried we might try to kill Dad. Reasonable enough. If looks were anything to go by, Taylor would have gutted him if she could.

The limo pulled away. Dad's two minions split up, the giant up front, the woman behind. He fell in beside us. We walked along in silence for a half block before he spoke.

"You two should not be out without an escort," he said. "It's dangerous."

"You mean it's dangerous for Riley," Taylor said. I was sandwiched between the two of them. "I'm hardly important enough to notice." Bitterness sharpened the edges of her words.

"I'm sure it seems that way," he said.

I could hear Taylor's teeth gritting at that response. I gripped her tighter, wishing Dad would just go back to whatever rock he'd crawled out from under. Dad. I kept thinking of him that way, but he wasn't my dad. Not the one I thought I'd known, and every time I said or thought the word, it felt like a lie. "What name are you going by these days?" I asked. "Not Sam Hollis. There's been no record of him since you vanished."

He nodded. "It was important that no one connect me to you. Any of you," he added.

"So what should we call you?"

That seemed to take him aback. "Brussard," he said at last. "Vernon Brussard."

"Vernon Brussard," I echoed. I wondered how he'd arrived at that, if it had any particular meaning. Then I dismissed my curiosity. Didn't matter. To me it was just a strange name for a stranger. Definitely better than calling him *Dad*.

"All right, Vernon. What do you want?" My forehead scrunched. "How did you find us, anyhow?" Then I rolled my eyes at my own stupidity. "Never mind. Stupid question."

Dalton had reported back to him, of course. I couldn't even pretend to be surprised. Vernon must have been waiting on us, knowing we'd walk past here eventually.

"I have some information that may interest you."

"What's in it for you?" Taylor asked.

He ignored that. "The FBI is not the only party with an interest in your friend, Clayton Price. Others have watched to see if his talent would reawaken."

How many people knew about Price's talent? Apparently he and I were among the few who'd been in the dark.

I shook my head. "I don't get it. What's the big deal? Lots of people have destructive talents."

"That is true, but his may be of particular value."

"Why?"

"It depends on what his talent actually is."

"You're dodging the question."

"I am," he agreed. "But for good reason. You haven't yet encountered his talent. It might be better if you don't have any preconceived notions about it. What I believe it might be is just an educated guess and that based on limited information."

"You know the story of his kidnapping," I said.

He nodded. "I've kept abreast of the case. We make a point of tracking powerful talents when they crop up on the radar. He may prove a powerful weapon. Or he may become an enemy."

"We?" Taylor pounced on the pronoun. "Who is *we?*"

"Interested parties."

"How very vague of you," she said.

"Now isn't the time," he replied.

"That's right. Just like mushrooms. Keep us in the dark and feed us bullshit," I said.

His mouth thinned. Obviously, he didn't find my comment amusing. It did, however, hit the nail on the head, and he knew it.

"I have come out of hiding to tell you all you need to know. All that is *safe* to know," he amended.

I stopped suddenly and faced my father. My heart thudded against my ribs. God, it hurt to look at him. I had loved him so much. But everything I felt, everything I remembered, might all be fiction. Probably was. I think that hurt the worst. I'd practically hero-worshipped him. I now second-guessed every memory. And even if they were all real and true, I knew now that his kind-father routine hid a much darker man, one capable of killing his daughter rather than letting her reveal her secrets. I couldn't reconcile that cold, brutal man with the loving father I remembered.

"So get on with it. Say what you want to say and then leave us alone."

He examined my face, his blue eyes darkening with emotion. It might have been pain, or regret, or maybe he was just hungry. I refused to care.

"Very well. In a nutshell, others are interested in Clayton Price and his talent and they will be coming for him now that the FBI has made a move. They won't want to risk losing him to insanity. You are watched as well, Riley. Soon, someone will come for you, too."

Vernon dug in his pocket and pulled out a brass key. He held it out to me. I didn't take it.

"What's that for?"

"Use it when you need me. I'll send help."

"Or you'll track me wherever I go."

"There's no active magic. You can tell. Look at it."

He was right. It was harmless. For now. "That doesn't mean it does what you say it does."

"True." He dropped the key into my pocket. "Use it or not, it's up to you. But I *will* come to you if you activate it."

I was tempted to throw it back at him, but I didn't. I couldn't even say why. Maybe it was just the residue of how much I'd loved and trusted him. I could always throw it away later.

"Is that all?"

"No. Be careful, Riley. Clayton Price was dangerous before and he's likely to be more so. His experience with the FBI might leave him unstable, or worse."

The idea sent razors spinning through my gut. My lips twisted. "Been there, done that. Thanks to you." I didn't give him a chance to respond. "If that's all you've got, then you can leave now."

He gave a faint shake of his head. "Oh no. We'll never be done. The two of you are my daughters, and whatever you think of me, I will always look after you." A smile softened the harshness of his expression. "You have both grown into strong, exceptional, talented women."

"No thanks to you," Taylor said.

"Of course it's thanks to me," he said. "Without me you wouldn't have the skills, the strength, or the knowledge you do."

"I guess Mom was nothing more than Kleenex," Taylor shot back.

His answering smile sent a chill down my spine. "Mel is and always will be brilliant and brave." Even so, he gave her no credit for raising us.

He turned his head slightly, and it was like a cloud lifted. I suddenly caught a glimpse of the real man. He might look mild-mannered and intellectual, like a college history professor, but beneath that veneer he was terrifying. Worse than Touray, who scared the shit out of me most of the time.

Price's brother was ruthless and brutal, but at least I understood him. He was driven by the need to protect his own. Underneath everything, Touray really cared. But where he was motivated by passion and the urge to protect, this man—Vernon Brussard, the stranger who was my father—was cold-blooded and calculating. To him, people were nothing more than pieces on a chessboard, even his own family. He'd tried to keep my talent from falling into the 'wrong' hands by killing me. In that split second, I saw the merciless savagery hiding behind the smile in his eyes and the jut of his jaw. This man wouldn't hesitate to use me or Taylor. A leopard didn't change his spots. He'd do or say anything to manipulate us. The fact that we were his daughters only cemented his belief that he had a right to use us. He'd made us; we belonged to him to do with as he pleased.

Or so he thought. I wasn't going to let him get away with it. I stepped back. "Stay the hell away from us."

"I don't think so. But I will say good-bye for now. Do be careful." He started to turn away. His limo had pulled up behind him. He looked back over his shoulder.

"While you're in the compound, you should visit section nine. You might find it interesting. Oh, and Riley, should you help Agent Arnow with her problem, be prepared. The stakes are much higher in that game." He touched his fingers to his hat in a little salute and then stepped inside the car. His two minions followed, and a moment later they drove away.

I looked at Taylor. She looked spitting mad. White dents framed her nostrils, and her mouth was a thin white line.

"We should go," I said. The hangar was only another couple of blocks. I started walking, my chest tight. Taylor caught up with me in a few steps.

"Of all the gall," she said. "He thinks he's going to get daddy privileges now that he's decided to return from the dead?"

"It's worse than that."

She frowned at me, clearly expecting a different response. "What do you mean?"

"I mean that he has plans for us."

"What do you mean? What kinds of plans?"

"I don't know, but everything he's done—he's like a farmer planting seeds and waiting for harvest. I think we're getting ripe for his needs."

"That's—" Taylor couldn't find the words. "What needs?"

"Nothing that ends well for us."

She digested that. "It's you he wants."

"Maybe it was a long time ago, but I think he's got his eye on you now, too. And Leo and Jamie and maybe Mel, too. All of you have talents and skills. I'm sure he's got uses for you."

She didn't answer as she considered what I'd said. Finally, as we turned into the driveway and approached the door of the hangar, she glanced at me. "What are you going to do with the key?"

"Keep it."

"Why?"

"Do you remember that fable about the frog and the scorpion? Where the scorpion needs to cross the river and the frog refuses because the scorpion will kill him, and the scorpion argues that that is stupid because if he kills the frog, he'll die too. So the frog gives him a ride and then in the middle of the river, the scorpion stings the frog and they both drown."

"What's that got to do with Dad and the key?"

"As he's dying, the frog asks why he did it. The scorpion says, 'it's in my nature. I can't help it.' Vernon is a scorpion. He's going to use us. It's his nature. We can count on it. It's as predictable as the sun rising in the east. The key will protect his property. Keep us from falling into the wrong hands. So we can trust that when we need him, he'll show up because he doesn't want anybody else to have us."

"I can see that. But you know, just because we want help, it doesn't mean he'll do it in a way that we like. He might rescue us from a burning building, but he'd leave everybody else we care about to cook."

"We won't let that happen," I said.

"How are we going to stop it?"

"We're going to play his game better than he does. And we're going to win."

If only it would be that easy.

Chapter 11

WE MADE THE FLIGHT up to Honigstock Peak without any hitches. It was on the southeast side of Diamond City. Getting there was weirdly silent, with no engine or rotor sounds whatsoever. All I heard was the whistle of the wind around us and the clicks and adjustments as Taylor took care of business. Usually we used headsets just to be able to hear ourselves think.

We had waited until darkness fell, then lifted off. We rose into the sky and shot west across the caldera. On the other side, we'd bank and come around on course. Taylor flew the Eurocraft with a deft touch. She wore a set of goggles that I assumed gave her night vision. I sat in the front seat beside her, watching the lights of Diamond City grow smaller. Heat blasted into the cabin space, fighting the exterior cold as snow began to swirl thick through the air. It was like flying inside of a snow globe.

"I can't believe it's so quiet," I said as we rose higher into the night.

"It's magic tech I commissioned awhile back. I can charge more for the flight tours and I've had movie people wanting to use my service. Got it installed a month or so ago, but I haven't really had a chance to use it. The nice thing is that it doesn't take a lot of power. The spells loop into one another and I only need a recharge every few weeks or so. It cost just about as much as the helicopter did, but it's totally worth it."

"Handy for tonight, anyway."

Taylor grinned. "Ain't it?"

She'd also shut off the helicopter's transponder and slapped a fake registration number over the real number. Even if we were seen, nobody would connect it to Taylor or me or Price.

As we climbed over the western rim of the caldera, the wind buffeted us, and we shimmied and bounced despite Taylor's expert handling of the stick.

As the snow turned blinding, I wondered how we were going to land. I figured GPS would get us to the right coordinates, but that wasn't going to get us safely down to the ground. Steep mountain ground with trees and snow. My foot pressed down on my invisible brakes. I made myself relax. Taylor had flown in wars, and she often flew rescues in the mountains in far worse conditions than this. She knew what she was doing.

I wasn't ready for when we abruptly started to descend after about a half-hour flight. I gasped as we seemed to rocket downward at a steep angle. The silence of the whole thing made it worse.

"Nervous?" Taylor flashed a grin at me. "Don't worry. I've got this." She was in her element.

She leveled off, and we slowed so that we were almost hovering. I could see patches of dark and light below that had to be trees and snow on the mountain. They spread outward and up and down on the left side of the helicopter.

"Bugs Bunny, this is Roadrunner," Taylor said into headset. "Go for coyote action."

Taylor watched the ground below out her window, the helicopter bouncing and swinging on the wind. All of a sudden we started dropping. My stomach rose into my throat, and my hands clenched on the sides of the seat.

We turned and spiraled down a ways, and then we dropped down to land. We jolted and scraped over the landing site, and the helicopter settled at an angle. Taylor began shutting it down, and I heaved a sigh, forcing myself to release my fingers from their death grip on the seat.

"Good flying," I said. "What was that Bugs Bunny business?"

"I had Jamie and Leo set off a couple of flares and drop them in my landing zone near the cave tunnel we're using. The heat was enough to show me where to land." She tapped the sides of her goggles. "Thermal imaging. I can see heat signatures with these."

Just then my door was pulled open. Jamie stood there.

"About time," he said. "Let's go."

I unbuckled my harness and slid out. He steadied me until I found my footing and then guided me across the clearing. Our landing zone was a semiflat shelf surrounded by trees on one side and a steep escarpment on the other. Buried boulders shouldered up through the snow. The helicopter sat slightly tip-tilted, rocking slightly. The skids settled unevenly across rocks and lumpy snow.

Taylor, Leo, and Dalton were busy installing three ground cleats to stabilize the craft. Dalton and Leo each carried one end of the first of three steel rods from where they lay on one side of the clearing. They were five feet long and about four inches in diameter.

Taylor indicated where she wanted it placed, and the rod sank down into the dirt and rock. When only a foot remained, the top flattened and formed two ears. Dalton and Leo fetched another while Taylor fastened down the rope she'd secured to one of the skids. They repeated the process twice more until Taylor was satisfied the Eurocraft wasn't going anywhere.

"I used quick release knots," she said as we pulled our gear out of the helicopter. "But all the same, keep a sharp knife handy in case. The knots might freeze, and if we're in a hurry, I want to be able to lift off quick."

The cave entrance was really a burrow, a couple feet across and less than that high. More than a little aware that everyone was watching me, I crawled inside, pushing my backpack ahead of me. No one could see my stomach clenching so hard it hurt, or the way my knees shook, or the sweat that broke out all over my body.

Inside, a covered lantern provided a light. Several duffel bags sat in a heap on one side of the narrow cavern. It was about eight feet across and went about twenty feet or so before darkness swallowed it. It smelled musty and earthy. Animal bones and bits of fur and feathers covered the floor, along with a thick mat of leaves and grass. If I had to guess, this was a bear house. I wondered where the residents were. Hopefully somewhere else and fast asleep.

"How did you get all this stuff in through that hole?" I asked.

"We didn't. We parked our vehicles a few miles away and came down a branch of this tunnel. Gives us two ways out in case we need it," Leo said.

Jamie crawled through last, dusting himself off. "I let Mel know we're on our way. We've got an hour before she and Agent Arnow go in."

"Better hurry, then," Leo said.

Dalton remained weirdly quiet, like a vulture watching us. I eyed him. I wondered if he knew Vernon had intercepted Taylor and me. I wondered just how much Dalton new about Vernon and his plans. One thing I was certain of, asking wasn't going to get me anywhere. He gave me a little nod. I had no idea what it meant. I turned away.

The three men hoisted the duffels over their shoulders. Leo led the way, with Taylor following, then me, Dalton, and Jamie bringing up the rear. Both my brothers trailed fingers along the walls. The sound gave me chills, like fingernails on a blackboard. It was about as bad. Both of them wore gloves made of what looked like chain mail, only very fine. At least the sound of metal scraping rock distracted me from my claustrophobia. I wasn't sure which I preferred. Either way, I was a basket case by the time we arrived at our destination.

It took us more than a half hour to get there. Mostly the passage through the mountain was natural. Jamie started on one of his geological treatises, and I didn't listen. I knew he was trying to distract me, and I was grateful, but I didn't really care about tectonics or rock solubility or anything else he was nattering on about.

We dropped downward. The cave system narrowed and widened with little warning. At one point, we had to elbow-crawl through on our stomachs. Taylor helped me stand after I came through, then patted my back as I leaned on my knees to catch my breath. One day I'd get over my claustrophobia, I promised myself.

The exit from our cave had been newly created. It wasn't that big, maybe three foot by three foot and narrower at the bottom than the top.

"It's the best we could do in the time frame we had," Jamie said apologetically. "The basalt is damned hard to break up."

I knew the technique. They'd push metal into the faults and cracks and then expand it, slowly powdering the rock and creating more faults and fissures until eventually they chewed it away. It was similar to the way that water wore at rock, but much faster. It was lucky that the big mine owners hadn't discovered what Jamie and Leo could do. They'd have pulled my brothers into their mining operations, whether they wanted to be miners or not.

Just like me.

I glanced at them. I wasn't the only member of my family whose talent put them at risk for kidnapping and modern-day slavery. Mel, too. Helping Price was going to lose her the protection of the FBI. She'd be a plum ripe for the picking.

Realization struck me like a fist. My family needed protection. My friends needed protection. Not just from Vernon or Savannah Morrell or the FBI. It wasn't until that moment that I truly understood Touray. His father had created his organization to protect his own, starting with his sons and stretching out to include all the innocent people in Diamond City. Now Price's brother was following in his father's footsteps. It was like an old-time lawman putting on the sheriff's star to protect a town from all the wild gangs of outlaws. He did what he did in the name of protecting his own. In that moment, I understood that I was going to have to do the same thing if I wanted to keep my own little tribe safe. Starting with Price and then Touray.

My laugh caught in my throat.

I'd just adopted Touray into my tribe. Whether he knew it or not, I'd just made him my responsibility. He was so going to hate that. Then again, I hated that in order to protect my family and friends, I was asking them to risk their lives. No, not asking. They'd volunteered. Because I wasn't the only one who wanted to protect the people I loved. I couldn't stop them. I didn't have a right to stop them. How the hell did I protect them when they were walking straight into danger? The fact was, all I could do was my part, trust them to do theirs, and hope to hell the plan worked.

Chapter 12

WE CRAWLED OUT of the cave right into a tangle of scrub. My brothers and Dalton had scouted the area earlier and had cut away branches to hollow out a space underneath. I followed Leo, who crab-crawled fifteen feet along the rock cliff until the scrub gave way to a pile of boulders and a stand of trees. Leo had left the lantern inside the cave, and the flashlight he carried was covered with a green filter. Hunters used them to keep animals from seeing them from the sides.

Beyond the trees, I could see the glow cast by the compound's floodlights. It was lit up like a baseball stadium. I could feel the pulse of magic the place put off. It was thick and heavy.

"How much time do we have?" Jamie asked Leo.

Dalton answered, "Twenty minutes until your mother and Agent Arnow go inside."

"Let's hustle, then," Leo said, then set off.

He led us through the stand of pines and scrub to just this side of a twelve-foot-tall perimeter fence. A trench filled with cement ran beneath it. Magic throbbed through it, and from the wires and insulators I could see, it was electrified. Cameras were mounted at intervals. The two closer ones had been turned upward toward the trees. On the other side there were no trees. In the distance—maybe fifty yards away—a blocky building loomed, its form dulled by the snow. Lucky for us there was snow. The cleared space meant no cover. A killing field. In the old days, that was so enemies couldn't approach a fortress without being seen, and so archers could shoot at them. I had to assume there was security watching the space, ready to kill. But with guns, not arrows. Hopefully they'd be too distracted by what Leo and Jamie did to notice us approaching.

"My null isn't going to help with the electricity in the fence," I pointed out.

"Won't be a problem. Once we get to work, there's not going to be any electricity going anywhere. After that, we'll make a hole in the fence for you," Jamie said.

They'd already dug down to the drainage pipe they planned to use to get close to the building. A hole was peeled back like something had burst up through the corrugated steel. Inside, the pipe's diameter was only three feet across, if that. I shuddered.

Leo swung down to stand inside. Taylor handed down a duffel, and he thrust it into the pipe ahead of him, then crawled inside.

"We're down to seven minutes before Mel and Arnow get here," Jamie said, jumping down. "Time to get to work." He looked at me. "We'll let you know when we get in place so you can hit the null. We'll do our best to take care of the shooters on the roof and knock out the lights, but be careful." With that he gave a little salute and a reckless smile, then ducked down after Leo.

We waited.

I was in no mood to talk. Instead, I crouched down behind a bush, watching the compound. It was nestled in a wide canyon with steep, tree-filled ridges circling around. Only one road in.

"What's with you and our dad?" Taylor asked Dalton suddenly. "How long have you worked for him?"

I glanced over. Taylor had her arms crossed and had squared off opposite Dalton. The light and shadows coming through the bushes and trees carved his features into alabaster and obsidian. Taylor's red hair darkened to the color of dried blood where her braid hung out from under her ski hat. I shuddered. What a depressing thought.

"Just over seven years," Dalton said.

Wow. He'd actually answered. Seven years. That was three years after Vernon had vanished off the face of the earth.

"How did you meet him?" Taylor asked.

"I was working for someone else. He asked me to work for him instead."

"Oh, please, spare me the details," Taylor said sarcastically. "You talk so much, I hardly can stand it."

Dalton actually smiled. "The story is boring."

"I'm not going anywhere." She glanced her watch. "At least for the next five minutes or so. Tell me your story."

Dalton's smile widened. "You're a good pilot," he said instead.

"I know. Don't change the subject. I'd like to know just who has my back going into that compound."

His smile faded as he turned serious. "I owe your father a great deal. He asked me to come and make sure you stay safe." He flicked a glance toward me. "All of you."

"Wow. He sent an army of one. It's like I'm surrounded by angels." Sarcasm didn't do a lot to veil Taylor's anger.

"He cannot interfere too much," was Dalton's irritating reply.

"Why not?" I demanded. "Who is he afraid of?"

He looked at me, his eyes rimmed in blue. "It is not for me to say. Ask him."

"He's not exactly forthcoming."

He shrugged. Not his problem. I gritted my teeth and turned to watch the compound again. I was done trying to get blood from a turnip. Though bashing Dalton with a baseball bat and getting blood the good old-fashioned way certainly had appeal.

Taylor hadn't given up. She had a captive audience and wasn't going to quit before she got some satisfaction. "What's in section nine of the compound?"

That seemed to confuse Dalton. "How should I know?"

"Because Vernon said we should check it out."

"I wasn't aware of that."

I looked at him again. He actually sounded sincere, and he looked more than a little annoyed. He didn't like Vernon keeping him in the dark, either.

"You know, I'm beginning to think you're just about useless," Taylor snapped, stomping away.

I smiled at Dalton's look of chagrin, which was followed by pure fury. He glared at Taylor like he wanted to strangle her.

"Look, they're here," I said as headlights swept up the entrance road and disappeared. There must have been a parking lot on the other side. From our position, I couldn't see Mel and Arnow get out and go in. I hoped they didn't run into trouble. They had the proper government clearance, and Mel had gotten someone in the upper echelons to help smooth their way in.

"How long before you think they'll get down to Price?" Taylor asked.

"As long as it takes, no more, no less," Dalton said.

Taylor glared. "Wow, maybe next you'll give us the big news that water is wet and snow is cold and oh, by the way, an avalanche will crush you like a bug."

"Do you ever shut up?" Dalton asked.

Taylor moved fast. Before I knew what was happening, she'd kicked him twice on the outside of the right thigh with rapid thumps. Despite the fact that Dalton had to be surprised, he responded almost as fast as she struck. He snatched at her. Taylor must've expected it. She collapsed into a one-legged squat on her right leg, gathering her left leg under as she twisted and thrust out her right. Instead of smashing him behind the front knee, she only caught his feet as he jumped into the air. It was enough to trip him. He pitched forward. Taylor rolled out from under him, rising into a crouch.

Dalton should have fallen onto all fours, his head and neck exposed. Instead, his fall turned into a tight shoulder roll. He gained his feet, spinning around to face Taylor. I tossed a pinecone between them.

"Ahem," I said. "Not to be a killjoy, but would you mind waiting to beat each other up until later? Maybe save your aggression for actual enemies?"

Of course, in my book Dalton *was* an enemy, but at the moment, a useful one.

Taylor took a long breath and let it out, then straightened out of her stance.

"Sorry." She said it to me, not Dalton. "Didn't mean to lose my temper."

"No worries," I said. In fact, it had been amazing to see her move. She'd learned a whole lot since the last time I'd seen her fight, which had been at some sort of class recital thing when she was fifteen. That had been right before Dad left.

I looked at Dalton. "You okay?"

He didn't take his eyes off Taylor. "I'll live."

"Good. I guess."

"Your concern is touching," he said, his lip curling in his favorite sneering expression.

"Did I sound concerned? Sorry. Didn't mean to. Next time, I'm likely to help Taylor out."

"She'll need it," he said, eyes narrowing until he looked half-asleep. "You won't catch me by surprise again," he said to her. "There *will* be a next time."

"Sure," Taylor said, bending to dust herself off. "Just let me know who to notify as next of kin."

His sneer disappeared as one corner of his mouth lifted in a reluctant smile. He didn't reply. He turned his back on Taylor to watch the compound.

I glanced at my watch. The whole episode had taken maybe two minutes.

Waiting became grueling. I almost wished the two of them would get into it again. Instead, Taylor had come to wait beside me. She remained silent and still as a shadow.

Worry clawed at me, but I forced myself to breathe and trust that Mel would be all right, and that this insane plan of ours would work. *We were breaking into the fucking FBI. I'll take $2,000 in the category of "Things I never* *thought I'd be caught dead doing," Alex.* A laugh at my own idiocy bubbled up inside me. I swallowed it. I was getting hysterical. I needed to keep my shit together. Not just for Price—for all of us.

A full ten minutes had gone by before a soft clanging sound came from the pipe. I looked. A piece of steel had elongated into a wand with a thicker ball at the end. It was tapping against the inside.

"I'm up," I said, unzipping my backpack and lifting out my null.

It was one of the big coffee cans—a little over forty ounces. I'd filled it with lead and melted it down into a solid chunk. I made a habit of picking up the lead balance weights that fell off cars. They made great nulls. Over the years, I'd collected enough of them that I was able to melt it into a solid chunk over a camp stove. The result was heavy, but it held magic well.

Even as I picked it up, I activated it. Power spread out from me in an invisible wave. It rolled out across the grounds, and I felt magic sucking down into it like water down a drain. It kept going past the main building and on outward, rising up the surrounding slopes. I felt it stop as the null reached its maximum circumference. At almost the same moment, it shut down, having sucked up all the magic around.

I dropped the expended null before zipping up my backpack. I slid it over my shoulders. "It's done. My null drained what spells were active, but there's likely emergency backups."

"Maybe you should have brought backups," Dalton said.

"Maybe I should have," I said. In fact, I did have one more big null, plus a handful of smaller ones. The big one wasn't nearly as powerful as the canister of lead, but it would likely shut down anything the feds were able to activate. Or so I hoped.

Only a few seconds passed before the lights surrounding the building went out. Simultaneously, the wires in the fence unraveled, opening a wide hole. We jumped through, me first, then Taylor, then Dalton. We ran across the open space. Dalton and Taylor were faster than I was and pushed ahead. I couldn't see anything, with the flying snow and darkness. A couple of inches had accumulated, and I wondered if we stuck out like sore thumbs on the white background. Half expecting to get shot, I was pleasantly surprised to arrive at the building unscathed.

Jamie and Leo crouched down beside the gray wall. Both pressed bare, flattened hands against the cinder block. They had faraway looks.

A gunshot ran out from on top of the roof. Dalton, Taylor, and I drew our weapons and pressed up against the wall, searching for the shooter.

"Missed one," Leo said. "Sorry. Wait . . . Got it."

He was referring to the gun, not the person. Hopefully he'd morphed the gun into handcuffs and shackled the guy.

Lights flashed on. The brightness hurt.

"Oh no you don't," Jamie said.

A second later the darkness returned. White splotches danced across my vision. I squinched my eyes closed and blinked, but they didn't go away.

"Backup generator is down," Jamie said. "All the circuits are fused. Melted down all the electronics."

"Got the guns I could find," Leo said. "Not a hammer or trigger will move. Still checking . . . Did you get all the cell phones?"

So the guards on the roof were still on the loose. They just didn't have guns.

"What about Mel?" I asked, though I wasn't entirely sure they would answer. Both were deep inside the metal runs of the building. Their focus was spread out across innumerable channels and inlets, skipping across desks and under floors, zipping through the electric lines and swirling around in lightbulbs. They were sorting everything, trying to understand what was what, and then pushing out beyond.

"No, no," Jamie murmured in response to whatever scene inside that he could hear or feel in his mind. "You should stay there. That's right. Those doors aren't going to open anymore. Cell phones are useless. I think we're good to go."

It took me a second to realize that the last was aimed at me. Or maybe Leo. Leo responded.

"Back out, then. Let's see what we can do to get inside."

I tried not to pace and fidget as I waited. A scrape of sound above us caught my attention.

"What's that?"

Dalton didn't answer. He looked up, and his eyes flashed to green. Once again, I wondered just what he could see. "Company," he said, raising his gun again and trotting away, weapon held up at eye level.

"Stay here and keep an eye on the boys," Taylor said to me, following after him.

I wanted to call her back, but I had to trust she knew what she was doing. After seeing her fighting with Dalton, I knew she could hold her own. Didn't keep me from worrying.

I held my gun ready as I stood with my back to the wall beside my brothers, who continued to work. I steadily scanned back and forth and upward. I wished to hell we had some bushes to offer us camouflage, which of course was the whole point in not having them. The feds wanted clear lines of fire in case of attack or, more likely, escape.

Movement beyond Leo and Jamie caught my attention. I stepped around them and crouched, bringing my gun up to eye level. Magic throbbed behind me in a sudden burst.

"Dammit," Leo swore. "What the hell is that?"

"Reinforcement between the cinder-block layers," Jamie replied. "Probably carbon fibers."

"What were they expecting? A dinosaur assault?"

"We're going to need the explosives. Take the rebar out of the walls. Let's see if we can build something to shape the blast. If we can blow everything out, we won't have to deal with as much rubble on the inside."

"It's not going to be much," Leo warned dubiously. "We can set up the interior side with a plate, but the carbon fiber reinforcement will probably interfere with the blast. It's probably pointless to even bother."

"But it might work. We ought to try."

I wanted to tell them both to shut up, but they probably wouldn't hear me. They were too intent on each other. Besides, they had to talk to each other if they were going to do their job.

I was so intent on eavesdropping that I almost didn't see the shape rushing at me from maybe a dozen feet away. It came out of the sweep of snow and shadows. Despite the fact that I was caught off guard, I didn't hesitate. Three shots center mass. The woman—I could make out curves now, and the soft edge of her jaw—jerked sideways and staggered as she bent over. She didn't fall. She had to be wearing a bulletproof vest.

Not giving her time to recover, I bulldozed her shoulder to knock her down, then put one foot on her neck, reaching down to pull her hands up behind her. She fought me, twisting, but her breathing was labored from the impact of the bullets. She probably had cracked ribs. Once I had her arms pushed up behind her back, she went still, except for the harsh drag of her breathing.

I didn't have anything handy to tie her up with. Note to self: bring zip ties next time I break into a federal building. I could have used my boot-laces, but I didn't want to let her go to fight them loose.

The crunch of footsteps warned me that someone was coming. I crouched beside my captive, one hand on her wrists. Dammit, I'd dropped my gun. I didn't dare search for it.

"It's me," Taylor called in a low voice as she approached. "Are you okay?"

I let go of the breath I hadn't known I'd been holding. "I'm fine. I need something to tie her with."

Taylor went to lean over Jamie and rifled in his coat pockets until she found what she was looking for. She returned with a spool of wire. Of course. Neither of my brothers ever left home without some supply of metal, and wire was handy for a lot of reasons.

She helped me wrap the woman's wrists.

"What do you want to do with her?" she asked, frowning down at the bound agent.

That's when I realized I'd almost killed a federal agent. This woman was technically a good guy. Many were corrupt, but how was I to know which weren't? And who was I to judge anymore? I was breaking a man out of federal custody—a man I knew was wrapped up with the Tyet. I wasn't particularly clean. If I'd killed her, who would she have left behind? A husband? Kids? Parents? Brothers and sisters?

I clenched my jaw. I'd known what I was doing going into this mission. I'd known I might be killing people, and I'd chosen to come. I hardened myself against the guilt and reminded myself that I was here to save Price and I'd do a lot worse than kill to help him.

"Let's move her next to the building out of the wind and the snow," I said. "She'll be okay until they find her." I hoped. She could just as easily freeze to death. At least she had on a coat and heavy pants. I picked up the knit cap she'd lost when I knocked her down and pulled it back down over her head. My gun lay on the ground beside it. I retrieved it and rubbed off the snow, checking it over to make sure it was in working order.

She looked up at us, her round face flushed and angry. "You won't get away with this. I've seen your faces."

"Perhaps we should kill you, then."

I jumped. I hadn't heard Dalton approach. He flicked an approving glance at me. Bile flooded my mouth, and I spat to the side. I had to be seriously fucked up to earn that bastard's seal of approval.

"Kill me if you want to," the captive agent said to us, though her voice shook. "You will be hunted down. There's no place you can hide."

I didn't know if she was being arrogant or naïve or just plain stupid. Of course we could hide. Or we could buy our way out of the situation if we had enough money and leverage. That was the way this game was played. All you needed was the stomach for it.

"Any others out there?" I asked Taylor, surprised at the calm steadiness of my voice.

"We caught a couple coming down off the roof. Knocked 'em cold before they saw us coming," Taylor said. Then grudgingly, "Thanks to Dalton. He can see a gnat from a mile away, seems like."

"Nice to have Terminator eyes," I said.

"Isn't it?" he said.

"How many more can we expect?" I asked, scanning the snow-blurred shadows for movement.

"That's it," Leo said, sounding worn to the bone. "It's the best we can make it." He sat back, putting his hand on Jamie's shoulder. "Let Dalton use the plastics."

For a long moment, Jamie didn't respond. Then finally his body jerked, and his shoulders slumped. He twisted so that his back was to the wall.

"We've got two layers of cinder-block wall reinforced with rebar and cement. Leo and I removed the rebar from a small six-by-six-foot section. In between the cinder layers is some kind of reinforcement—probably carbon fiber, if I had to guess. There's also about a foot of cement sandwiched in there with it." His tired gaze fixed on Dalton. "We managed to put a steel plate on the backside of the blast zone to help focus the energy. We didn't have any luck getting shielding inside the walls. Can you blow it?"

"Yep," Dalton said. "Give me a hand."

I wasn't sure who he was asking to help him, but I stepped forward. My brothers were exhausted, and I wanted to give them a chance to recover. Taylor could watch for any more attackers.

Dalton squatted down beside one of the big duffels and began pulling things out. He started with a roll of tape and what looked like a bunch of white plastic sausage links all hooked together to make a good twenty-five-foot length. Orange and black lettering spelled out *Detagel, High Strength*. I'd seen the stuff before. They used it in the mines. It was stable and readily available. I hoped it would work. Dalton seemed to know what he was doing. I decided to trust him. On this, anyhow. It's not like I had a choice.

"Hold this," Dalton told me as Leo pointed out where they'd removed the rebar and placed the interior steel plate.

I grabbed the end of the Detagel tube-rope and held it in place as Dalton taped it down, following the outline Leo had given. He used the explosives to make an oblong circle about three feet wide and five feet tall. He pulled out another length of explosives and zigzagged down the center, filling it in.

"That seems like a lot," I said.

"If it is carbon fiber inside, we'll need it," Dalton replied, pulling out some other equipment, including a set of sound-deadening earmuffs. He slipped those around his neck, then plugged several things together and fastened them to the explosives. He started walking away.

"Come on," he said to everyone.

Leo and I grabbed our gear and followed. Jamie and Taylor helped the agent to her feet and hustled her along.

Dalton paced down the length of the building. When we reached the corner, he peered around it, then went around. He stopped and motioned us past. "Get up against the wall."

We obeyed. Jamie and Taylor pushed the agent down to sit against the wall.

Dalton fished his cell phone out of his pocked and pulled the earmuffs over his ears. He dialed and looked at us. "Cover your ears."

He did a silent countdown on his fingers. Three . . . two . . . one. The explosion ripped through the night. The building shuddered, and pressure from the blast swept down the side of the building like a hard wind.

Abruptly, it was over. My ears rang, despite covering them.

"Let's move," Dalton ordered, yanking off his earmuffs and shoving them into his duffel.

"What about her?" Taylor asked, pointing at the trussed FBI agent.

"Bind her legs and leave her. They'll find her before she gets too cold," I said. Hopefully we'd be long gone by then.

I hurried after Leo and Jamie, who'd jogged back the way we'd come. A fog of cement and rock dust filled the air.

"Nice," Jamie said, sticking his head inside. He started to crawl through. Then, "Ow! Okay, watch yourself. The edges of the carbon fiber are sharp."

Before Leo could follow, Dalton made a sound and hoisted himself into the wall. I could hear the sounds of kicking and the loud clang of steel hitting the ground, along with the rumble of falling rocks.

"Are you okay?" Leo called in a low voice.

"Come on," Dalton said.

Leo clambered through. I motioned to Taylor. "Go ahead."

She climbed through, and I followed, one hand carrying my backpack, the other my gun.

The wall was close to three feet thick. The outer cinder blocks had blown out, leaving a hole a good twelve feet wide or more. The interior cement had held up much better, thanks to the carbon fiber grid layer down the middle of it. The hole in that was smaller, and sharp bits of the grid clawed out from the remaining cement. Rubble filled the hole, and I had to crouch to get through.

On the other side, the cinder blocks had vanished and most of the rubble had blown into small chunks and powder, thanks to the blast shield Leo and Jamie and made. The massive plate of steel lay on the floor, looking as if a meteor shower had pounded it. In the center, a seam had torn open, about three feet long and a few inches wide.

Dust filled the air and clogged my eyes as I stepped down. Leo grasped my wrist to help steady me. I glanced around.

We stood in a nondescript hallway. The floors appeared to be polished concrete beneath the layer of dust and crumbled cement. The only lights were those Leo, Jamie, and Dalton had slid onto their heads. Jamie handed one each to Taylor and me.

"Where now?" Dalton asked.

Everyone looked at me. I was more absorbed in what they couldn't see. Price's blue and burgundy trace wrapped around me in comforting ribbons. It was still vivid and bright. I wanted to touch it, to see for myself how he was.

I dropped into trace sight and reached into the bone-chilling cold of the trace dimension to take hold of Price's trace. Wild rage, pain, hate, and terror assaulted me. It clamped down on my mind, flattening me beneath it. I couldn't breathe. I heard a deep-throated sound, like a snarl. It came from my throat.

"Riley?" Taylor turned toward me.

"Get away from me," I snarled. I put my hands up. I'm not sure what I meant to do. I'm not sure *I* meant to do anything. The maelstrom of Price's frantic emotions twisted around me, yanking me under into a vast ocean deepness. Somewhere within the building, his hands came up, and mine followed suit. Power flooded him and crashed into a wall of pure terror.

He was afraid of himself.

This was seriously bad.

Chapter 13

I SHOOK MYSELF, trying to divide myself away from Price's emotions. I'd never tangled up in anyone like this before, but then, I'd never been in love with anybody before, either. I didn't know if he could feel me, but I wasn't going to let go of his trace in case he could. I didn't want him to think I'd abandoned him. Right now, that would be worse than anything else I could do. Especially given the fact that he was about to go nuclear. Literally.

"Riley?" Taylor asked.

"I'm okay," I said. I'm sure they believed that, the way I was standing there all frozen and my voice sounding like my vocal cords had been scraped with a rusty razor. "Price is starting to cascade. I've got to help him. I can't wait for you."

"Do what you need to do," Jamie said, and Taylor and Leo nodded, though both looked tense. "We'll track Mel and Arnow and catch up with you. Be careful. He'll have guards."

Dalton scowled at me. He didn't know my trick for traveling through the trace dimension. He was about to see it. Vernon was going to want me more than ever after this.

"Be safe," I said, and reached into the trace dimension again, concentrating on Price's location. Finding him, I let myself tumble into the searing cold.

Inside was a wonderland of brilliant color streamers that went on forever in an ocean of velvet black. I took a second to find my equilibrium. The last time I'd been here, my mother had been waiting for me, wanting to tell me something. I'd been too much in a hurry then to stay and was in the same boat now.

The cold pushed into me. Living things weren't meant to come here. If I stayed long, I wouldn't be living. I focused on Price's trace. I was counting on the fact that I'd nulled the magic out of the building to have gotten rid of whatever barrier had blocked me before.

Relief throbbed through me as I shot through to Price. In just seconds, I pulled myself out of the spirit dimension and into his prison cell. I staggered as my feet found the floor. I caught my balance and turned, searching for Price.

He stood braced in a corner, his face twisted, his teeth bared in a snarl. He was naked. Bruises covered him, and his hands were hamburger—like he'd been punching the walls. Blood trickled from scrapes on his shoulders and arms and smeared his face. I suspected he'd done most of the damage to himself, trying to batter down the walls. He panted, his chest bellowing with the effort.

"Price?" I could barely hear my own voice. The power emanating from him smothered sound and air. Rainbow trails pulled at the corners of my vision. He was in a full-on cascade, and there was no good way to stop it that I knew of.

I'd never witnessed a cascade, but I'd heard enough to know that the end result would be disastrous. Basically, Price's magic was surging inside him, with no outlet. He'd opened the spigot on it, whether he meant to or not, but he'd also bottled it up. Now it was building, like too much air in a balloon. Or maybe more like Mentos in a bottle of Coke. Sooner or later, he'd pop. Sooner was more likely. That would be ugly enough if he was an ordinary talent, but he wasn't. The fact that he'd knocked down a mountain as a child meant he had to be something else. Something unbelievably strong and dangerous. The breadth of his destruction could be biblical.

I didn't have any kinds of nulls here that would suck down the kind of power he was manifesting, plus I'd been in such a hurry to get to Price that I'd left my pack with the others. I needed to help him get it under control before he did something seriously awful, like taking out this part of Colorado. If he even could gain control at this point.

I wiped my palms on my thighs and stretched out a hand to him. "Price. It's me. Riley. I'm here. I need you to calm down."

His dark sapphire gaze flicked around the room and eventually settled on me. His muscles bunched, his jaw jutting. He lurched toward me, fists raised.

"Get the fuck away from me, bitch," he rasped. "Go to back to hell where you belong."

I recoiled before I realized he didn't believe I was actually there. My heart galloped in my chest. His face twisted. His eyes darted and flickered as if he saw things I couldn't. Probably he could. A dreamer could have locked him into a hallucination. For him, it would feel real.

"It's really me," I said. "I'm Riley." Yeah, because repeating myself was totally a winning argument. I bit my lip. I hadn't thought I'd have to prove myself to him, which was idiotic. I should totally have anticipated that, given that they'd be screwing with his head. I had no idea how to convince him. Anything he knew about me could have been plucked from his mind by an FBI dreamer, which meant it was impossible to come up with something only he and I knew about to confirm my identity.

He moved so fast I didn't see him coming. His hand closed around my throat, and he slammed me back against the wall. He held me there, his fingers curling into my windpipe like he'd rip it out. His face pushed close to mine, his nose pressing up against the skin below my ear. He sucked in a deep breath.

My body responded before I could think. Thank goodness for all those training drills when I was younger. I scrunched my shoulders high and pressed my chin hard against his hand. I grabbed his wrist, digging my thumbs into the tendons. He was impervious. Abruptly, I changed tactics. Keeping my chin clamped against his hand, I reached across with my left hand and grabbed his wrist, keeping it locked to me. At the same time, I used my right hand to grab his arm above the elbow, pushing sideways so that the joint strained backward. I pivoted my hips, shoving with all my might. I kicked my leg out to drive his leg out from under him. If he didn't let go, his elbow would break.

I wasn't all that sure he was in a state of mind to care.

Abruptly, he released me and staggered sideways. Before he could snatch me again, I attacked. I was too close to the wall to twirl a round-house kick into his kidneys. Instead, I punched him there. I heard the breath huff out of him. I kicked the side of his thigh. I was aiming for the knee. Ten pounds of pressure on either side of the joint was all it took to break it. Or would have if I hadn't missed. Even so, the thigh kick was enough to drop him to the floor. I knew from experience it hurt a hell of a lot.

Unfortunately, Price didn't give in to his pain. He bounded to his feet and swung around. I held up my hands flat before me to forestall him. Miraculously, he paused.

"It really is me," I said. "I came through the trace to get you."

He glared at me from beneath his lowered brows, his black hair hanging across his eyes. His unshaven jaw was dusted black, highlighting the hollows and contours. He looked like he'd lost twenty pounds. His skin stretched tight over the planes of his muscles. Veins and tendons stood out in relief. He took a step toward me.

"Riley isn't here," he gritted between clenched teeth. "You are some FBI bitch made to look like her. If you're even here at all and not just in my head."

"Why can't I be Riley?" I demanded. "You have to know I'd come rescue you."

"No. Riley would never be that stupid. If anybody's coming for me, it's Gregg." He scowled, as if annoyed that he'd been made to talk so much.

"He couldn't make it, as it turns out," I said. "Besides, I totally would have come for you whether you or he wanted me to or not. If there's one thing you should know about me, it's that I don't abandon people I love. Hell, I don't even abandon people I barely like. Anyhow, I love you and I *am* here. For real."

"I don't think so. Get the fuck out of my head!" He balled his fist and punched himself just above his ear. I winced. He did it again.

"And you call me stupid," I muttered.

"What?"

"I said, you call me stupid, but you're the one hitting yourself in the head. If you really want to crack your skull like an egg, you probably should get down on the floor and whack it on the cement." I glanced around. "Or the corner of that table, though from the looks of you, you've already tried bashing yourself to death."

His cell was a square of concrete. All of it looked like it was made to be washed down and disinfected. Smears of blood here and there explained why. A drain in the center of the floor told me I wasn't wrong. The only furniture was a steel table bolted on one side of the room, about five feet or so off the wall. Underneath was welded a locked steel box. No doubt to keep the essential torture tools handy. Up in the middle of the ceiling was an eye-in-the-sky camera, probably with microphones to catch everything Price said. It was totally blind and mute now, though, thanks to Leo and Jamie.

I fixed my attention back on Price. Luckily he hadn't taken advantage of my momentary distraction to attack me. I drew in a breath and let it out slowly. Right now he was my enemy, and I had to remember that. He *would* hurt me if he could. Maybe kill me.

"Is it helping?" I asked. I waved a hand toward his head. "The whole bashing yourself in the noggin thing?"

"You'll never get what you want from me," he said.

"I want to get you out of here where you're safe," I said. "And I wouldn't mind having those two weeks you owe me." Not that that was going to happen soon. "What about giving me the benefit of the doubt? That I'm really Riley, that I'm really here, and that it's time to escape? Couldn't hurt, could it?"

His bark of laughter startled me. "You don't think I'm that stupid, do you? We escape"—he put air quotes around the last word—"and when we're supposedly elsewhere, I spill all my secrets to you?"

He had a point. I frowned. What could I do to prove myself?

"Shit," I muttered. I wanted to pace, but I didn't dare turn my back on him. I worried my upper lip between my teeth. I still held his trace. Could I do something with that? I ran my fingers down it.

"What was that?" Price jerked upright, his eyes widening. "What did you do?"

I smiled. "What I do. I'm a tracer, remember? I'm touching your trace."

I should have known it wouldn't be that easy. Immediately, he began shaking his head.

"Right. That tactic is more clever, I'll give you that. But I still don't believe you."

He was bound and determined not to believe me. Not that I could blame him. The FBI was out to break him, and he had to assume everything that came at him was a ploy. I had to do better.

Maybe I should just drag him out through the spirit dimension. Maybe the trip would prove it. And if it didn't? He was still cruising for an overload, and it was going to happen soon. If anything, the air in his prison cell had grown thicker and heavier with magic.

Well, if just running my fingers over his trace had startled him, what if I . . . ?

I yanked hard on his trace, then jumped back when he jerked toward me.

"Christ!" he yelped, and for the first time, his angry armor cracked and I not only saw but could feel his shock and terrible fear. Immediately, his expression closed up and his emotions shut back down. "I'm done with you," he said and turned his back on me. "You're not here and you're not worth my time or attention."

I took the moment to scan Price from head to foot. Despite my frustration, I was overjoyed that he hadn't lost his mind. They hadn't broken him. Even naked and mentally tortured as he clearly had been, every inch of him oozed pride, toughness, tenacity, and explosive energy. Not to mention incredible stubbornness.

Most of me wanted to take the moment to punch him, knock sense into him somehow. I would have if he wouldn't have cracked my skull in return.

It occurred to me I could have Leo and Jamie build a cage around him. No, Price was too close to full-on cascade. I needed to get him out of here before he totally lost control. Too many people could die otherwise, including and especially my family. That meant pulling him through the spirit dimension to somewhere he couldn't do a lot of harm, and where the FBI wouldn't find us.

The only viable option I could think of was my house. I couldn't take him out into the wilderness. He wasn't dressed for the cold. At least at home I had monster nulls that could help contain his power when he went off like Mount Vesuvius. Hopefully I wouldn't end up like all the statues in Pompeii.

"Have you thought about the possibility that I might really be Riley?" I asked, taking one last chance on convincing him. Having his cooperation would be a lot more helpful than fighting him. "I mean, if I am actually who I say I am, and I'm here to rescue you, then you're wasting time. I haven't asked you a single question. I haven't tried to control you. Think about it."

He spun around, and his expression was feral. As in, insane rabid wolf. All he needed was a little bit of foam to complete the picture. "I told you to leave," he said in a flat, implacable voice. "Now I'm going to make you."

I stepped back. Big mistake. He leaped at me. I ducked under his out-stretched arm and jammed my shoulder under his hip. I pushed and rolled around his back at the same time.

One thing about Price is that he's smart and he's got crazy good fighting skills. He'd anticipated my move, and instead of losing his balance, he put all his weight on his other leg and twisted out of my way. I crashed through the hold and fell forward, catching myself on my hands in something like a downward-facing-dog yoga pose.

Before I could recover, he picked me up and slammed me down onto the steel table. My head bounced, and the breath whooshed out of me. I jerked my feet up to my chest, intending to jack them into his stomach even as he jammed his forearm against my throat. Instantly, I gagged at the pressure on my Adam's apple. Panic flared. I clawed at his face.

I've got curves. And by that, I mean I've got plenty of boobs and what I've been told is a luscious ass. At the moment, my boobs were seriously getting in the way of getting my feet up high enough to pry him off. All the same, I levered one of my feet up and got my toe under Price's jaw. I kicked out as hard as I could. He lurched backward. I rolled off the other side of the table, coughing and gasping and keeping the table between us.

"Helluva way to treat your girlfriend," I said. Sort of rasped in between the coughing. "I'm not sure I want to spend two weeks alone together after all."

He lunged at me again. "Bitch!"

He vaulted over the table, and I dodged around the end. His fingertips caught my collar. I twisted free and got the table between us again. The black of his eyes had swallowed the blue. Whatever reason he'd been clinging to seemed to have vanished. Worse, the pressure of the magic in the room had doubled, and the rainbow colors prismed through the air all around me.

"I will kill you, just like every other time I've killed you," he said in a singsongy voice. "Maybe this time you will learn that I will *never* let you use Riley to get to me."

I don't know what would have happened next if Dalton hadn't shown up. One second he wasn't there, the next he appeared just inside the door. Before Price realized he was there, Dalton chopped down on the back of his head with the butt of his gun. Price crumpled.

I scrabbled around the table and fell to my knees beside him and pulled his head up onto to my knees. Blood smeared one of my hands. Words clogged my throat. I stroked his face.

"You're okay. I'm with you. I'm going to get you out of here."

Abruptly, the steel door melted away, and my family stepped inside. Mel came first, followed by Leo and Jamie. Arnow was next and finally Taylor.

"Are you okay?" Mel asked.

I nodded.

"Jesus, Riley! What the hell did he do to you?" Jamie rushed in and gripped my chin, tilting it to see my neck. His hand shook with fury.

"I'm fine. A dreamer's been at him. He doesn't know it's really me. He thinks I'm a figment of the FBI's imagination."

Jamie's faced hardened, his upper lip curling. He said nothing. I couldn't tell if he was still pissed at Price or the FBI. Didn't matter.

"Get some clothes for him and some shoes. I've got to get him out of here before he goes nova."

Dalton responded, swiftly disappearing out of the room.

"Nova?" Leo repeated.

"The cascade is peaking," I said. "I don't know how he's held on this long." I would have thought knocking him out would have released his stranglehold on the magic altogether. Then again, he'd been suppressing his talent for a long time. It was probably something he did automatically, on a gut level. Like breathing.

The others exchanged looks.

"Give me something for his head, would you?"

Taylor handed me a stained microfiber cloth from her pocket. She'd grabbed it at the hangar. I pressed it to the blood leaking from Price's head. That's when I caught sight of the other woman through the doorway. She stood back in the shadows of the outer room. She was tall, with dark hair. That's about all I could see of her.

"Who's that?" I asked.

I didn't hear the answer. Price's eyes flickered, and he stiffened. His eyes opened and met mine. Time stretched as I waited for him to decide what to do.

"What happened?" he asked finally.

"Dalton hit you on the back of the head."

He frowned. "Dalton? The asshole working for your dad?"

"That's him."

"What's he doing here?"

"Helping to rescue you. Spying for my dad. Who knows what else."

He reached up to touch my neck. I was pretty sure I was wearing a black-and-blue choker necklace of bruises. A flicker of something flashed through his eyes, then vanished. Anger returned. His hand pulled back. I half expected him to hit me.

He twisted his head and glanced past me. "What are they doing here?"

"I told you, they came to help me break you out."

Scowling again. "Where's Gregg?"

I didn't know if I ought to tell him, but maybe it would motivate him to believe me. To believe *in* me. Inwardly, I snorted. Like I was Santa Claus or Big Foot or something. "Savannah Morrell has him."

His eyes widened, and he rolled away onto his stomach and then up to his feet. "What?"

I got up, the microfiber rag wadded in my fingers. "After you were arrested, he and I got pulled into a trap. I got away. He didn't."

I wrapped my arms around my stomach. Guilt balled in my chest. That I got away. That Touray hadn't. That I hadn't stayed to help him. I drew in a breath and blew it out. If I'd tried to help him, I'd have been captured and no one would be out to help either of the two brothers. At least I was free and could organize a rescue. Sometimes retreat was the smartest thing to do.

To my surprise, Price grabbed my shoulders and jerked me to him. "You're okay?"

"Asks the man who tried to choke you to death," Jamie said. "Let go of my sister and step back or I'll rip your head off." His tone was utterly calm and utterly cold. He meant every word. I guess that meant he'd decided to blame Price for hurting me.

Price ignored him, his attention riveted on me. He brushed my throat lightly with his fingertips, but his expression remained shuttered. I had no idea what he was thinking. At least he seemed to be leaning toward believing I was actually who I claimed to be.

Snaking steel curled between us and wrapped his torso, arms, and hands. His fingers straightened and his arms dropped to his sides. Price fought the pressure, but though his muscles strained, he was completely incapacitated. He didn't seem to notice. He kept his gaze fixed on me like I was his lifeline. Or maybe it was the predator in him, fixing on his prey with single-minded intent.

At that point, Dalton returned with a blue jumpsuit, a shirt, and a pair of loafers and some socks.

"We have to go. Now."

"What's going on?" That was Arnow. She was back to looking more like her professional self, this time with a sleek designer pantsuit. Her hair was pulled up in an elegant chignon, and she wore a pair of stiletto heels.

I wanted to roll my eyes. Who wore heels like that on a mission? But then again, this was her professional agent look. I supposed if she'd shown up in boots and fatigues, someone might have twigged to the fact that she was up to no good. Of course, in my experience, she was *always* up to no good, no matter how she was dressed. Her very presence should have set off warning bells.

"There's a small army on the way. Someone managed to call in the cavalry before everything shut down. They'll have to come from the city. Your people's diversion has kept them busy til now," Dalton announced out of the blue.

"How do you know?" Leo asked skeptically.

Dalton gave a little shrug, and I knew exactly how. Vernon. And they were clearly in real-time communication. I exchanged a look with Taylor, and she nodded sour agreement.

"He's probably telling the truth," I said. "Pull the cage off Price. He can't go outside without clothes and shoes."

Leo and Jamie didn't argue about accepting Dalton's word. The cage drew back and shrank into a waist-high tube. Dalton handed Price the bundle of clothes, finally breaking the lock of Price's stare on me. I just wish to hell I knew what he was thinking. Did he really believe I was me? Or was he just playing along for the moment?

Didn't matter. Getting him out of here was the goal. I'd worry about the rest later.

While he dressed, Mel beckoned to me. She eyed my neck and brushed her hand over the side of my head. "Are you okay?"

Given that she read emotions, she knew I wasn't. All the same, I nodded. "Totally fine."

She smiled as if expecting that answer. She looked at Price. He'd pulled on the shirt and zipped the jumpsuit over it. *FBI* was printed on the back of it in yellow. The narrow confines of the tube made it impossible for him to get the shoes on. I wasn't even sure they'd fit.

"He's terrified," Mel said. "And angry. Every time he looks at you, he's swamped with helplessness and love mixed with doubt and hatred and that spikes both the terror and anger to new levels. He's started to feel guilty as well and that's pushing him right over the edge."

"He doesn't believe I'm me. He can't yet."

She nodded. "The guilt may mean he's starting to change his mind."

I'd thought the same thing. At least I'd hoped. "I've got to get him to my place where I can use my nulls to control the explosion of magic."

She frowned. "Is that wise? You'll be alone with him. If he decides to attack again, he could kill you."

"He won't," I said, with more certainty than I felt. "He loves me. He'll figure it out. Besides, I can't let him go into full cascade here."

"Ready?" Dalton asked before Mel could answer.

Price straightened and set his hands on the top of the tube to lever himself out. He hissed and yanked them back. Streaks of blood smeared his palms. The top held a knife edge.

"Shit, Jamie. What were you thinking? Let him out."

My stepbrother didn't look remotely apologetic. He folded his arms over his chest and stuck out his chin defiantly. "Fucker hurt you. He deserves what he gets."

"He doesn't even know I'm real. It's not his fault." I looked around for something to bandage his hands. "Is there a first-aid kit?"

"Here," the dark woman said, pulling the yellow-and-red box off the wall in the outer room and bringing it to me. She cast a sidelong look at Price as she did.

She was older, probably in her late forties or early fifties. Her hair shined black with artful reddish highlights. Polished pink fingernails tipped elegant fingers. Her face was sharply drawn, and though she'd put on covering makeup, dark half-moons underscored her eyes. She was taller than me, probably about five foot nine, and was dressed in black wool slacks and a dark green sweater. Everything about her screamed sophistication and money. I had no idea who she was or why she was here. Something about her was familiar, but I couldn't place it. Or maybe it was the intensity of her gaze that threw me. Like she could see inside me, like she was measuring me.

"Thanks," I said, giving her a frowning nod before I went to help Price. The metal tube imprisoning him remained, though the top edge had now been rolled into a soft edge. I glared at an unrepentant Jamie and then set about wrapping Price's hands. I itched to take him out of here, but he might not let me give him first aid once we were at my place. His hands needed tending now.

I carefully didn't look into Price's face as I ministered to him. I wasn't sure I could handle it. I loved him so damned much, and he didn't even know I was me. That hurt. And pissed me off. A totally unreasonable and juvenile part of me demanded that he should recognize me no matter what. That there should be some essential quality, some elemental, crucial connection that let us know each other anywhere. I rolled my eyes at myself. *Oh please*. We weren't living in some sappy movie, and his failure to know me most definitely wasn't his fault.

I opened the first-aid kit. Taylor started to come over to hold it for me, but Leo pushed her aside and grabbed the box. Apparently, he thought Price too dangerous to get close to. For her, at least. Taylor's teeth gritted together loud enough for me to hear, but she stood back. Mel touched her arm, and they bent their heads together, talking quietly.

I pulled out what I thought I'd need and turned to examined Price's hands. He held them fisted, and blood dripped onto the floor.

"Let me see," I told him.

He uncurled his fingers, and I gasped.

"Fuck, Jamie. You cut him to the bone."

My brother didn't bother answering, which was probably smart. He wasn't going to be apologetic, which meant I'd have to kick him in the balls. Silence kept us reasonably civilized and focused.

I kept swearing as I packed thick gauze pads across Price's right hand and wrapped it tightly with a bandage, then repeated the process on the other. By the time I finished, blood was already soaking through the first bandage. All the while, I was aware of Price's gaze drilling into the back of my head and the way he held himself still, hardly breathing. He never said a word, never flinched.

Finally, I stepped back. "That's as good as it's going to get until you can see Maya." She was the best tinker I'd ever met. She'd healed me on more than one occasion. Wouldn't she be surprised *not* to be treating me this time? I almost smiled.

"Here," Dalton said, holding out his hand. He dropped a necklace into mine.

If I hadn't been so happy to see the heal-all, I would have rolled my eyes at him. He seemed to carry an endless supply of them. I'd meant to invest in some for myself, but I hadn't yet had a chance. I slid the chain over Price's head and activated it. Instantly, he quivered as the wormy magic delved inside him.

"Time to go," I said.

The tube surrounding Price melted away. Jamie wasn't giving in so easily, though. Loops of steel circled Price's wrists and pulled together, handcuffing him.

I growled. "Don't be an ass. His hands are still practically hamburger. Let him go."

"He'll be healed up in a minute and we're not going to take any chances." This time it was Leo who replied. "He's too dangerous." He looked pointedly at my throat.

"This isn't his fault," I argued. "They've fucked with his head."

"He's not safe, either," Leo declared. "Any more than a dog provoked to kill. I'm not going to let him hurt you again." I opened my mouth, and he raised his hand to forestall me. "I'm not changing my mind, so get used to it."

I looked at Taylor, Jamie, and Mel. All of them sported the same set expression. No support for me there. I didn't know how I was going to cut the damned things off at home, but I'd figure something out.

"Change of plans for me," I announced with an encouraging nod from Mel. "I've got to take Price out of here to my place."

Before anyone could respond, the magic in the room swelled. Rainbow colors solidified. I could barely see. The trapped energies boiled. Panic roared through me. *Don't let Price lose it now! Not now, not with my family so close!*

I whirled around, hoping I could find a way to calm him, or channel the eruption of power. As if.

He wasn't looking at me. He stood still, his expression melting into confusion. I turned to see what had riveted his attention. The woman who'd handed me the first-aid kit. He stared at her like she was impossible. Not so much a ghost as the Wizard of Oz or the Loch Ness Monster.

I turned to look back at him. His shackled hands came up, reaching out. "Mom?"

Chapter 14

MOM?

I may have stopped breathing. I turned to look at the woman. Now I could see why she looked familiar. She and Price shared the same bone structure, the same high cheekbones, lips, raven hair, and straight brows.

"Are you really here?" Price asked, and there was a wealth of hope in his voice. He scowled. "Or is this a trick?"

"I'm here," his mother confirmed, making no effort to close the distance between them. Her eyes had narrowed, and she looked anything but happy. Price read her coldness. His hands fell. He looked like he'd been kicked.

"The FBI brought you here, didn't they?" He asked, his voice lifeless.

"They thought I could help," she said with a little nod.

"Help them to break me."

I could tell he wanted her to deny his words, to say she'd come to help him. She didn't.

"I promised I'd help them however I could. They needed to see you for what you are so that you can finally be destroyed."

His head tipped. "What am I, exactly?"

I reached out and gripped his arm as the magic around us seemed to spasm.

His mother's face contorted with a mixture of powerful emotions, then smoothed back into a mask. "You are an abomination. A demon from the depths of hell. Satan's own spawn."

Each word was a bullet. Price flinched as they struck, his eyes widening. But his mother wasn't done.

"I tried. Oh, the Lord above knows how much I tried, but there was no saving you and no stopping you. You needed to be destroyed. I knew it when I gave birth to you and every day after. I tried everything, but your father didn't believe me. He said it was just your talent manifesting early, that I'd see how wrong I was, but I wasn't wrong. You carry the very soul of the devil inside of you."

I couldn't help but stare. Was this bitch for real? Yes. Her eyes had lit with the fervor of her screed, and she meant every word.

"I tried everything, even taking you to an exorcism in South America, in one of the holiest places on earth. You destroyed it!" Her voice rose. "You slaughtered everyone. You're evil and you need to be destroyed!"

She stabbed a finger at Price, her whole body shaking. He just stared. I had a bad feeling he was buying the crap she was selling. Soaking it in like a dry sponge. The magic around us flickered wildly.

"What a fucking bitch you are," Taylor said, coming to stand in front of Price as if to protect him. "With a mother like you, I'm surprised he *isn't* some sort of demon, which he's not. *You* are certainly an evil witch."

"Do you think it easy to kill your own child?" Oriana Price demanded. She looked at Jamie. "You see how dangerous he is. That's why you tried to cut off his hands. That's why you bound him. *You* know what I say is true."

Before Jamie could respond, Price spoke. "She's right," he rasped. "I killed so many." He closed his eyes, his face white as milk.

He was remembering that long-ago trip to Belize. I was sure he was replaying the long-forgotten memory in his head. But he'd been three years old, dragged to the back end of nowhere, in order to have some religious fanatics exorcise his God-given talent. What had they done to that terrified boy? I couldn't imagine, but it had sent him into such a frenzy of fear and horror that he'd unleashed disaster just to protect himself.

"He protected you. Otherwise you wouldn't have survived," I said furiously, turning on his mother. "Yet you call him evil. You know what evil really is? It's a mother who takes her toddler son from his home and family, gives him to strangers, and encourages them to inflict who knows what kind of horrors on him. Then you have the gall to show up here thirty years later to do it all over again. From where I stand, you're the only one in this room who has the track record to claim the title of Spawn of Satan, so you can just go to right back to hell where you come from," I said.

I wondered if Touray or his father knew that she'd been behind Price's kidnapping way back when. I doubted it. I didn't know their father, but I couldn't imagine Touray wouldn't have taken some revenge for Price's suffering.

I turned to face Price. "Forget her. She's batshit crazy. You're one of the best men I've ever met."

Price looked past me at his mother. His eyes widened, and he grabbed me and yanked me toward him as he leaped past Jamie and Taylor, shouting. In the same moment, gunshots blasted. Time slowed. I straightened and whirled in time to see Price stagger back. All the magic that had hung so thick in the air exploded. The last thing I saw as I catapulted through the air were his eyes. They'd gone totally white. I curled my arms over my head to protect it and braced to hit the wall or the ceiling or the floor.

Only I didn't hit. I settled down as if on a pillow. Time sped up again. The floor rippled and shook. Walls flattened. I twisted to stand up, but something held me down. Debris flew through the air, and I flinched from it. It bounced away without touching me. Chunks of masonry, dust, chairs, and tables from the outer room. None of it landed on me. Again I struggled to get up. I couldn't. It was like I was in a cocoon. I couldn't twitch a finger.

Magic tumbled around me in frothing waves. Their strength built higher. A sound started low. It grumbled and snarled and turned into a roar until it wrapped me like a massive tornado. All around me the air whirled. Debris came at me and flew past, leaving me unhurt. Soon a mound built over me. Blind panic hit when the darkness closed and I could no longer see.

I lost it. I couldn't think, couldn't calm down. Later I would remember I could have just dropped into the spirit dimension and escaped that way, but my claustrophobia had me in its teeth and I couldn't think of anything else.

I must have passed out eventually. Maybe I hyperventilated. Or maybe I just went catatonic. When I noticed myself again, I was in a state of total immobile hysteria. My heart raced, my chest ached with jagged cramps. I was so high on adrenaline, my heart felt like it was about to blow. Panic-sweat soaked my clothes all the way through. If I'd had the room, I could have made sweat angels on the ground. As it was, I lay there, feeling the terror mounting higher as I returned to awareness. It should have plateaued or my body should have gotten bored with feeling all that fear and not having anything to do with it. It didn't. I was on overload and heading for meltdown. Tremors shook me like a baby's rattle. A thin layer of nothing held a mound of crushing death above me. When would it give? When would it fall on me and I'd be buried alive?

What had happened?

The question was stupid. Price had happened. And his mother. Oh God! She'd shot him. I hadn't seen where the bullet hit. Fear for him roared up inside me. Maybe she'd missed. I remembered the way he'd jerked back. No, the bitch had been less than twelve feet away from him. Even Elmer Fudd couldn't miss at that range.

I had to get out of here. I lay facedown, with my head twisted to the right, my hands curved up toward my face. I pushed up with all my might. Nothing. Why I thought I'd be able to get out now better than before, I had no idea. Logic wasn't actually something I was using at the moment. I pressed my head into the cold cement floor and closed my eyes. As fear rose up over me again, I forced myself to count breaths inside and then out, and I didn't let myself think of anything else. Slowly, I found myself relaxing. If you could call ratcheting down from overload to just completely terrified. I kept breathing. It's not like I was going anywhere.

That's when I remembered I could travel through the trace dimension. Oh, for fuck's sake. I was a total idiot. Instantly, I opened myself up to it and tried to fall inside.

Nothing happened. I didn't know if the cocoon was stopping me or my immobility. Okay, then. How did I get into the trace dimension if I couldn't actually move? I took stock. My nulls. I had one tattooed on my belly and one on my scalp. I had used them both recently and hadn't fully recharged them. Even at full strength, I didn't think they could take down the magic-formed cocoon or the magic storm raging around me. The rest I'd brought with me were in my pack. Fat lot of good they did me there. That left just the spirit world. Or waiting. Since the last one seemed more likely to end in death than not, I decided I had better make option one work for me.

The nice thing about having your mind occupied with a goal is that fear stops being quite so all encompassing. It wasn't gone, but at least I was back in my head's driver's seat for the moment.

After contemplating a few minutes, I decided my only option was to open the door on the spirit world inside myself and travel through the spirit world that way. Easy peasy. And for my next trick, I'd fly to Mars and back, and then jump a tornado to Munchkinland.

The trouble was, I didn't know if what I wanted to do was even possible, much less how to do it. I took a breath and let it out and focused my attention on the problem. I could open myself to the trace, which meant I was halfway to getting into the spirit world. I could summon my magic. Could I use it to pull myself into the trace dimension? To open up a door?

I'd never done anything like that before. Usually I channeled my magic into an object, most often creating nulls. I didn't have a lot of other things I *could* make. Other times I was able to pull magic from a spell, unwinding the power, then channeling it into a null. I couldn't throw magic the way movie wizards and witches did. I relied on touch to move the magic from me to an object. That, of course, was the problem. I couldn't move, and I was cocooned inside hard air, or so it seemed. My trace sight told me it was made of magic. The optimist in me held on to the hope that the cocoon was proof some part of Price knew me, that I could reach him.

I chewed my lips and tasted dust. I expect I was covered with it from head to toe. Now that I thought of it, it itched at my eyes and tickled my nose. I sneezed, then twice more in quick succession. This whole situation was turning torturous. Now something felt like it was crawling up my back. An ant maybe. I pushed myself up against the cocoon and wriggled. The crawling sensation went away. For now.

I was wasting time. I didn't want to fail, and most of me thought that I would. Trace magic just wasn't meant to be an active power. It was passive, the kind that waited for its prey to walk into it before it chomped. An alligator rather than a lion. Right now, I needed lion power.

You're the strongest tracer in living history, as far as anybody else seems to know. If anybody can travel through their own trace, you can. I told myself this and kept repeating it in my head so that the piranha doubts couldn't grab hold. I had to get out and stop Price. My family's lives were at stake. Price's life was at stake. Not to mention the FBI agents imprisoned in the building, and who knew how far the damage would go.

I summoned magic into me. Normally, I'd let it flow through, but this time I held it. Before long I got light-headed. My body felt fizzy, and tickling warmth swirled down my arms and legs and up through my head. I squinched my eyes shut as the carbonated feeling hit them. Not entirely comfortable.

The pressure built inside me. How much would I need? How much was too much? I decided to err on the side of blowing open a door versus not succeeding at all, and took as much as I could hold.

Now for the tricky part. Which is to say, the part where I played mad scientist and experimented in the hopes I got it right and didn't kill myself in the backlash of failure. Or even success, for that matter.

I'd kept myself open to the trace. I felt the spirit dimension waiting just beyond. Could I send magic through my trace and somehow use it to pull myself inside? I focused on my trace ribbon and sent magic shooting down it. I wasn't sure what I thought would happen. Like I said, mad-scientist time.

I braced myself. Nothing. The magic dissipated out along my trace, like pouring ink into water. I needed to anchor it somehow so that I could pull myself along. Could I flare it out somehow to catch on the edge of the spirit dimension, like a grapple? Though it seemed completely impossible to me, with nothing to lose, I tried anyway. I concentrated, pushing the flowing power to divide and spread. I put all my strength of will into my working. I about fainted when tendrils of power answered me, unwinding from each other and spreading out into trace space. My heart thudded.

I pushed the strands outward, trying to curl them into hooks. The result looked like tangled spaghetti. That wasn't going to cut it. I focused on one of the tendrils, straightening and then curving it back on itself. By the time I was done, my entire body ached and I was sweating like a horse. Worse, the other four energy tendrils had returned to the flow. Fine. I only needed one good hook to dig in and hold.

I whirled it in a circle, feeding more energy into it to lengthen the line. I panted as holding the energy grew harder and harder. I felt myself shaking. Or maybe it was the rest of the world. The floor continued to buck and rear. I had no idea how much time had passed.

I scrunched my eyes tight and bit my lower lip. I clenched my whole body and strengthened my effort.

To no avail. I made a grunting sound of pure frustration. There had to be a way to get the fuck out of this cocoon. *Think, Riley, think!* If only I could grab hold of my trace—

Wait. My forehead furrowed. God, I was stupid. My trace was nothing more than a magical umbilical cord. It was anchored inside me, body and soul. I was *always* touching it. Travelling along it should be one step easier than using my hands to grab it. So why did it feel like I was about to jump into a blender full of broken glass?

Damn, but I wished I knew what I was doing. I wished that my mother had lived to teach me. I could visit her for a few minutes at a time in the spirit world, but that didn't make for a good classroom. Plus if my dad—Vernon—wasn't lying about Mom being a grifter, and that was a big *if*, then I couldn't really trust my mom either.

I determinedly pushed away that worry. None of that mattered at the moment.

I sank into myself, searching for my link to my own trace. How had I never tried this before? Maybe because it felt a little touchy-feely stupid. Like one of those new-agey programs of self discovery. I snorted. Okay, maybe they weren't so stupid. If I'd actually ever tried one, I might have learned something useful. I had given meditation a shot once or twice. This felt a little bit like that. 'Course I'd never been any good at it. Firefly thoughts kept buzzing into my head and distracting me. Like the fact that my boobs were killing me. Or that I was getting a crick in my neck. Or that I really wanted a jug of sweet, creamy coffee. I fought them off and concentrated on the power rushing into me. And out.

That last fact was crucial. The point where it left me was the intersection of me and my trace. *Good thinking*, I told myself by way of encouragement. *Now find it and get inside. You've totally got this.* Easy as pie.

Pie, by the way, is a lot harder than it sounds. Unless you're eating it. That's easy enough.

God. More firefly thoughts.

I followed the flow of magic down inside me. I couldn't exactly see it. I felt like I ought to have been able to, but it was blurry and out of focus. The pull was inexorable, once I let myself fall into it. It whirled me around and carried me along, inward and through the middle of myself. The sensation made me nauseous and champagne fizzy at the same time. I turned inside out, and my skin and flesh held me together. My bones electrified, and I felt incandescent. Then I hit the intersection where my trace grew out of my essence.

My entire being jolted with something so primal, so deeply essential and basic, that I felt it on a plane of existence that I could only think of as my soul. I think I might have screamed. I don't know. It wasn't pain. It might have been pleasure. The intensity was so fierce that I felt every molecule of my body freeze. A small nova went off inside, spreading a shockwave of heat and ice and joy so thin and fine it was almost agony.

I stayed suspended there in that moment, in that space where I pierced through the root of myself, for I don't know how long. Time didn't matter. Only the feelings that radiated out and came crashing back, the ripples warring and growing more powerful with each expansion and contraction. I could have stayed there forever. I was drugged. High as a kite, as the stars themselves. I was a star. A sun. The whole damned universe.

I forgot everything. Nothing else mattered. This was *divine*. Touching God. Touching the very spark of creation. It couldn't be anything else.

Cold. It seeped into me, turning sharp and knife-edged. It sliced down into me, down into that space where I hung enraptured. It didn't hurt. I gathered in the feeling, letting it temper and increase the glorious feelings that had come before.

That's about the time my brain kicked in. The part that wasn't orgasming from my little trace masturbation. Cold meant I'd tapped into the spirit dimension. I'd opened a door. Or at least a window. Maybe a tiny hole. It didn't matter. I'd done the hard part. Now all I had to do was go through to the other side.

Turned out that going through was nothing. Dragging myself away from the rapture of communing with my own trace was another something else altogether. Most of myself dug in, wanting to remain in that amazing place of between, where I felt light and bright and free and so incredibly euphoric. Blissful. Joyful. There were no words to truly describe my ecstasy.

The determined little wart that was my brain reminded happy Riley that Price needed help. That my family needed help. That the world as I knew it was coming to an end.

Happy Riley didn't seem to give a damn, though. All that drama was too far away and so very small in the grand scheme of the universe. Warty brain smacked happy Riley alongside the head and grabbed her by the hair, then proceeded to drag her down from Orgasm Mountain and dump her into the frigid ice of the spirit dimension.

Arctic cold slapped my face. I reeled as I collected myself. Glorious sensation continued to reverberate through me, but my mind was clear. I looked around.

The velvety purple black of the spirit dimension surrounded me. A jungle of jewel-toned trace ribbons flowed across it, tangling and trailing in every direction as far as the eye could see. Silky tatters of opalescent energy floated through like ghosts. They probably were.

Holy crap. I'd actually made it.

Cold continued to press in on me, but unlike my last two trips through, it didn't instantly sink its thorns deep into the marrow of my bones. I felt somewhat insulated, though the cold would chew through soon enough. I glanced down at myself. I looked like a watercolor painting. Not transparent, not like my mom when she'd appeared to me here, but still wavery and not quite real. I was wrapped in green light the color of oak leaves. Curls of silver swirled through it like smoke. I blinked. I seemed to be inside my trace. It was protecting me from the deadly chill of the spirit world. Not forever though. I knew I couldn't stay here too long, all the same. Not that I planned to. I was going to get out right now.

I'd already decided where I was going. Given that I didn't know how far-reaching Price's destruction was, I had chosen to return to the mouth of the cave and make my way back to the compound and hope there was something left. I didn't let myself think that Price had killed my family. I had to believe he'd protected them the way he'd protected me. If not—

I shoved that thought away and turned my attention back to the task at hand. Ordinarily, I would take hold of my trace in my hand and follow it back to wherever I'd been that I wanted to return to. I supposed now I needed to just push myself along the inside of my trace until I found the right spot. I pictured one of those message systems where you put your message in a tube and sent it rocketing along to its destination.

I started to push off.

"Riley?"

I stopped, twisting around. My mother stood—floated really—right behind me. Her skin glowed with mother-of-pearl color. I could see right through her. She looked the same age as she been when she died—just about the same age I was now. We looked a lot alike, except her hair was more auburn than copper. Taylor looked more like her than I did. There was some irony for you.

"What are you doing here? Are you *inside* your trace?" Her eyes widened.

"I was trapped. This was the only way out."

Her gaze sharpened. "Trapped?"

"My boyfriend cascaded and then lost it. I ended up in some sort of protective magic cocoon. This is my way out, but I need to get back and help him."

She shook her head. "It's too dangerous. You need to stay away until he drains or stops on his own."

"I can't. I wasn't alone. Leo, Jamie, Taylor, and Mel were with me. Plus some friends and a whole building full of people."

"Christ." She came closer and peered at me through the veil of my trace. "They are alive at least."

I hadn't realized how scared I was that Price had killed them. So scared I'd forgotten to *look* and see for myself. I shuddered with reaction. "Thank goodness."

"Thank your boyfriend," Mom said. "That he's managed that kind of control during a cascade eruption means that maybe you *can* help him. You'd better go. Don't try to travel through the trace to him. It could be very dangerous."

"How?"

Her head tilted in a way that seemed really familiar. Then I realized. The gesture reminded me of me. "Dangerously dangerous," she said with a little grin.

Now I knew where I got my sense of humor. "That's helpful," I said, rolling my eyes. I wonder if I got that from her, too.

"Do you really have time for a magic lesson? I'm telling you it would be a bad idea. Deadly even. Don't do it. Get back to the physical plane. Now, get going."

I nodded acknowledgment and yet didn't move. "Dad—Vernon— said you were a grifter." I blurted the words, then bit my lips as I waited for her response.

Her head tipped to the side. "I suppose I was, as much as anything," came her unexpected answer.

"What does that mean?"

"I have a lot to tell you. You were supposed to come see me."

"I haven't had time. And I had to heal up from—" I broke off. How did I explain that I'd had to have my thumb reattached after a sociopath cut it off, and then I'd been kidnapped by my father's henchman? To get away, I'd nearly killed myself. That was last week. This week was looking busier. "Anyhow, I'd planned to come back and see you, but then Dad showed up and all this happened with Price. My boyfriend," I added, realizing she didn't know who he was. "Plus I nearly got kidnapped again by Savannah Morrell. Oh, and this FBI agent I hate has asked for help finding some of her people. I said I'd help her."

Some people have simple to-do lists. Fix dinner, pick the kids up, go to work, clean the bathroom, grocery shop, blah blah blah. Mine read more like a comic-book hero's. Or villain's.

I could see my mom trying to sort out that deluge of bizarre information. Finally, she waved her hand dismissively.

"I have things to tell you. Before it's too late."

"Like about being a grifter." I don't know why that bothered me so much. It's not like she'd been hiding it from me. She'd been dead. I'd only discovered her here in the spirit world a week ago, and we'd not exactly had a big heart-to-heart conversation.

I was starting to shiver as the cold worked its way through the insulating walls of my trace to find me. I clamped my teeth together as they started to chatter.

She gave a half smile that was both ironic and shrewd. "I was what I was. It kept a roof over my head and food on the table. I couldn't let anyone know who or what I really was. Same as you. I make no apologies, and regrets are useless. Anyway, I gave up grifting when I married your father. I never hid my past from him."

Same as you. I knew so little about her, and what I did know had come from Vernon, whether he told me things or injected fake memories into my brain. But this much was true. She knew what it was like to have to hide, to fear that someone would discover her and either enslave her or kill her. In that, we were exactly alike.

I frowned as I realized that there was something in the way she changed the emphasis in that last sentence. I itched to be on my way, but—

"You did hide things from Dad, though."

Her smile faded. "I did. But now it appears those secrets are unraveling, and you are the one to pay the price."

I wrapped my arms around myself as cold wrapped my spine and wriggled through my veins. "What do you mean?"

She shook her head. "Not now. You have been here long enough, even protected as you are. Just don't wait too long to return. With your father back . . ." She looked grim. "I don't like this."

"Why?"

"I would not trust him," she said, the words coming slowly, almost unwillingly.

"Why not?"

She cocked her head at me, then gave a little nod, as if convincing herself. "You are the last of the Kensington line. Zachary Kensington was your many times great-grandfather. I believe your father is aware of this. I believe he knew I was of that blood when we met. I believe our meeting was no accident." She finished with a tightening of her lips. A bitter smile. "Go now. Come see me again. Soon."

With that she simply vanished. I stared at where she'd been. I didn't know what to think or how to react. Why would the fact I was related to Kensington matter to anyone?

Before I jetted off into Distraction Land, I caught myself. My mom's news didn't change what was happening with Price and the danger to everyone I loved. It was just another mystery to deal with later, providing I lived long enough.

I turned my attention to getting where I needed to go. I pushed off, sliding through my trace again. I arrived so fast that I almost shot past the spot. I reversed the process of getting into my trace, ignoring the solar burst of bliss. Well, I tried to ignore it. I slowed, taking more time than I should have to pull myself through and out.

I exited my trace more easily than I expected. All of a sudden, I was back in the frigid air of the Colorado winter night. Actually, I sprawled facedown on a pile of rocks and snow. I lay there a moment, letting myself adjust to the pain. It probably ought to have worried me that I didn't feel cold at all. I was too numb from the spirit dimension. Finally, I groaned and worked on standing up. It took a few tries. My knees hurt something fierce, and a rock wedged into my ribs like an iceberg under the *Titanic*.

When I managed to get to my feet, I swayed. My head spun, and a warm trickle of blood ran down my cheek. I touched my face and sucked in a quick breath. The cut was a good two or three inches long and extended from the middle of my right cheek into my hair. I scooped up a handful of snow and pressed it against the wound. Hopefully the cold would stop the bleeding.

I ached like I'd been used as a punching bag. When this was over, I wanted to spend a week in my bathtub. I snorted. When this was over. As if that would happen anytime soon.

I glanced around. I had arrived in the stand of trees and boulders just beyond the cave entrance, exactly where I'd been aiming. Somehow I'd remembered there being fewer rocks.

That's when I became aware of the sound of wind. The clearing I stood in was still as death. Not a breath of air stirred. And yet—I could hear the roar of the wind, like a tornado.

Price.

I dropped my handful of bloody snow and started running.

Chapter 15

BECAUSE I'M JUST that sort of brilliant, I'd figured out that Price's talent had to do with air or wind. Also, water is wet.

I was unprepared for the strength of his talent, even knowing that when he was three years old he'd wreaked Armageddon across a mountain. People do exaggerate.

Not this time.

I ran through the trees. It was eerie. Nothing moved. Not even snow fell. Magic saturated the air so thick I could hardly breathe. It blinded my trace sight with opaque rainbow shimmers. I'd never experienced anything like it.

At the edge of the trees, I stopped. Rather, something stopped me. I ran into a wall of air. Inside was a whirl of dust and debris. I couldn't see more than a foot in front of me. It was like staring through a window into the heart of a tornado. It's entirely possible a Kansas farmhouse whirled by, maybe a tin man and a scarecrow.

I pressed up against the invisible wall. It was hard as rock, just like the cocoon that had held me. I jerked back as a chunk of something battered just above my head and vanished into the spinning mess.

I was impressed. Despite cascading and erupting like a volcano on steroids, Price had managed to control his talent. At least enough to contain the disaster inside this wall and protect me. And protect the rest of my family. For now. I scowled at the murky darkness in front of me. How much longer could he hold on? I had to get to him and help him stop the cascade somehow.

The idea of going inside the air wall was obviously not the brightest. I didn't have a choice. Price had to be stopped, and I was the only one left standing to do it. I was the only one he might listen to. *Might*. If he was willing to believe I was really me. I grimaced. Time for him to get his eyes opened.

Getting inside was the first hard part. I could try to tear a window into his wall by sucking down power, but I had no good place to put the magic. I couldn't just release it into the air or the ground. I had to create something with it. Maybe if I found a big boulder or something like it, I could channel the energy into the rock and create a massive null. Plus, he'd likely just feed more energy into the wall. Which meant I'd pretty much need to take the whole thing down.

I chewed my lower lip as I considered. I'd have to outlast Price. Given this stunning display of his talent, I wasn't sure I could. I was probably the strongest tracer alive, but he was something else altogether. Manipulating the elements took enormous power. I'd never actually seen an elemental talent before. In the early days, they usually ended up dead. They were too scary to let live. Nowadays, either they kept themselves well hidden, or they were enslaved to a Tyet organization or a government. I wondered if the FBI suspected what he was. But no, they'd have grabbed him much sooner if so.

Given that FBI reinforcements were on their way, I needed to find a way through sooner rather than later. That's when I remembered the pipe that Jamie and Leo had used to cross under the fence and up to the building. Just the thought of crawling through it made my body clench and my heart jump into high gear. No choice. I turned along the wall and started jogging through the trees, not letting myself think about what could go wrong.

I reached the hole. It gaped at me. I didn't even have a light. If I did this, it would be in pitch-darkness, and who knew if the other end was even open or if it had been covered over by Price's maelstrom.

Before I could talk myself out if it, I jumped down inside. The pipe was about three to three and a half feet across. Leo and Jamie must have sized it up to help them get through. I lowered myself down onto my stomach and began crawling. My brothers had flattened the corrugations in the bottom of the pipe, making it more comfortable, leaving the ridges in the sides to give purchase for feet.

The noise of the storm above roared, echoing down from ahead. Hopefully that meant the exit was clear. I clung to that thought as I wriggled along. Before long my elbows, knees, and toes ached and throbbed. Even flattened, the bottom of the pipe was hard and held an unreasonable amount of rocks and sticks. The floor was muddy, with water pooling here and there, adding to my chill.

I kept my eyes closed, imagining I wasn't inside an underground metal tube. I don't know if the events of the night had already numbed me to fear or if I actually convinced my head that I wasn't in a really long coffin, but I managed to stay relatively sane and to keep moving. Maybe it was just knowing that people were counting on me. My family was counting on me.

I dropped into trace sight, but the thick rainbow magic made it impossible to check anybody's trace. I scooted faster.

Once again, I was totally soaked in sweat and mud by the time I reached the end of the road. I couldn't imagine how bad I smelled. I felt the push and tug of the wind before I reached the end. I stopped a yard or so from the opening, which actually still was open, bonus for me. Fingers of wind scooped down inside the pipe, shoving me back. I spread my legs and braced myself, refusing to give ground. I tried to remember what was ahead. The FBI building was probably ten feet from the exit hole. Or it had been.

What was I going to find? Would I even be able to get through the maelstrom to find Price? In the darkness, I snarled with fierce determination. I'd come too far not to. Hell, I'd crawled through a fucking hole in the ground. There was no way I was going to lose this game now. I had his trace. Even if I couldn't see it, I could feel it. That meant I could find him anywhere. I just had to hope I didn't get pulverized by a flying house on the way. I wouldn't want to end up like the Wicked Witch of the East. Though I could have used a pair of ruby slippers right about now.

It would be a whole lot easier if I could just travel through the trace to him. But Mom had said that would be very bad. I had to believe her. As plans went, running through a tornado seemed pretty stupid, and yet I couldn't think of any other options. Maybe I'd get lucky. Maybe the building was still standing and I'd be able to crawl inside and gain some protection that way. Right. Because the last time Volcano Price had erupted, he'd scraped off half a mountain. A building was totally stronger than a little mountain, right?

I was fucked.

Get on with it, I told myself, and then decided to stop thinking so hard and just do it.

I crawled down to the opening. My ears popped and gritty wind sanded my skin. I squinched my eyes to slits. Wind pummeled me. The still sane part of my brain balked. Was I really going to do this? This was suicidal. What choice did I have? I asked myself. As if in answer, an idea sparked. I could try one other thing. I wriggled backward down the pipe, out of the wind's immediate reach. For once being in the narrow confines felt safer than being out.

I reached into the cold of the trace world and grabbed Price's trace, wrapping it around my hand. A landslide of emotion crashed over me. Fear, exultation, fury, joy, hate, exhilaration, guilt. The torrent filled me. Inwardly, I clawed to hold on to myself. It took all I had, and I knew I couldn't last. Surely if I could feel him, I could make him feel me? I collected myself around the little stubborn wart in my brain that had saved me before. I focused, sending a sharp pulse down his trace, at the same time yanking on it as I had before.

Nothing happened. I did it again and then twice more as desperation mounted.

I could feel it when Price became aware of me. Curiosity colored the maelstrom of his emotions. The next thing I knew, the air in the pipe thickened. A cataract of rainbow energy poured inside from the hole ahead. My mouth went dry. Air rushed over me and under me. It pressed inward, molding to my body. I clutched down on Price's trace as my ribs compressed and my breath leaked from my lungs.

My claustrophobia returned with a vengeance. In the dark, being squished from all sides, panic jumped into the driver's seat. I wriggled and fought, but I couldn't move. I couldn't breathe. I did the only thing I knew how to do. I ripped magic out of the air, dragging it into me until I felt incandescent. I held it as I reeled in more. I thought my skin would split. I kept drawing it in. I didn't stop until I felt my mind clouding from lack of oxygen.

I gripped Price's trace and sent all the collected magic shooting along the ribbon in a blistering gob. I poured all I had into that fiery mass. I wasn't sure what it would do to him. Not that I was thinking of that. Instinct and primordial desperation had me. I didn't know my name. I didn't know where I was. All I knew was that I was going to die and I had to fight.

Somewhere far away I felt the mass of magic hit him. I felt the predator surge inside him, focused, determined, and ruthless. He didn't recognize me. What little reason I clung to cringed. He was coming for me. Ha. Like he didn't already have me trapped.

The pipe ahead ripped open. Metal screeched, and the steel around me shuddered with the force. It unzipped above me, exposing me to the storm above. Wind coiled around me and raised me upward, holding me upright above the ground.

I could still feel the rush of emotion through Price's trace. It's an odd thing to be totally terrified of the man you love. I wondered if this was how abused women felt. But no. Price was no abuser. He had honor, and courage, and he loved me. He had protected me from his power, and he still was. Debris continued to whistle and spin around me, but it never hit. In fact, it seemed to be sifting out of the air, like it was too heavy to be raised.

Once again, I marveled at Price's control. By all rights, he should be dead right now. His magic should have shredded him. Yet he'd managed to harness it. How the hell had he suppressed this kind of power? *What* had they done to rip the lid off?

Not that it mattered. I was dangling in midair with no way down and nowhere to go. The last thing I needed to worry about was how this had happened.

Abruptly, the sound of the howling wind silenced. I hadn't realized how loud it was until it was gone. All around me, chunks of stuff fell out of the air and thudded to the ground. A hail of broken junk. Hopefully no dead bodies. Or body parts. I remained fixed in the air. A spider pinned to a display. I swallowed. My throat felt chalky. My tongue was sandpaper. I tasted copper. I must have bitten myself.

The tornado continued to rage beyond the clearing where I hung. A gray dust-bowl ghost appeared out of the settling dust. Price. The coveralls we'd found him were shredded and stained with blood. His own. Grime coated him like he'd been through a cloud of volcanic ash.

His eyes were still white. I couldn't tell if he was sane. I couldn't read his expression through the mask of dust. He stopped a few feet away, looking up at me. He didn't speak.

"Mind setting me down?" I asked. Whispered. Between the fear constricting my throat and the dust I'd swallowed, my voice was toast.

His expression didn't change. Neither did he let me go.

I drew a slow breath and let it out. "Price? Baby? Let me down," I said gently.

I didn't go in for endearments as a rule. Price liked to call me *baby*, and even though I consider myself a powerful, independent woman, I totally ate it up. Made me go all hot and gushy inside, like one of those chocolate lava cakes. The only thing I ever called him was *Price*. I couldn't remember ever even using his first name, much less a *honey* or a *sweetheart* or *snookums*. Calling him *baby* now was a risk. Seeing's how he still might not believe I was me, it might just piss him off, and he'd whack me to a pulp on the ground.

He stood stiff as a statue, his hands clenched at his sides. I struggled against my invisible bonds, but the best I could do was twist a bit and wriggle my fingers and toes. It's a wonder I could move my jaw enough to talk.

I considered trying to suck the magic out of my bonds, but Price still poured power into them. I could channel some of it into the two nulls tattooed on my skin, and maybe some of the trinkets I carried on me, but I doubted I had enough space to put it all. Once I started channeling, I couldn't break the stream until the magic ran out. At least, I never had done that before. I had no idea when Price would run dry. Or if he'd stop on his own. I wasn't all that sure he would stop. Or that he could. *That* was a scary fucking thought.

On the other hand, he'd shown a lot of control. Maybe all he needed was motivation. I sure as hell couldn't tell him how to turn off the spigot. It was supposed to be an instinct. Like breathing or blinking. He clearly had known how to turn himself off once, demonstrated by the fact that he'd shut himself down when his mother had taken him to South America for whatever exorcism she thought the priests could perform. Bitch. So Price had stopped himself once, which meant he ought to be able to stop himself again. He just had to remember how. All I had to do was give him a push in the right direction.

As ideas went, the one I got was ninety percent brilliant, ten percent suicidal. Or maybe it was more ninety percent suicidal. Anyhow, it was an idea, and it could work.

Or not. I decided not to think about that.

I reached out to the magic cocooning me, and I pulled away a thread. Magic flowed into me, cool and hot at the same time. I channeled it down into Price's trace, pushing it back out toward him.

When it didn't rebound back at me, I grabbed more magic, drawing as much as I could. I dumped it into his trace. He recoiled and backed away from me. I had his trace, though. He could go to Timbuktu, and I'd still be feeding him his magic. Now that I started, I couldn't stop the loop. Only he could, by shutting down his magic.

A blast of power sparked over my skin like a bee attack. I let out a yell. "What the fuck is that?"

"Stop," Price said, his black brows a solid bar above his white eyes. "What are you doing?"

Well halle-fucking-lujah. I'd made him talk to me, if nothing else.

"I can't stop," I said. "Not now that I've started. The ball's in your court for that. We're going stay on this merry-go-round until one or both of us burns up, or you put on the brakes. I'm voting for the second one."

His face worked, his mouth twisting as he raised his fists up and ground his knuckles against the side of his head. He uncurled his fingers and slid them through his hair, gripping and pulling. His entire face contorted, and his body tightened as if he hauled against a great weight.

Nothing happened.

He gave a gasp and stared at me. The edges of his eyes were rimmed red. With the white, he pretty much looked like a demon straight out of hell. "I can't."

"Don't give me that. You did before. When you were a kid. Plus you've been controlling it this entire time. Hell, you don't even believe I'm really Riley, and you've been protecting me from your power this whole time. You've got this. You just have to do it."

Because *Just Do It* is the best advice of all time. Sort of like, *don't have that stroke*, or *just tell the bully to leave you alone*, or better yet, *tell the sun to set in the east for once*. I tried for something more dire.

"If you don't reel it in, you're going to die." I didn't point out that I would die, too. I wasn't all that sure he wouldn't think that was a benefit.

"How?"

I could see that asking cost him. I could feel it in the surge of hatred in his trace. Nope, he didn't really trust me yet. Maybe he never would.

I let the pain of the possibility wash over and through me and away. I couldn't afford the distraction. "I don't know. It should be instinct."

Price made a growling sound, and I couldn't blame him. I was zero-for-two on the helpful advice front. I scrabbled to think of something actually useful. How did I shut down? I snorted at myself. When it came to channeling magic, I couldn't. But was that true? Maybe I just hadn't figured out how, same as Price.

"Maybe this is all in my mind. A scenario to train me to use my power so you can use me." His upper lip curled.

"So now I'm not only not myself, I'm a figment of your imagination?" It was like a bottomless pit of uncertainty. I couldn't win. As far as he knew, there would always be a chance his perceptions wouldn't be real. That in reality he was still trapped in the cell and everything he was experiencing was nothing more than a dreamer fucking with his brain.

"It's more likely than Riley actually being here, don't you think?" he rasped.

"More likely than me showing up with my family, with Dalton, with Special Bitch Arnow, all of us trying to rescue you? Right. That doesn't sound anything like me. I would never commit a risky assault on an FBI compound to rescue my boyfriend before the feds fucked with his head. Instead, I'd probably be—what? Hanging around at the diner? Or maybe sitting on the couch at your place, surfing the satellite for game shows until you were released? Maybe your brother and I would be out bowling and drinking piña coladas together. I swear, it's like you don't even know me. If the FBI really had invented this little movie for you, they'd have created a scenario starring Touray and a couple hundred of his militant minions. If your federal buddies included me at all, I'd probably be hanging out in the getaway van, delicately chewing my freshly polished nails while I waited nervously for you to be rescued. Or maybe I'd be wrapped in rope on a railroad track while the Evil Villains waited for you to come running. I sure as hell wouldn't be crawling through a fucking underground tube or letting you strangle me."

He stared at me, his face blank. With his white eyes and the dust masking his features, I couldn't read his expression. Finally he spoke. "You're late."

Hope stabbed through my heart. "Excuse me?"

"You're late. To rescue me before the FBI fucked with my head." He knocked his knuckles against his forehead.

I licked my lips. "Does that mean you believe I'm really me?" I couldn't read anything from his trace. His emotions were too confused.

He ran the tip of his tongue around the ridge of his teeth. After what seemed like a week, he gave a sharp, decisive nod. "I do."

And as he spoke the words, a spike of uncertainty surged through his trace. He didn't really believe. But he wanted to, so that was half the battle.

"Great. Now put me down."

"You shouldn't have come," he said, and now it was easy to read him. I didn't need trace for that. His entire body screamed condemnation and fury. "It was too damned dangerous. Shit, Riley. Look at me. Look at what I've done. I can't stop." His hand jerked toward the winds raging beyond our little bubble. "I can't—"

He jaw knotted. I heard his teeth grind together. "Tell me you were lying, that you can stop whatever you did and break away from me."

"Nope." I met his gaze. "I wouldn't if I could. Either we get out of this mess together, or we go down together."

"God damn it, Riley! This isn't a game."

"I never thought it was. But here's the thing. I know you'd risk everything to save me, even if you weren't really sure I *am* me. On the other hand, you might not do enough to save just yourself," I said. "Now you'll have to get us both out alive. Or not."

The tendons in his neck tightened and pulled taut. "When this is all done, you and I are going to have a serious talk," he said, glowering.

"Can't wait. Why don't you get on with your end of things?"

His eyes narrowed. "You sound awfully sure of me."

"You've never failed me yet."

His gaze fixed on my neck. I expect the bruises ringing my throat had turned ugly already. "Haven't I?"

I made a dismissive sound. "Not that I've noticed. So why don't you get on with hitting the kill switch on your magic?"

I wasn't going to say anything to Price, but I was beginning to feel the strain of feeding his magic back to him. I could still keep it up for a good while, but I was mentally and physically exhausted and travelling through the spirit dimension wasn't exactly a walk in the park. I definitely had limits, and I was starting to feel them.

"Riley—"

"No," I said. "You've got this. I know you do. Don't overthink it. Just do what comes naturally."

"None of this comes naturally," he rasped.

"Fake it, then."

He just stared at me. "That's it? Your best advice to me is to just do it and fake it? That's all you've got?" The left corner of his mouth quirked slightly.

"All right. Imagine your power is a really big light switch and switch it off."

He grinned. It was gone in a second, but I could feel a shift in the fear and tension roiling through his trace. It wasn't as thick. Not only that, but I felt his trust in me strengthen.

"Your advice is getting worse by the second."

"Just wait until I get to the old standbys like picture everybody naked and eat your Wheaties and wait an hour after eating before you go swimming. I'm full of helpful hints like that."

He smiled again, and this time it lingered a moment longer. Then his expression hardened. He closed his eyes and drew a long breath, his arms hanging down at his sides. He exhaled, then breathed in again. And then again.

Nothing happened.

I bit my lips to keep myself quiet. He didn't need distraction, and I didn't have anything useful to offer. Except maybe . . . "You can do this. I know it."

"Glad one of us does," he muttered. Strain etched his voice.

"Don't be a pansy," I said. "Suck it up."

His eyes opened a slit. "That's not helping."

"You didn't like touchy-feely encouragement. I thought I'd go for tough love."

"How about you shut up and let me concentrate?"

"If that will help."

"It couldn't hurt." He closed his eyes again.

Again I could feel that lightening in his trace. Maybe I was a distraction, but I was also helping him feel more in control and less vulnerable. More like himself.

"You know that if you can't shut this down, we won't ever have sex again," I said.

His eyes popped open, and he glared at me. "Not. Helping."

"I just thought you might want some motivation. I mean, beyond the obvious."

He gritted his teeth. "I hate to ask. Obvious?"

"The part where we won't be having sex because we'll be dead. But no pressure."

"Right. *That* obvious. No pressure at all." He squeezed his eyes shut, but a smile ghosted over his lips.

Again I waited. My heart skipped madly. My stomach twisted into corkscrew knots. All of a sudden, I had a crazy urge to go to the bathroom, and my nose itched. Stupid body. I hated feeling helpless. Being helpless was far worse.

But Price could do this. He *would* do this. Because he never failed, and more importantly, we had too much at stake. Both of our families needed help, and then there was us. We hadn't had nearly enough time yet. We'd barely gotten started. We needed more time.

His chest rose and fell, the rhythm growing faster. His body clenched tighter than a fist. Still nothing. I raked through my mind, hunting for some little tidbit that might help.

"Set me down."

It took a few seconds for his eyes to flicker open. "What?"

"Set me down. Let me loose."

Scowl. "Why?"

"Because I have to stop feeding magic back to you, and I need something else to tie it to."

"Why?"

"Because then you'll eventually run dry."

He eyed me suspiciously. "And if I don't dry up before you're exhausted and played out?"

"That won't happen."

"Because you're superwoman?"

"Because I won't stop until you do." I said it with fierce determination.

"You're delusional."

"I'm desperate," I corrected.

"So am I, but that doesn't seem to matter much, does it?" Bitterness dripped from his voice. "Have you considered that my running dry could very well kill everyone that I've protected thus far? That's"—his attention turned inward—"more than sixty people. I'm still feeding those protections. If I can't figure out how to shut myself down while still leaving those intact, they'll all die."

His words were utterly devoid of emotion, but that only told me how much the idea of killing so many people—innocent people—tortured him. That and the fact that he didn't let me out of my little hard-air prison.

That meant my idea was a nonstarter, which left me with only one other option to help. One very crazy, very stupid, very desperate option. It probably wouldn't even work.

Price scowled at me. "What's whirling around in that bull head of yours?" He gave a sharp shake of his head and wagged a finger at me. "No risks, Riley. You've already put me through hell on that front too many times. Not again."

I just stared at him, my throat too tight to speak. He must have seen what I was feeling.

"Riley," he warned hoarsely. "Don't. Whatever you're thinking, for my sake, please don't."

I shrugged. Price started toward me, fear etching grooves around his mouth. I didn't wait for what he might say. He couldn't talk me out of it. Instead, I closed my eyes and fell down inside myself. This time I wasn't going to travel through *my* trace. I was going to travel through Price's.

Chapter 16

I DROPPED DEEP inside myself, same as before. Instinct told me that I could only help him from within. I could show him how to shut off his magic. The trick was getting inside his trace. There was only one way to do that, if it was even possible.

I didn't think about the wisdom of what I was about to try. Wise or not, I was going for it.

I needed to have an out-of-body experience. Short of killing myself, I wasn't sure how to detach my spirit from my flesh. Yet that was the only way to make the jump from me to Price.

I dove down within, to the root of my trace. I found the bliss and ignored it. This was where my trace fastened into me. What if I cut through it? Would I be able to escape my body?

I pulled hard on the energy from Price, turning it inward and focusing it like a knife. I'd never thought to cut through trace before. Typically, trace magic was more defensive. It wasn't meant to strike out in any way. *Time for this old dog to learn a new trick*, I thought.

Holding the energy so it didn't feed forward wasn't easy. All of my senses seemed to ripple and spasm, like I was trying to breathe water and my body knew it wasn't natural. I figured that if this didn't work, it might kill me, in which case I could do what I needed to. That's me. Always looking for the silver lining.

Ugh. *Focus, Riley*, I told myself. *No more firefly thoughts.*

With that, I settled into the task at hand. I pushed everything else away, and concentrated on the energy building inside me. I saw it in my mind's eye—blue-white heat and scarlet smoke. I made a hammer of hard gray light, and began to beat at the energy, shaping it into the knife that I needed. At first, the blows merely caused the power to flicker and bend, returning to the original shape like water. I ordered the power to harden, to let me hit it. Somehow it obeyed. I struck at it, over and over as more and more power fed into me from Price. I couldn't let the extra leak off without ruining what I'd managed thus far.

When I could do no more and I felt like I was going to shred apart from the pressure of the magic, I took the knife and slashed at my trace. I didn't want to sever it all the way, just make an escape hole.

The pain was as intense and all encompassing as the bliss had been. Nothing could have prepared me for it. Not just pain, either. A nothingness, a gray emptiness slipped inside me. It deadened what it touched.

Urgency drove me to leap through the hole I'd made. Without my attention, the energy knife dissolved. I let the magic continue on its way back to Price. It would hit him in a massive punch. Hopefully he could handle it.

Price's burgundy-blue ribbon looped all around me. I paused to look at myself. There wasn't much to see. Without my spirit, there was just a blank spot attached to a long streamer of green and silver. Some of that energy bled through the hole I'd left in my trace, clouding in the brilliant string jungle of the spirit realm. It looked like a stain. A thin strand of trace continued to follow me, looking about as strong as a spiderweb.

I tore my eyes away and took hold of Price's trace. I felt like quicksilver, with no weight to drag me down. Urgency spurred me. I flung myself along his trace ribbon. I hadn't gone far when I hit turbulence. I clung to his trace as I was tossed, twisted, and dragged in a storm of wild currents pulling me in all directions at once.

I fought against them, focusing all my energy on my task. Energy curled around me like tentacles. Thousands of invisible hooks scraped at me. It was like being stuck in a bramble bush. My attention blurred, and I felt myself hesitating. My focus unraveled. Bits of myself unwound and confettied away, pulled by forces I couldn't see. I snatched at them to smooth them back down, to little avail.

I couldn't tell if the attacks on me were intentional. Had I just swum into a school of trace-eating piranhas? Was there some spiritual crocodile trying to drown me before it ate me? Or was this just business as usual in the spirit realm?

Whatever was happening, I wasn't going to make it to Price if I didn't either hurry up or fix the problem. Fighting didn't seem like an option. It would take too much time and energy to create another knife, and who knew if it would even help.

I bumbled forward. It felt like I was bleeding from every pore. Shimmery strands of myself floated out like a corn-silk halo around me. I felt thin. Price's incandescent magic ran through me like a river of flames. I pushed myself into the torrent, feeling his power crackling about me. It flared up, searing me. At least, I thought it was. I couldn't feel anything.

More tentacles looped around me, but then slid weakly away. They didn't like Price's power. Then something weird happened. Petals of hot magic swept over me like hands, smoothing out the ragged tears in my spirit and collecting me back to wholeness. How? Price?

Or someone else? Too many questions and no time for answers and no one to ask.

I crashed into Price. The collision sent shockwaves rippling through me. I'd already decided what to do and now corkscrewed around where his trace transected flesh, sliding through his skin, muscle, and bone and into the core of his being.

I'd sent my spirit without my body, and now nothing stopped me as I curled myself into that place where Price's trace rooted in his being and simply nudged inside.

When I'd gone through that same node inside myself, it had been ecstasy. This was violation.

His entire being contracted violently away from me. Energy exploded, tearing and twisting. I fought to retreat. Price's trace thinned and faded to a water wash of blue and pink. A tremendous sense of horror flowed through it. Debilitating nausea and weakness surrounded me, leaching into me everywhere I touched him.

Dear God, what had I done?

With every passing second, his trace faded, turning to stagnant brown, then puke yellow.

Price was dying. I was killing him. I had to stop it.

Why hadn't our touching affected me in the same way? I had no time to think about it. Pulling back wasn't helping. I pushed up close and into him, reaching out all the magic I had to wrap around him. Opal filaments spun out of me like spider silk. They stretched and wove together as fast as I could think. They circled around his churning center. I fed all my love into the magic. I spun out soothing coolness and green forest silence. I thought of running streams and the safe coziness of my house. In every pulse of power, I promised sanctuary. More than that, I opened myself to him, inviting him to know me, to know how much I loved him, how much I admired him, how proud I was to know him.

Hesitation. Then inside that little bubble, he surged, enveloping my spirit. He surrounded me, clinging and burrowing. The shock of it shook me. If I hadn't known it was him, I might have shattered under the connection. I had no armor. Every part of my soul was exposed, raw. He smothered me, drawing me into himself. We wove together, separate, but somehow also one.

His wildness tempered. His trace flared bright, like ruby wine under a bright spring sky.

Riley? What have you done?

His words vibrated into me. They resonated like the plucked strings of a harp.

Wonder. Exhaustion. Bleak fear. Hopelessness.

I've come to help you.

Come? Then, *How?*

Hell if I knew. But we were entwined. I could feel his emotions. If I tried, I could feel the grime on his skin and the grinding pain of his many wounds. I pushed my senses out, filling him, letting him feel everything that I was.

Oh fuck.

It sounded like a prayer. Like ecstasy.

Parts of him contracted, and fire built between us. He touched and lingered in me. I tried not to notice the friction. The sensations were almost too much to bear. I'd never felt anything this powerful, this intimate. So far beyond flesh, and yet the pleasure was primal and excruciatingly profound.

Still I could feel he was on the ragged edge. His power was enormous. He pulled it in from outside himself as well as inside. Air was his tool. He could snatch the winds from the skies and suck the oxygen from a room. He could make walls of nothing and turn thin air into a battering ram.

I'd never known anyone with such capacity to wreak havoc. Total devastation. If word got out, everybody would want him.. Same as me. How was that for irony? We were going to be competing for the top of everybody's most-wanted list. The couple eternally being hunted together stays together? Be still, my heart. It was like a Hallmark card.

All the same, I'd rather face the world with Price than alone or with anyone else. If we could get out of this mess in one piece. Or hell, a few pieces was probably survivable.

This isn't hurting you, is it? Anger edged his worry. *Don't risk yourself for me.*

I don't know. And bite me. I'll risk what I want for whoever I want, especially you. Deal with it.

He tried to pull away from me. Yeah, I was going to let that happen. He and I were too intertwined now. I had him in a spiritual headlock. We'd both need to willingly unwind from each other.

Dammit, Riley! This isn't what I want! I need to know you're okay.

I will be. Just as soon as we get your magic under control. I'm not going anywhere until then, so you may as well just stop arguing and focus on the problem.

When this is over, you and I are going to have a serious talk about boundaries.

Sure. And when you convince me you wouldn't dive headfirst into a wood chipper for me, then I'll agree not to do the same for you.

That shut him up.

Now for the hard work. I explored inside him, learning his body, feeling my way out to the tips of his fingers and toes. I sank into a depth of emotion I'd not known he felt. He kept it hidden from me. For the first time I really understood the extent of his fear, his rage, and his love for me. The last was breathtaking. It was too big to hold. Wonder made me ache. How I had earned that sort of love? How could I begin to deserve it?

What's wrong?

What do you mean? I asked, feeling like I'd been caught with my hand in the cookie jar.

I can feel you. You went into electric panic mode.

Electric panic mode? What's that?

Think of it as 'Riley freaks out about God knows what and does something incredibly stupid and dangerous.' What happened? What's wrong?

Nothing.

Bullshit.

Really. It's nothing. I just . . . I don't know what the hell you're doing with me. The humiliating words came hopping out of me without my permission. I couldn't stop them.

Instead of answering, he tightened up on me, trying to see for himself what I was thinking. Luckily, we hadn't reached the point of mind reading. Here's hoping we never did. He might find out for sure what a total nut job he was sleeping with.

Explain, he said finally.

We don't really have time—

Price gave a mental sigh that I felt all the way through me. *Let's get this over with, then. Rest assured, we will talk about this later.*

As far as I could tell, there wasn't much to talk about. I mean, I had a little bit of an inferiority complex regarding him. Didn't mean I wasn't going to hold on to him with all my might. I wasn't going to go all self-sacrificing and tell him to find someone who better deserved him. She might not even exist, and if she did, I'd probably kill her in a jealous rage. So I'd have to step up.

It's really not that big a deal, I said.

I'll decide that for myself.

Fine. Since that settled it, I turned my attention back to shutting off his power. *Concentrate on the flow of magic.*

I felt it circling through him and pouring in from outside. As I saw it, there were two problems. Teaching him to quit drawing power was one. The second was whether or not everything he'd controlled at that point would collapse. I had to help him manage both.

After I finished a null spell, if it was activated, it worked independently of me. I didn't know if Price's magic would do the same. Given that he didn't know what he was doing, he might have the capacity, but might not have built the spells that way. He might need to constantly feed them. If they were spells at all and not just shaped wind that would dissolve as soon as he let go. That's when I remembered that my body was still hanging in thick air a few feet away from Price. If that cocoon failed, I'd fall about six or seven feet, maybe a little more. Mentally I shrugged. It was just bones and bruises. I'd survived worse.

I pushed my senses into his again. I felt his energy tremble and then surge against me, like a key into a lock, like he was coming home. He *needed* me. That revelation made my heart swell Grinch-style.

I let myself go, concentrating on the current of his magic. It was like riding a river of flames. Price's exhaustion was palpable. I don't know how he'd held on this long without collapsing. His desperation hammered at me. He didn't want to kill anyone. Didn't want to hurt innocent people. The idea drove him to the edge. It was a vicious circle. The more he feared, the higher his panic and desperation flared, and the more he feared.

It stopped now.

I pulled him along with me, weaving the threads of our spirits into a tighter, finer cloth until I couldn't imagine how we were going to manage to separate. I'd figure it out later. One catastrophe at a time.

I sought the center of his power. I'd always known where to find mine and how to simply do a little mental twist to open the spigot and turn it off. Mostly it wasn't hard. Except when I was channeling power from another source. Then I had to wait for it to run out and hope my strength held out. That reminded me. How long had I been channeling Price's power back to him? I didn't feel the exhaustion that I should. That was bad. Separating from my body had made it impossible to judge my own health. As soon as it hit my brain, I tucked the thought far away from where Price might pick up on it. Then I hurried.

The heart of someone's power is just the place where you connect to it. Where it gathers inside you. I like to think of it as a reservoir. All you have to do to tap it is open up a floodgate. Maybe you open it a crack, maybe you fling it wide and let it all go at once. From what I could discover about Price, he'd opened his as wide as it could go. Instinct had given him the ability to control the power he released, but he needed help closing it up and tying off the magic so whatever he'd created wouldn't just disappear. At least I hoped. He was another species of talent altogether, and I had doubts. Big ones.

When I came to the place where his magic lived inside him, I found out how right I was. There was no lake of power. Instead, it was as if Price was made out of magic. More than that, he drew more in from the outside. From the air and the wind and the shifting pressures and the jet stream and gravity—I had no real idea. But it flowed into him through his skin and coiled inside him, shining bright, like a faraway galaxy.

Ignoring the fact that I had no idea what to do, I dug in. I'd told Price to fake it. Fake it till you make it. Maybe I should have that tattooed on my ass. It was fast becoming my motto.

I reached out through our closely bonded spirits. I made myself not think. Thinking right now was my enemy. I wanted to feel. I wanted Price and me to be completely in sync. I needed to find that hidden instinct that told him how to manage his magic. The only way to do that was to get beyond thoughts.

The trouble with not wanting to think, which is perfectly doable otherwise, is that random little thoughts burst into your head and insist upon staying there. I ignored them the best I could, and tried to feel Price's toes. Silly trick, but the physical was always a dodge for the mental. I became aware of his physical aches and pains. Some of them really hurt. I pretended I couldn't feel them. I floated on his being, letting his senses tell me things.

What are you doing?

I about jumped out of my skin when Price spoke. His skin. Whatever. I'd not forgotten he was there, obviously, but I'd been so intent on my goals that he startled me. *Searching. Can you be quiet? I'm close, but I have to concentrate.*

Can I help?

I'll let you know.

His tension rose around me, and his magic churned higher, responding to his emotions. *Are you being careful?*

No. *Of course I am. Now, just relax and let me work.*

Telling someone to relax mostly pisses them off, and Price was no exception.

Seriously. Relax if you can.

You make it impossible.

I make you that hot, do I?

You twist me into knots and make me want to strangle you.

I could feel the instant he remembered that he actually had tried to strangle me. Guilt washed over him. Over us. It sent me spinning. I could barely think. All I knew was that smothering shame and remorse. It was so not helpful.

I felt myself being torn away from the source of his magic. Panicked determination speared through me. I flung my magic out in a desperate effort to reach my goal. It wasn't enough. Bleak anguish pulled at me. It wasn't just about me. His mother. His brother. The people who might die. Who might be dead. The destruction. He was sinking down into a quagmire of magical overload and self-hatred, and like a drowning man with a lifeguard, he was dragging me down with him.

I launched everything I had toward his magical core. I let go of everything that kept me grounded. I stretched, pulling taut like a rubber band, strung between two opposing forces. I refused to give up. I was too close.

I wrapped myself around the magic I was feeding back into Price. It seared. I boiled and charred. I rode the flow into the swirling galaxy of magic within him.

I could feel Price now, more than ever before. This joining was like nothing I'd ever felt. It was beyond orgasm, beyond words. I touched him in primitive ways. Everything I was lay open to him. It was divine. It was the closest thing to touching stars that I'd ever experienced.

Now everything was easy. I worked totally by instinct. I guided him to that inner knowledge to control his power. I showed him how to feel what it was like to consciously direct his magic, to control how much flowed through him, to turn off the sweep of incoming power. As he learned, the bleakness in him receded, and his confidence and strength returned. No one likes to be helpless, but for Price, it was like death. Like Samson having his hair cut off. It was betrayal by his body and by everything he thought he was.

I felt his relief and his joy and the surge of gratitude just before I died.

Chapter 17

I'D NEVER DIED before, so I didn't know how it was supposed to go. I recognized it, though. The heat of my spirit cooled, and the colors of my trace faded to gray. It felt papery and thin. A husk. Oddly, I didn't feel much different. My spirit separated from Price's like ash blown on a breeze. The spirit world dug hooks into me. Nothing hurt. I didn't feel anything. I wondered if something had happened to me, like a heart attack or a bullet. Or had I just forgotten to breathe?

Even as those questions rolled through me, realization began to hit home. I had *died*. The big buh-bye. Gone off the earth. Never going to go home again. Never going to talk to my family or be with Price or go to the diner and hang out with Patti. I wasn't going to help Arnow; I wasn't going to find Touray. I didn't have to worry about the Kensington blood in my veins. Part of me thought that last was funny. How bad was that going to piss off Vernon?

Words and thoughts tumbled through my head—or whatever passed for a head when you're dead—and I embraced them. Underneath was a morass of feeling so dark and so awful that just knowing it was waiting made me want to run.

But there's no running from death. No running from the loss, from things unfinished, things unsaid, and things undone.

I'd failed.

That one thought echoed through me, growing and aching. I went free-falling into a pit of grief and a thousand other whirling emotions. Reverberating through it all was the fact that everything was over. I was too late for anything I had left undone.

I sank under the waves. Down and down. It's not that I gave up; there was no giving up. There was no trying to save myself. No fighting back. There was nothing to do at all. Game over.

What would happen next? Would I go to heaven? Would I stay in the spirit plane? Or maybe I was going to hell? Did heaven and hell even exist? Maybe I'd be reincarnated. Maybe I'd stick around and watch over my family for the next millennium. Watch over Price.

The idea drilled a fiery hole through my heart. Not that I had one anymore. Still, it hurt. To think about watching over him as he grew older, found another love, had children, became a grandfather . . .

If I could have, I would have wept. Wasn't death supposed to be a release of some kind? A trip into bliss and forgetfulness? But no. The truth was I didn't want to forget. That idea was so much worse than having to watch Price go on without me. My memories were all that I had left of myself. If I lost them, I lost me. I'd be erased.

I was so bogged down in the thorny tangle of emotions that I didn't notice the gray of my trace picking up a tinge of green.

Something jolted through me. I jerked like a fish on the end of a line. Was I getting dragged into the afterworld now? I yanked back, decision hardening in my mind before I could even think it through. I wasn't going anywhere. I was going to be that creepy ghost haunting my family and lover. I'd watch out for them.

Again the jerk, and something else. Sensation, almost physical. But that was impossible. Unless—

I wasn't dead yet. Not all the way, anyhow.

I pulled myself up out of the pit of despair. It was like climbing up a cliff without a rope. Except I actually had a rope—my trace. It still felt papery and thin as a hair, but a slight suppleness had returned. A hint of sap hiding in winter-parched bark.

Returning to my body was like crawling into a pine box. It felt splintery and rigid. Instead of bliss when I passed through my core, it was ash and jagged glass.

I fitted myself back into my flesh. Instantly I became aware of pressure on my chest.

"God damn you, Riley. Don't do this to me. Fight. Come on!" Price's voice sounded ragged.

Abruptly, the words cut off as he pressed his lips to mine. He pinched my nose shut and blew air into my lungs. My chest expanded, and it *hurt*. I made a sound that was barely a sound. He heard. He lifted away.

"Riley? Baby, look at me. Please, open your fucking eyes."

That didn't seem like a lot to ask, yet I couldn't obey. A rhino seemed to be sitting on my eyelids. Without a word, Price went back to blowing breath into my lungs, then switched back to chest compressions.

I'd been in pain before. I've broken bones, been battered and bruised. But this? This was like standing still while Muhammad Ali used me for his personal punching bag. I felt broken ribs grating and bending. I curled my fingers and lifted my hand, pushing at Price's shoulder. If you could call the butterfly tap a shove. Still, he stopped. He caught my hand and lifted me up against his chest. He pressed a bristled cheek against mine.

"Come on, baby. Don't run out on me. You still owe me two weeks."

Dampness splashed onto my forehead. Tears. I struggled to open my eyes. I managed a sliver. Price pulled away and grasped my jaw in a gentle grip.

"Come *on*, Riley. I need you. I love you. Fight for me. For us."

I managed to open my mouth a crack and made a whimpery sound. He heard.

"That's it. You can do it. I've got you. Take a breath."

That's when I realized I hadn't breathed for myself. I sucked in and instantly started coughing. Then crying, because my chest hurt so damned bad. At the same time, pure, undiluted joy exploded in my skull, sending sparks dancing through my blood. A storm whirled in my heart. Price held me, crooning things that I couldn't hear. I didn't care. He was here. I was here. We were both alive.

But not free. Not yet. And my family? The people in the FBI compound? Price had cocooned every last one of them, and because he hadn't set them up as separate spells, he was still supplying the energy to keep them intact. We weren't out of the woods yet.

My joy quieted as reality intruded. It didn't go away, though. I don't know if it ever would. For seconds or minutes, I'd lost everything. I was never going to take my life for granted again. Even excruciating pain in my chest made me want to laugh. Even agony was so much better than being dead.

I caught my breath. Price pulled me against him, putting his arms around me tightly and burying his face in my neck. It hurt, but I didn't care.

"I thought you were gone."

He sounded tortured. Just like I felt.

"So did I."

"Don't do that again."

Like I could promise that. Instead, "We have to find the others."

He let out a breath and then stood, lifting me in his arms. They shook, whether from exhaustion or emotion, I couldn't tell.

"I can walk," I said, though I wasn't actually that sure.

He sniffed and nodded, his face a grim mask of dust, blood, and streaks of mud where his tears had tracked. "I don't want to let go of you."

I nodded. I didn't want to let go of him. But he wasn't going to be able to carry me either.

"We'll have time later," I promised, though we both knew chances were better than good that I wouldn't be able to keep it.

Wordlessly, he bent and set me carefully on my feet.

I took a step, and his hands tightened as I started to sag to the ground.

I locked my knees and pushed myself back upright. Biting my lower lip, I took another step, then another and another, until I was walking unaided.

Dust still hung thick in the air, though the winds had stopped.

"You okay?" I croaked. I tried to swallow, wishing for water or anything wet. My throat felt scratchy and sore and swallowing just made things stick together. I coughed. My chest and ribs protested with an instant starburst of fire. I wrapped my arms around myself and doubled over.

Price caught me against him and stroked my head and back. "Easy, now."

I let myself enjoy his touch for fifteen seconds or so, then pulled back. As I did, I sucked up some of the dust off his clothes. I coughed and sneezed at the same time. The resulting pain sent me to my knees. Price lifted me to my feet and steadied me. By then I was whimpering and crying and getting really annoyed that I was wasting the water of my tears when my throat was so damned dry. The air was still and frigid, and the tears froze on my cheeks and crusted my eyelashes.

Price was swearing, an unending string of profanity, growing more creative and vulgar as he went. If I could have, I would have joined him. I couldn't catch a big enough breath for that. Instead I made myself stop crying and shuffled forward. This time he held me around the waist, and a good thing, too, or I'd have face-planted more than once.

"What's that?" I asked, when a rattle of rocks broke the silence. Price didn't answer. More rocks, louder this time, clattering together. I waved at the dust in the air to clear it, which did no good at all, much to my unreasonable irritation.

"I don't know."

"Are your cocoons still working?"

When Price didn't answer, I turned to look at him. His mouth twisted with concentration.

"Price?" I prodded. "Are the cocoons still working?"

He nodded. "I don't think I can last much longer, though."

"Let's hurry, then." I sorted through my family's trace, finding Jamie's and Leo's. If we could find them before Price's magic failed, they'd be able to reinforce the rubble and then dig people out.

They were together, probably in the torture chamber where the FBI had held Price. We had to get to them. I stumbled and tripped across the field of rubble, twisting my ankles and holding my arm across my chest to help keep the bones from moving. It didn't help. I fought through my cloud of agony, doing my best to just ignore it. I couldn't let it distract me. Anyway, pain was temporary. Fucking awful, but temporary. I kept telling myself that as I dragged myself across the remnants of the compound.

I'm not saying my experience in the aftermath of Price's destruction was anything like the same, but I wondered if this devastation was a little bit like what the people of Manhattan saw when the World Trade Center collapsed. Price had dismantled most of the FBI building. A twisted skeleton of the steel infrastructure rose ghostly through the cloud of dust, wires and rebar hanging like broken spiderwebs. Given the damage, I was surprised at how little debris covered the ground. I wished I could see more. I knuckled my eyes and pulled up the neck of my shirt to cover my nose and mouth.

What had happened to everyone in the upper levels of the building? What about the woman we'd knocked out and left outside? Had Price protected them? Or had they all died? Bile burned my throat. I wanted to think that this was their own damned faults. They'd brought Price here. They'd driven him to the brink of insanity. They'd only got what they'd asked for. And yet—I couldn't blame them. Not all of them anyway. Not even most of them. Neither could I blame Price. He was a victim. Basically, this whole disaster was the result of awful arrogance and complete stupidity. They'd been so sure that they could control him.

You're the one who pulled down all their protections. No, I rejected that. Even if we hadn't shown up, I don't know that their binding spells and nulls would have been nearly enough to contain Price. I'd seen the heart of his magic. I couldn't imagine that they'd been prepared for that.

Even if the FBI had good enough containment, I'd do it again in a heartbeat. They'd been torturing him. It was wrong. Evil. Nobody deserved that kind of treatment. That the law rationalized and permitted it was just damned malicious. Wicked, vicious, and full of hate. But even if the law was right and just, I'd do whatever it took to get Price out.

Something crystallized in my brain then, the world around me grinding to a halt.

When I'd lost my mom, I'd started holding myself separate from people. Sure, I loved my family, but I'd made sure to do it on my own terms. Keeping a safe distance, just in case one of them should decide to leave me, too. I couldn't let myself feel the pain of that kind of loss again. When my dad had vanished, it about broke me. I don't know if it had been deliberate—if the tampering he'd done in my head had made me retreat back behind my walls, or if it was my own way of armoring myself. It didn't really matter. I'd done it.

The first chink came in the form of Patti. Over the years, I'd built a deep friendship with her, despite myself. Patti didn't take "Back off" for an answer. I'd also eased back into closeness with Leo, Jamie, Mel, and Taylor. I'd kept my barriers up, but I'd opened a few tiny windows for the people who mattered to me. Especially Mel, who was always there for me, always supporting me, always loving me no matter what sort of crap I threw at her.

Then Price had arrived on the scene. He'd chiseled relentlessly through the rest of my defenses. Inch by painful inch, I'd dropped my barriers against emotional invasion. The only way to love him was to let him inside, and I found out that I loved him more than I wanted my own safety. Something I'd proven again in the last hour or so.

It wasn't until this very moment that I realized that no matter what my father had done to my mind, he didn't own me. I was my own person. I'd broken down the walls he'd built in my head. He couldn't erase who I was at my core. I'd found a way out. While it was certainly true that I'd never totally erase his influence, so what? I was in charge of myself now. I chose my own path, for good or for bad. More than that, I was proud of who I was. *I'd* made me. *I* was responsible for who I was and who I had become.

Just me.

Ever since I'd walked into Mel's house to find my father sitting there so smugly, I'd doubted myself. I'd wondered how much of what I believed or thought or felt was really real. How much was me, and how much was some construct he'd injected into my head?

Now my doubts were gone. However this version of me had come to be, I knew exactly who I was. A surge of triumphant pride flooded me as I felt a weight I hadn't known I was carrying fall away.

Feeling more confident than I had in a long time, I set my feet in motion again. Price stayed beside me, one hand under my elbow to steady me, even though he was staggering like a drunk.

I found a door hanging drunkenly from a jamb. It stood alone, a set of stairs littered with debris leading downward just beyond. Leo's trace flowed down them. I followed. Before I could go more than two steps, Price wordlessly circumvented me, leading the way into the murky darkness. He kicked aside chunks of cement and other bits of the building, reaching back to grasp my hand firmly as I slowly descended after him.

We went down two flights and reached a closed fire door. I leaned against the wall as Price heaved a pile of rubble out of the way. Finally, he managed to open it about eighteen inches. I eased through, and he followed. The emergency lights that had been activated after I nulled the building's spells down illuminated the darkness.

On the other side of the fire door were more steps going down, and another closed doorway leading out into the building. There was relatively little damage here, except that the doors had been sealed shut. It looked to be the work of Jamie and Leo. Beyond, someone hammered against the steel door. There were no windows to see how many people were trapped or who they were, but I was glad to hear signs of life. Price was too. He closed his eyes, and his lips moved in something that looked like a prayer.

We continued down, following the trace. Price kept our pace slow. His feet were a bloody mess. They left a trail of red prints behind us. Each landing was alike, insomuch as the door into the building was sealed shut and voices and hammering sounded behind each. I couldn't help grinning each time as relief jetted through me. On the fourth level down, which was apparently level six, the door was gone, and the trace trail led through it. It wasn't until that moment that I remembered Price's mom.

I spun around and caught his upper arms, ignoring the throbbing pain of the movement. "Your mother."

The look on his face was utter heartbreak. Abruptly, he jerked away, his muscles tightening into steel cables. His expression hardened. "What about her?"

What about her? She'd come here to help the FBI destroy him, and all he could say was "What about her?" I led with the obvious. "She tried to shoot you."

"She did shoot me."

I blinked at that. Then my stomach flip-flopped. Despite the fact that he had no reason to lie to me and it was ridiculous to think so, I denied it. "No. You'd be bleeding more. I was inside you. I'd have known." But of course, I hadn't known. It hadn't occurred to me to look. "Where?"

Price shrugged and then thought the better of putting me off. "Thigh."

To see it I'd have to strip him mostly naked, thanks to the jumpsuit. I crouched to see the wound for myself. He let go of my wrists. The hole was practically invisible beneath the thick dust. The bullet had gone into the interior of his right thigh. Close to the femoral artery. But no, if he'd been hit there, he'd be dead now. I made myself let go of my sudden panic and gave him a crooked smile.

"At least it wasn't too serious. It didn't bleed much."

He grimaced. "I'm holding it closed."

Of course he was. It was going to take awhile to work my brain around his potential. "Neat trick," I said, straightening up. His mother's shot must have been what released his magic, his instinctive need to preserve his life. "Handy."

I kept my face expressionless. When he stopped being able to hold the wound closed, what then? If his femoral was hit, then he'd die in a matter of seconds. Maybe he'd have a minute. We could tie a tight bandage, but I had no idea how long that would hold, especially since it was going to take awhile to get out of here.

Unfortunately, Price could read me like a book.

"What's wrong?" he asked.

"Did your mom take parenting lessons from Lizzie Borden?" I turned and started walking. Time was more my enemy now than it had been before.

"Lizzie Borden killed her parents with an ax. Not quite the same thing."

"It's the best I can do. I'm not up on famous murderous moms. Maybe if I read more Stephen King." That won a flicker of a smile. It vanished as quickly as it had arrived. "Maybe we should make a New Year's resolution. Give up near-death experiences. It would make life easier for each other."

"It's March," he pointed out. "A little late. Or early."

"Never too late to make positive life changes." I slid my hand into his. His fingers clenched around mine as if he clung to a lifeline. I welcomed the pain.

"All right. I so resolve," he said.

"Amen, brother."

"How do you do at keeping your New Year's resolutions?" he asked after a moment.

"As of this instant, I just started nailing them a hundred percent."

We fell silent. I knew we were close to our destination when we reached wreckage again. It was like a bomb had gone off. Emergency lighting illuminated the destruction. Shattered furniture and computers mounded together, piled against rubble and stumps of walls. Holes gaped in the ceiling where the tiles hung down or had disappeared altogether.

I picked my way across. We'd been underground when Price went off. How had he ended up on the surface without collapsing the entire underground of the building?

We'd not gone far before we found ourselves facing a wall of rubble. I could feel frigid air brushing down over the top of it. My breath unfurled white from my lips. The trace trails we followed went through the rubble.

"We've got to climb over. They're on the other side." I said it, but I didn't know how we were going to manage it.

"It'll kill us. That stuff is loose. One thing gives way and we go down under an avalanche. Besides, with your injuries, you wouldn't get three feet up."

He was right on both counts. "What other choice do we have?"

He let go of my hand and rubbed both hands over his face. I felt magic gathering.

"Can you do this?" I asked. He was past exhausted, and holding on to control with his fingernails. Using his magic had to feel like pushing shattered glass through his veins.

"I will. You showed me how."

I'd shown him how, but I hadn't given him superhero strength.

His jaw hardened into stone. His body tightened, his muscles bulging with effort. Despite the cold, sweat beaded on his forehead. Rock grated and rumbled. I resisted the urge to step back, setting my hand on his lower back to remind him I was there.

The grating sounds increased and turned to rolling thunder. Dust swirled into the air, and bits of wood, metal, stone, and other debris crumbled down the side of the mounded wall, bouncing across the floor. Several things pelted me in the legs, and one hit hard enough to bruise. I hissed through my teeth, but otherwise kept quiet. I didn't want to distract Price.

Slowly a hole opened up in front of us. It started small and pushed up and outward until it was about four feet across. Tons of debris sat above it. Nothing fell from it. A layer of thick air held it tight from falling. The inner edges of the tunnel fluttered loosely, grating and rumbling, but it held steady.

"Go!" Price said hoarsely. "I can't hold it long."

Sweat had mixed with the dust on his face and turned to rivulets of mud. His eyes gleamed pearl white and his mouth twisted into a grimace of effort. He looked like he wore a devil mask.

"What about you?"

He shook his head, his face screwing tight. "I'm sorry. I can't—Go." The last word dripped despair. At himself, for not being stronger, at me, for having to go alone without him, without help. He was running on fumes. He probably wouldn't be able to hold the tunnel long enough for me to come back. Which meant he also wasn't going to be able to hold the cocoons either. Once they evaporated, everybody he was protecting in there under the rubble might be crushed. Neither was he going to be able to hold his wound closed.

"Go," he said again.

"Your wound." I protested.

"I'll manage. Go. I can't hold the opening."

I hesitated in an agony of indecision. Then I turned and started toward the hole. They needed help now, and Price and I were the only ones who could give it.

I slipped and slid over the tumbles of building wreckage. My ribs screamed as my foot skidded over a loose piece of stone. I twisted, falling to one knee and catching myself on my hands. Blackness clouded my vision as steel teeth chewed through my chest. Behind me, Price drew in ragged breaths, panting faster as the strain on him grew.

I struggled to my feet and staggered onward in an Oscar-worthy impression of a shambling zombie after a plague apocalypse. I'm sure I looked like one, too. I tried not to think about what I was about to do. Even though the tunnel wasn't that long—maybe ten feet across—it pegged my claustrophobia meter into the red. In fact, I'm pretty sure the dial was just spinning, I was so crazy scared. It's one thing to crawl through a pipe that you imagine could cave in on you; it's another thing to go through one that is actually fighting to collapse. Worse, it was on its way to the winner's circle. I just had to get through before it lost cohesion. Before Price ran out of juice.

Even so, once I stood in front of the hole, I couldn't move. The whole thing shifted and scraped, chuckling with demonic voices, promising to crush me, smash me into spaghetti sauce, and devour me.

I told myself to just rush through. Like I was capable of rushing. At this point it was all I could do to stay upright. I eyed the fluttering, shifting tube. I wanted to get through. God only knows how much I wanted to. I couldn't.

Then I didn't have a choice. Something scooped me up and rocketed me through. I had this image of me sitting in a barber chair and suddenly zooming down a moving sidewalk. Very George Jetson. It swept me through to the other side before I had a chance to even think.

Instantly the invisible chair dissolved. I crumpled to the ground. I may have screamed. I know I started swearing, and my eyes were leaking unceasingly. I refused to call it crying. I wasn't crying, dammit. I was exhausted, stretched to my limits, hungry, hurting, and terrified, but I absolutely was not crying.

I took my bearings. Two walls of the cell still stood. I tried to remember the layout of the space. I thought those walls had been behind Price when he blew. If so—I turned. Where had I been standing? My stomach lurched. About six feet under a pile of rubble, if I was right. A lighter layer covered the floor, though I had to guess it was still two feet thick at least. Too much for just what he'd knocked down locally.

I looked up, following the current of cold that poured down from overhead. A massive hole punched through the levels above. I could see stars glimmering through the slowly settling murk. A weirdly calm voice in my head noted that Price must have escaped to the surface that way, lifted on his wind.

I considered what was left of his cell and the room beyond. Price still held the tunnel open. Given the wreckage, I didn't think we'd have a quick escape. Much of the covering layer of debris had come from Price's escape hole. Everything else had been pushed into the encircling wall. I had no idea how deep the floor's layer of rubble went. Two feet, maybe more. Enough to crush someone to death.

I staggered to my feet, searching for Leo's and Jamie's traces. Their metal talents would help rescue everyone else and stabilize the escape tunnel.

I found Leo first. I clambered across to the point where his trace emerged from the wreckage and started to dig. Every moment was pure pain. I bent and lifted a bit of masonry and dropped it behind me, then did it again. My chest screamed. My muscles shook with strain. My vision narrowed to small points, and my hearing turned muffled. My head filled with the overwhelming thud of my blood pounding through my heart.

I knew I hadn't any time, so I didn't stop. I was moving too slowly. I couldn't make myself speed up. I'd reached my limit. An angry sound burst out when I lifted a chunk of masonry only to cause more rubble to tumble down into the hole I'd made. I wanted to pause to catch my breath, catch my balance. Instead, I bent again to my task.

I uncovered Leo's cocoon. Not just a cocoon. Thin steel mesh traced under the inside, following the contours of the air bubble. It would support the rock when the cocoon collapsed. I would have cried with relief if I wasn't out of tears. At some point the waterworks had shut off. Given that I felt like dried-up leather, I expect I ran out of spare liquid.

The surface of the cocoon felt like roughened plastic, and I had to remind myself that it was only air. I rubbed away at the dust on the surface and found myself looking at cloth through the holes in the mesh. I needed to find Leo's head. I stepped down on top of him and dug more.

For once I had good luck and soon found his neck, then his chin, then his entire head. I bent over him, rubbing away the grime from his cocoon. He looked okay. He had a couple bruises on his chin and forehead, and blood trickled from his swollen nose. He'd broken it. He lay on his back, one arm across his chest, the other arm up around his head. His eyes fixed on me, flaring with emotion.

"Can you hear me?" I croaked, then coughed, because I wasn't hurting nearly enough. When I caught my breath and straightened back up from my curling crouch, I looked down at him again. "Can you hear me?"

He gave the barest nod and then made a sound that could have been a yes. His air prison was too tight to allow him to speak.

"The air cocoons are going to go away. Price is almost done. You'll have to hurry to help me dig out the others when it goes. I'm going to look for Jamie."

I didn't wait for a response. I climbed out of the hole, scrabbling up over the uncertain pile of wreckage. I tore my pants as my leg skidded down. Distant pain flared in my knees. I clambered to the top and found where Jamie lay, about fifteen feet from Leo. If anything, the rubble seemed deeper here. I didn't let myself think about it. Urgency clawed at me.

I'd been expecting the tunnel collapse, so I shouldn't have startled when it finally crashed down. It gave with a tremendous grinding noise that sounded like thunder. I jumped and staggered, bending to catch myself with my hands as the ground beneath me shook and settled. Dust billowed, and I pulled my shirt up over my mouth. It was sticky with sweat and filth, but it kept me from coughing.

Grating and swearing from behind me made me turn.

"Riley?"

Leo. I closed my eyes in relief so deep it made my head spin. Instantly, they flashed open. Dear God. If Leo was out, then the ground settling hadn't just been from the force of the tunnel's collapse. The cocoons had collapsed.

"Help me! Jamie's under here!"

I started to dig, but Leo's magic was faster. Threads of metal spun out and under the rocks, then lifted them up, throwing them off and me with them. I fell backward, but a curl of flat steel looped around me before I could hit. It straightened and set me on my feet.

I lunged forward, up over the lip of the hole holding Jamie. Unlike Leo, he'd not built a cage around himself. Maybe he'd been knocked unconscious. He sprawled on his side, his legs spread like he had been running. Bits of rock chips and wood splinters sprinkled across him. I knew he was alive. His trace told me. Even so, I stared at his chest, needing to see him breathe.

"Riley, help me find the others," Leo said behind me.

I remained rooted.

"Riley!"

I jolted and slowly eased around. The ground felt floaty and weirdly soft.

"Help me find Taylor and Mom."

Leo held out his hand, and I took it. Tension and worry carved haggard lines into his face. He stepped closer and put his arms around me. I leaned into him, whimpering a little. It took me a second to drop into trace vision and focus. I'd have thought I'd pegged out on all possible fear and horror. I was wrong.

"Oh no," I rasped as my throat knotted. "Mel's hurt."

That was an understatement. Mel wasn't just hurt. Her trace was more gray than not. She was mortally wounded. She and Taylor lay near one another. Dalton and Arnow were there, too. A few feet away, closer to Jamie, I found trace I didn't recognize. It was a thin blue with red clumps like warts. Price's mom.

I pointed locations out to Leo, who pushed his metal framework under the rocks and lifted the weight of them off, then one by one, mounded the covering wreckage upward. The rubble rolled off, with the sound echoing off the walls. Leo and I staggered over to the lip of the hole. He held my hand to help balance me. Taylor lay facedown. Dalton sprawled over her. They'd lucked out, with an overturned desk giving them shelter from the worst of the crushing rubble. Mel had not fared so well. She lay twisted, facedown, hips awkwardly turned sideways. Nothing looked wrong except for a puddle of blood that spread from beneath her head.

"Mom!" Leo leaped down beside her, reaching to pull her into his arms.

I wanted to warn him not to, that her back could be broken, that she probably had internal injuries. But it was too late. Even before he touched her, her trace went entirely gray.

I went still. A soft whimper escaped me. Grief flooded me. Grief and no little guilt. I'd failed her. I shouldn't have let her come. Shouldn't have asked so much. Inside I clenched tight so I wouldn't shatter. What would I do without her?

"Mom? Mom? C'mon. Talk to me. Wake up." Leo's voice stretched thin and high as he held Mel against his chest, rubbing her back and cupping her cheek. Her head fell back. "No!"

I couldn't tear my eyes away. This had been me less than an hour ago. Price had brought me back. But not Mel. Her body was broken. She wasn't coming back.

I couldn't even begin to figure out how to deal with all that. I steeled myself and made myself go past him to Taylor and Dalton. Both had begun to move. I tried to help, but I had no strength to offer. I was made of tangled yarn.

"What happened?" Taylor said, sitting up as Dalton pushed himself off her.

He helped Taylor up. She swayed, and he put a steadying arm around her waist. She pulled away. Her attention turned to Leo, who sat on a pile of stone, cradling Mel against his chest, his head bowed.

Taylor went white beneath the grime. "Leo? Mom? Mom? Mom!" She scrabbled to climb out of the hole. Dalton helped shove her up. She fell to her knees beside Leo, snatching one of Mel's dangling hands. "Mom? God, no! Please, no!" She broke into harsh sobs.

Unable to watch, I returned to the hole where Jamie lay.

He hadn't moved, though now I saw his chest rise and fall. I couldn't do anything to help him. If I tried to crawl down, I'd end up standing on him.

I stood there and stared down at him, feeling beyond lost. The brilliance of his trace told me he wasn't seriously injured. Not life threatening anyhow. Blood clotted above his left ear. That worried me. Head injuries weren't so easy to heal, even with the help of a dreamer. The brain tissue could be fixed, but the mental damage was harder to mend. *Impossible*, a noxious little voice whispered in my head, the same one that had noted Price's likely escape route. *Impossible to fix.* I bit my lips until I tasted copper, refusing to consider the possibility.

I remained where I was until a moan caught my attention. I tipped my head, listening, and when it happened again, I knew. I remembered. Anger swept through me, righteous and cleansing. It strengthened me.

I hobbled to one of the last two holes we hadn't bothered to check yet. I looked down inside. Price's mom was sitting up, her hands pressed to her forehead.

"Now you see," she rasped "He's evil. The child of Satan."

If I could have, I would have spit on her, then buried her again, this time for good. Unfortunately, I couldn't muster any saliva, and Leo had made sure the debris wouldn't refill any of the holes. My jaw locked so tight that I almost couldn't speak. Finally the words pushed out.

"If that's true, then you are Satan."

She gave a bark of harsh laughter. "God has given me the wisdom to see the truth of my son's evil and I have begged his forgiveness for birthing such a monster. But it is not enough to have penance for my sins. I must stamp out the demon taint that I allowed to enter this earth. I am not alone. I will call down an army of God's purest soldiers, and I will see that abomination scorched to ash and you as well, for you are Jezebel returned to this realm to turn the righteous against God." She lifted her arm to point accusingly me at me.

Yeah, and maybe God works in mysterious ways, and he made Price just the way he wanted him to be. I didn't bother to say it. As much as I wanted to, you just can't argue with stupidity. Instead, I curled my lip and turned my back, just in time to see Arnow crawling up over the top of her prison.

Like the rest of us, she looked the worse for wear. Her hair hung in a tangle around her shoulders, and she carried her heels in her hand. In the other, she held a folding knife. She'd shredded her coat and wrapped each foot in the fabric to make makeshift shoes. She got over the lip and stood up, pocketing the knife. Her gaze flicked over the scene, lingering on the tableau of Mel, Leo, and Taylor, then moving on to stop at me. She picked her way over to stand next to me.

"If you want, I'll help you kill her," she offered, jerking her chin at Price's mother. "She could use it, and given that I'm not a big fan of your boyfriend, that says something."

"Price went to a lot of trouble to protect her," I said, more than a little tempted. It's not like he'd miss her, but then again, just because I hated my dad didn't mean I wanted him gone. If only because I still had questions and he was the only one with answers. No doubt Price felt the same way.

"Suit yourself." She made an attempt to dust herself off and then gave up. She glanced at Taylor and Leo, who were clutching each other with Mel in between. "Sucks. Sorry." Arnow actually sounded like she meant it.

"Thanks."

We stood there for a moment before she started fidgeting. "What happened?"

"Price razed everything from the ground level up. I managed to get out to help him get under control and we came back in for you."

She nodded, her gaze running over me, taking in the way my arms wrapped my ribs to help brace them, and the way I listed to one side. She looked away, scanning the space we were in. "How did you get in? Where is he? How do we get out?"

If there's one true thing to be said about Super Special Agent Sandra Arnow, she's practical. And efficient.

"Price made a hole in the rock. He's on the other side of that berm. Hopefully Leo and Jamie"—my voice cracked—"hopefully Leo and Jamie can make a door out." Hopefully Price wasn't bleeding to death.

She nodded again. "Where is he? Jamie?"

I nudged my chin toward the hole where he lay. She went to look. Then she turned around and crossed over to where Leo and Taylor mourned Mel. She walked like a cat, picking her way with ridiculous grace and ease, almost like walking on a cloud, despite her nearly bare feet. She shouldered past Dalton.

"Not to make light of your grief, but your brother is injured and we need to get the fuck out of here. If we don't kick on the afterburners, we'll all end up in jail. Personally, I'd rather not. So could you two get your heads back in the game before the next shoe falls?"

And the Arnow I knew and despised was back. Tactless and rude.

And also, at least for now, right.

Taylor twisted around so fast I thought for sure she was going to punch the FBI agent. She restrained herself, scrubbing her hands over her cheeks and leaving behind muddy swirls. She stood and shoved Arnow out of the way and headed toward me. "Jamie?"

I pointed. "He's unconscious. It would be best if Leo could lift him out."

I heard footsteps over the scrape and rattle of cement. Leo came to stand on the other side of Taylor. He still held Mel close against his chest. Tear tracks runneled through the dirt of his chiseled face. He'd always had that faintly hungry look, his cheeks high, his eyes set deep, his jaw sharp as cut crystal. Covered in grime and torn by grief, he looked like a survivor from a disaster film. His eyes glittered with emotion. He stared down, his brow furrowing, his cheeks sucking in.

Odd rustling and clicking sounded from the hole. I crept closer to watch. Leo let out a little *chuff* sound and I could hear his teeth gritting as he clenched his jaw tight with effort. Slowly Jamie rose up on a bed of what looked like chicken wire. Copper wires reached out and caught on the sides of the hole, walking him over on millipede legs.

Taylor crouched and touched his neck. "His pulse is strong and steady."

"He took a hard hit to the head," I said.

She reached into a pocket and pulled out a little flashlight and flicked it on. She pushed open one of his eyes and examined it, then the other.

"His pupils aren't blown. That's a good sign."

I had no idea whether she had any idea what she was talking about. Chances were she'd had some medical training overseas. Or maybe she was studying to be a doctor on the side. Fuck if I knew, a fact that bothered me a lot. Another thing about her I'd overlooked. Another damned thing to feel guilty about. Like I didn't have enough.

A shadow flashed in the corner of my eye, and something thudded against my breastbone. I looked down. It was a necklace. A silver chain sported a green-and-pink crystal point. Fluorite, maybe. Or watermelon tourmaline. I wasn't a stone expert, but I'd hung out with my jeweler brothers enough to pick stuff up. Long, deft fingers picked it up from my chest and shoved it down the neck of my shirt. Instantly the healing worms started wriggling through me, followed by a wave of heat and nausea.

Dalton slung two more over Leo's and Taylor's heads, then crouched and did the same to Jamie. He glared at Taylor as he straightened. If looks could kill, she'd have chopped him to pieces. She started to pull it off her head.

"Use it," he said.

"I don't need it."

"You need it enough and we have it."

"What if one isn't enough for Jamie?" She yanked it off her head.

Now it was Dalton's turn to look murderous.

At that point, I doubled over, doing my best not to throw up, if for no other reason than it would hurt like hell. The sensation of wriggling magic dug deep into me, and since I could do nothing else, I let it. *Quite wise of me,* I thought, and then suppressed the hysterical giggle that bubbled up inside. I was losing it. Going off the rails of the crazy train.

Vaguely, I heard movement and people talking around me. None of it seemed to make a whole lot of sense, but then my brain was entirely distracted by the things happening in my body. My ribs and the muscles around them moved into place and sort of clicked together, which went beyond repulsive right into gruesome. Healing heat cascaded over me in sheets of fire. I panted and gripped my knees tightly as my body shook. Dizziness overwhelmed me, and I swayed sideways, losing my balance. Before I could fall, hands caught me, holding me against a solid male chest. I stayed there, mostly because I couldn't move.

Even without seeing his face, I figured it had to be Dalton. Leo already had his hands full. Dalton lifted me like I weighed no more than a wad of paper. I felt like one, too. His heart beat strong beneath my ear, and he smelled of sweat, dirt, and something herbal, like rosemary or sage. One arm held me around the waist, while he pressed the palm of the other against my back. I continued to twitch and shiver through the healing. My teeth chattered. I jumped like an electrified frog when he spoke, his deep voice rumbling through his chest.

"We don't have time for that. Leave her. She would not want you to risk yourselves to take out her body."

It took about ten seconds for me to process his words. In the meantime, Leo was swearing at Dalton and telling him where he could stick his head in graphic detail.

The healing worms started to inch out of me, like maggoty witch fingers withdrawing from my flesh. I pulled out of Dalton's impersonal hold. He kept his hands on my shoulders to steady me.

"Thanks," I said, and that's when I noticed it no longer hurt to breathe and the fire wrapping my chest had gone out. I met his silver gaze. "Thanks," I repeated, trying to sound more like I meant it.

From the way his mouth tightened, I hadn't succeeded all that well. "Don't mention it."

I decided to take his curt advice and turned away. My heart leaped. Jamie was sitting up, with Taylor steadying him. Leo still clutched Mel's limp body, and Arnow was fiddling with the fabric swathing her feet, binding it tighter.

"Is he okay?" I asked Taylor.

"He is fine," the brother in question replied with a rasp.

"It's hard to say," Taylor said, ignoring him. "He's always had mashed potatoes for brains. I can't tell if it's any worse now or not."

"I take offense to that," Jamie said. "Why don't you two be useful and help me up?"

"Why don't you be useful and start cleaning my toilets for me?" Taylor retorted, but got to her feet and reached out a hand for him. I did the same, and we hauled him upright.

His gaze flicked to where Leo held Mel's body. The expression bled away from his face, leaving it utterly cold and scary angry. "We should go," he said in a clipped voice. "Give me a minute to make a stretcher to carry Mel."

"It's foolish. It'll just slow us down," Dalton said, and I realized that they'd been arguing over this while I'd been off in healing land.

"I hate to say it, but he's right," Taylor said.

"I'm not leaving her behind," Leo declared, and where Jamie was icy, Leo burned like an inferno.

Both wanted blood for Mel's death. Blood and revenge. I looked away, making a strangled sound. If not for me, none of them would be here. If not for Price, Mel would be alive.

"What's wrong?" Taylor asked, looking at me. I'd managed to capture everybody's attention.

"Price got shot," I said, because that was also true and my guilt wasn't worth talking about at the moment. "Maybe in the femoral. He's on the other side of this wall."

"Jesus Christ," Jamie muttered, and metal bits whipped over the ground toward him like clanking tumbleweeds. Others shot up out of the rubble like bullets. The rest of us stood back out of the way, and in under a minute, he'd created a stretcher.

As Leo laid Mel down on it, Arnow nudged my arm.

"What do you want to do about Mommy Dearest?"

"Leave her," I said.

"You're sure? Leaving enemies behind to stab your back isn't particularly smart."

As much as I'd come to hate the woman, as much as I wanted for her to be dead and Mel alive, I couldn't kill her. Neither could I let anyone else do it for me. Whatever else she was, she was Price's mother, and he'd wanted her protected. "Let's go."

Jamie and Leo stood with a hand on each other's shoulder as they opened up a new tunnel through the rubble wall. Both were exhausted, but thanks to Dalton's heal-alls, they weren't fighting pain and physical damage. All the same, they were both drenched in sweat by the time they were done, and Jamie shook like an aspen leaf in the wind.

Dalton and Taylor brushed both of them aside when they tried to pick up the stretcher.

"You couldn't carry a tune at this point," Taylor told Leo when he tried to protest. "You've done your part. We'll do ours."

She and Dalton took the stretcher through first, then Jamie and Leo followed. I had a staring contest with Arnow, and she won, so I went next, and she brought up the rear. Maybe she figured if she didn't follow me, I might not work up the courage to go through. She was probably right.

I heard Price's mother saying something as we left, but couldn't make out the words. Everything sounded muffled. A blanket of numbness had dropped over me. I'd withdrawn into an emotional space where I didn't have to feel. It was totally artificial. I knew it. But I clung to the relief all the same. I needed to be strong. I could break down later.

Luckily, that made going through the death tube much easier. Even though I could sense terror bubbling angrily through me, I didn't actually experience it.

I reached the other side and immediately looked for Price. He slumped over on his side. Leo and Jamie had already started toward him. I wanted to call them off, but they only hoisted him into a sitting position. His head lolled and tipped back. Streaks of drying blood ran from his nose. More drenched the torn legs of his coveralls. It looked like he'd lost a gallon.

Numbness shattered. I made a sound like a wounded cat.

"Here." Dalton tossed a heal-all pendant to Leo, who snatched it out of the air and dropped it around Price's neck. In the meantime, Jamie tore a strip from his shirt and tied it around Price's leg.

By the time I got to his side, Price's eyes had flickered open. They were back to his normal sapphire. His gaze moved slowly over everyone until he found me, and then he smiled weakly.

My brothers pulled Price to his feet. He sagged between them, but they drew his arms over their shoulders and slid supporting arms around his neck. Price's head hung down.

"Let's get out of here before we can't," Arnow said, spurring everyone to get moving. She stood in the doorway, waiting.

As they passed out of the room, Jamie and Leo paused and

half-turned. Without exchanging a word, they released the metal webbing that held the rock tunnel open. It collapsed with a grinding roar and a puff of dust, sealing Price's mother on the other side.

It wasn't a death sentence. Someone would find her before she died of thirst or from the cold. But they weren't going to make the rescue easier for her. I couldn't help the angry triumph I took from that.

Arnow fell into stride beside me, her wrapped feet making a *shushing* sound on the floor. She didn't say anything, but I could feel her darting looks at me.

"Spit it out," I said as we reached the stairwell leading up. Dalton and Taylor had already maneuvered the stretcher onto the back zig of the stairs. Price had begun to move on his own. Leo and Jamie continued to brace him, guiding his zombie steps up. His feet had stopped bleeding, at least, thanks to the healing pendant.

"You know that this is only the beginning, right? You'll all be fugitives now. Criminals. Every LEO will be after you, and they'll want you only marginally less than the scumbag Tyet honchos out there. They'll all be coming for you."

"Not exactly news," I said, even though her saying it out loud made it real in a way it hadn't seemed before. "What's your point?"

"Have you got somewhere safe to go to ground?"

"Yep." My house in Karnickey Burrows would keep us under the radar, at least for now. Though it would be crowded for all of us, and I wasn't letting Dalton or Arnow in or telling them where it was. Later we'd have to figure something else out. But that could wait until Price and I rescued his brother.

"Are you sure?" she asked doubtfully.

"You don't have to worry. I don't plan to get killed or captured." I trudged up the stairs, exhaustion leeching all my strength.

"The best laid plans . . ." she pointed out.

I sighed. "We'll be fine. Then we'll get Touray. Then I'll help you." I glanced at her. I asked the next question reluctantly. I didn't really want to know. "Do you think they'll be okay for a little while yet?"

She shrugged, but tension pulled tight around her eyes, belying her casual tone. "Maybe. Probably. I hope so. Anyway, believe it or not, I wasn't thinking about them. I was thinking about you."

Sure she wasn't. I totally believed that. 'Cause I was born yesterday and fell off a turnip truck right after. I didn't say it.

We climbed some more. By the time we reached the fifth level, Price was walking mostly on his own. He'd not spoken since he'd seen the stretcher with Mel's body. He kept his head down, his shoulders hunched.

I knew he was bleeding from the guilt over Mel. No magic pendant would cure that. Leo and Jamie continued to frame him, lending him support when he stumbled.

"You've quite a family," Arnow said, so softly I almost didn't hear her.

The corners of my mouth turned in a smile. "They are amazing. More than I deserve. I—" A ball of emotion filled my chest, and I broke off.

"They use that against you. Your enemies do. Family. Friends. It's one thing to get yourself into trouble, another to drag the people you love in," Arnow said in a bleak voice. "It can break you."

"Yes."

"Don't let it."

I glanced at her and then at Mel's stretcher.

"Is that even possible?"

She shrugged. "I'd like to think so. I hope so. For your sake, anyhow."

"Because you need me to find your friends."

"Because you don't deserve it."

I snorted. "What the hell do you know?"

"I know I'd be honored to be your friend."

That had me gaping.

She chuckled, dry and mocking. "Don't worry, I don't expect it."

"That's good," I said, more out of reflex than anything else. My brain was still reeling from her declaration. Friends? Me and her? I guess stranger things had happened, but I couldn't begin to imagine one just at the moment. Maybe me thinking of Touray as family. That was pretty bizarre, but no, this was even more so. And weirdly, I was tempted to believe her. She'd sounded like she really meant it. I shook my head. I didn't remember hitting it, but I had to have a head injury to even consider believing Arnow wanted to be friends.

The others had reached the top of the hole where Price and I had entered. They gazed around. The dust still hung in a low cloud, but higher up it had begun to settle. The ghostly shape of the building's remains stood like a skeleton above us. Arnow and I picked our way through the rubble on the stairs and joined them. I looked at Price, who still stood between Leo and Jamie. He stared at the wreckage. His arms dangled loose at his sides. I put my hand in his. No matter what happened, he wasn't alone. His fingers tightened hard on mine.

"He's not going to get far without shoes," Leo said, motioning toward Price's feet. "Plus the cold will take his toes." He glanced at Arnow. "She's not much better off."

"I'll manage. I'm not going to hold you up," Price growled.

Leo ignored him. He bent and unlaced his boots, pulling off both socks and jamming his bare feet back inside. He held the socks out. "Put these on."

Price looked like he wanted to protest, but he said nothing, let go of me, and took them. Jamie did the same thing for Arnow. She pulled them on over her wrappings.

A whirring slithery sound broke the heavy silence of the destruction and made me jump. A few seconds later, electrical wires, pulled from the carnage, snaked over the ground. The copper slid out of the colored plastic insulation and wound around and under Price's wool-clad feet.

"Lift your left foot."

Price complied.

"Now your right."

The wires coiled and wove together to create a kind of sandal, with a thickly matted sole he could walk on. The project was repeated with Arnow.

"That should do it," Leo said.

"Let's go, then," Dalton said.

For once I was in a hurry to get inside a cave. I felt exposed, like we were being watched. Like even now, guns held us in their crosshairs. I'd rather be under a billion tons of rock than out in the open.

Once again Leo and Jamie fell in beside Price. I frowned; it was beginning to look like they were guarding him. Arnow and I brought up the rear. Just inside the tree line, or what I supposed was the tree line, were the shattered remains of the building. Its carcass mounded in a wall and circled around into the darkness following the edge of the now-vanished barrier Price had created. Most of what was left was no bigger than my fist, like the entire building had gone through a blender. Price's superhero name: Vitamix Man. Need a building knocked down? He's your guy.

Leo and Jamie made another tunnel in the rubble and led the way through. As I waited for my turn, I dropped into trace sight and turned to look behind us.

"Oh shit," I whispered.

In the city, which is my normal habitat, I am surrounded by trace. It is everywhere, like mounds of tangled yarn blocked only by buildings, and even then they are covered with the tracks of those who built them. In the wild, there's always trace, but it's usually a loose weaving of colored ribbon. For me, it's a little like looking at an aurora borealis. The black goes on forever, and the colored weavings extend as far as I can see. The city becomes a brilliant explosion of light.

Only this time, what I saw was a line of massed traces circling around the compound and inching down toward it. But that wasn't what scared me. Just behind that leading edge of colorful trace was another line, this one of gray death, like those who were now descending on the compound, had slaughtered everything in their path and then moved on.

"What is it?"

Arnow put a hand on my arm and gave me a little shake. I realized she'd been asking, and I'd not heard.

"Company." I turned toward the tunnel, and looked up. More descended over the ridge above us. We were surrounded. Had they found the helicopter? The cave passage? I didn't even know who *they* were. And who were the first *they* that had been slaughtered up along the ridgeline?

I scrambled through the tunnel, my heart revving into high gear again. My exhaustion sloughed away beneath the tide of adrenaline. I slid out the other side and lost my footing, landing on my hip and side. I barely felt the pain in my agitation. Arnow helped me up. Leo and Jamie let the tunnel collapse behind me.

"We're surrounded," I said as everyone looked at me. "Coming over the ridges of the valley. What's weird is that there's a lot of dead trace, like there was a first group and the second overtook them and killed them." I shook my head. "A *lot* of dead trace. A small army. And a bigger one coming now."

Silence and an exchange of baffled looks met my announcement.

"FBI maybe?" Taylor was the first to speak.

"Which one?" I asked. "First group or second?" I had a feeling it had been the first. The second was bloodthirsty and didn't care about whoever got in their way. Feds tended to care a little more. Which meant we were screwed if the second group got a hold of us.

"Does it matter?" Dalton said. "We've got to move. Now."

I'd wondered if the second line might be my father's people. Now I knew they weren't. Dalton wouldn't run from them. A chill ran down my spine. Even though I didn't trust Vernon, he was a known evil. This other—could it be the people Oriana Price had promised were coming? I voiced the question out loud.

Price's head jerked around to look at me. His face was carved in austere lines, and his eyes were sunken and hollow. I couldn't read his expression, but then, I didn't need to. I knew he was swimming in guilt and recriminations. I knew he felt like an anchor dragging us all under.

"If so, what do they want?" Arnow asked.

The obvious answer was us, especially Price. Before I could blurt that out, she continued.

"Mommy Dearest said her people wanted you dead," she said to

Price. "But if so, then why didn't they just napalm the place? Hit it with bombs? Coming in like this, in force, says these people want you alive. So maybe she lied, or maybe it's somebody else. Maybe whoever it is is after something else altogether. But if they *are* here for you, then they've got to be fairly confident they'll be able to take you down. Likely they've got a mountain of nulls or binders and a lot of firepower."

"All the more reason to get the fuck out. Move it!" Dalton ordered.

We all jumped to obey. Dalton and Taylor led the way with Mel's stretcher. Leo and Jamie went next.

"Are you coming?" Arnow asked as I bent to pick up a rock.

"In a minute," I said, considering it. If our pursuers had a tracer—which they would, and probably a good one—we needed to null out or we'd be followed and captured in nothing flat. But the trace was already laid down. Nulling it now wouldn't help. I needed to reel it up. Which wasn't possible. Unless I could find a way. Given how many impossible things I'd done already tonight, this had to be a piece of cake.

I moved down and sat under a tree, my back to it. Arnow watched me impatiently.

"What the fuck are you doing?"

"Trying to keep them from following us," I said absently. "You should shut up now. Go tell the others to keep going. I'll follow when I can."

She said something crude and also anatomically impossible, and then stormed off. I focused on the power inside me and drew it up. God, but it hurt. I'd overused my power to the point that the slightest working hurt. This was going to be a lot more substantial than that.

I took a breath and let it out, closing my eyes as I sorted out how to get rid of the trace we'd already laid down. Since learning to travel through the spirit dimension, I'd discovered that nulling didn't do away with trace, it just hid it. So maybe what I wanted to do was hide the trace we'd already laid down, not actually destroy it.

I reached into the icy spirit space and gathered up all our trace, including what we'd laid down when arriving. I twisted all the strands around the rock as an anchor and also as a conduit for my power. Then I started building the null.

I let myself sink entirely into the process. I dug for power. It moved like sludge inside of me. I reached deeper, searching for the source of my magic and dragging it out of myself. I didn't know how much it would take, but I had to make it enough. I sucked whatever energy I could out of the protective nulls on my belly and head. I hadn't had a chance to recharge them, but a little was better than nothing.

As I sank deeper into my work, the world spun away. The rock in my hands was the only island of solidity. I couldn't feel the snow under my butt or the tree against my back. My eyes weighed too much to open, even if I wanted to.

Deeper and deeper. I drove down relentlessly, searching for every little scrap of power I could muster. The null glowed in my mind's eye. Was it enough? I didn't think so. It didn't feel any different from one of my normal nulls. It needed more. And I needed to tie the power to our trace. I started weaving them together. That's when I realized how it could work. Elation bubbled through me.

Bubble may be too strong a word. It oozed as best it could, like tar through beaches of salt and sand.

I set about creating spirals along each of the trace ribbons. I soldered them into the null and spelled each one to spring out as soon as the null was activated. They'd fling outward as far as the magic had strength to send them. Where the coils slid over someone's trace, it would disappear.

After I finished the spells for the direction we were going, I turned it back to where we'd come from. Sooner or later, our pursuers would find our trail, but if they didn't know we'd crossed the wall, or which direction we'd gone when we came up out of the underground, it would take longer. We needed that time to get away. I needed to make this work.

Only I'd reached my limits. Hell, I'd gone way past them, and if I didn't tie off the null soon, it would explode in my hands. I'd be dead, and the whole attempt would be useless. The trouble was, I could tell that it wasn't enough. I couldn't stop yet. I *had* to find more power.

I don't know when I realized that magic was building around me. I could feel it in the air against my skin. I snatched at it, pulling it in. It had a flavor. Like Leo, sweet, biting, metallic. More flowed round me. Jamie. A different metallic, and sour with heat. And more. This time I didn't recognize it. It burned me almost, but with a cold so deep it hurt. The taste was like summer berries and winter wine. It had to be Dalton. Price was out of gas, and neither Taylor nor Arnow had any magic to offer me.

I grabbed what was given and poured it into the null. Its magic swelled. When it reached the level where I thought it would do the trick, I tied it off before letting go of the others' magic.

While passing out at that point seemed like a good choice, I wasn't allowed. I found myself on the ground, with angry people all around me arguing in loud whispers. My hands wrapped the rock in iron claws.

"Shut it!" someone said louder than the others. Arnow. Her voice chopped through the other voices like an ax. "Bitch at her later, but right now, see if that null she made can be activated and let's get the hell out of here."

Someone lifted me up into a sitting position.

"Riley? Can you stand up?" That was Taylor.

I made a sound like gargling marbles.

"Someone will have to carry her. Should you make another stretcher?" That was Arnow. Funny how she was in the thick of things. Couldn't trust her at all, and yet she was still helping. She *had* said she wanted to be friends. Plus she needed my help. And she wasn't too eager to get caught here, either.

"Can you get the null?" Jamie. He sounded rough, like rusted gears.

Someone pried up my fingers.

"Got it," Leo said. Immediately after, I was pulled up and over someone's shoulder in a fireman's carry.

"Are you sure you can manage? You're in bad shape." Taylor again.

"Just go." Price's voice rumbled above my left ear where my head dangled upside down against his chest. "I won't let anything happen to her."

"I'm activating the rock," Leo said, and as soon as he did, an electric rainbow ran through me all the way down to my core.

"Jesus! What the fuck was that?" Dalton, and he didn't sound pleased.

I was, though, because he never lost his cool and I'd managed to break it. Points for me!

"Whatever she did, it feels like it's working," Arnow said. "Let's get going before it stops."

That jolted everybody into action. Price strode beneath the trees, his sandaled feet crunching in the snow. The silence of the night echoed in my head. It was so quiet. Except for us, the world might have been dead.

Twigs scraped along my shoulders and caught in my hair as we pushed through the bushes into the cave. Once there, we paused again.

"They're bound to have found the helicopter," Taylor said without preamble. "They may be already pushing down into this cave, depending on how good their tracking is."

"We left our vehicles farther out," Leo said. "I doubt they cast their net that far. And thanks to Dalton, we camouflaged them, plus set up trigger alarms. If anybody discovered them, we'll know before we get there."

"On the other hand, if they did find them and then followed you into the caves, that won't do a lot of good," Arnow pointed out.

Even though I couldn't open up my eyes to save my life, I could hear

Leo's shrug of dismissal. "We ran wire along the cave path. Jamie and I will know if anyone's there."

"It's either that or going undermountain back into the city," Jamie pointed out. "We can find our way—we've both spent years exploring the caves and mine systems. It'll take us days, though, and even if we had that kind of time, we're bound to run into booby traps and mine guards. Without water, food, and shoes for Agent Arnow and Clay, I don't see that we've much choice."

It's about that time that I remembered the key in my pocket. Vernon had said I could use it to summon him. He'd help us. No doubt he would. But at what cost, especially now that Price had found his power? No thank you. Anyway, I couldn't have moved to get the key if I wanted. Not that Dalton couldn't summon Vernon. I couldn't forget that he was my dad's henchman. Loyal only to him, not to us. A snake in the grass, a fox in the henhouse, a turd in the pool. We simply could not trust him.

Having settled on a goal, we set out again. Nobody spoke except to offer guidance in the darkness. I couldn't even muster any fear of being under a billion tons of dirt and rock that was about to collapse on us. That was a better prospect than getting caught, and was I too damned tired anyhow.

I'm not sure how long we traveled. Forever it seemed. Price never spoke to me. His breath rasped in the quiet, and his feet made a scraping sound that reminded me of fingers on a chalkboard. I was entirely uncomfortable, and all the blood rushed into my spinning head. Plus I was cold. Aching cold. The kind you feel right before you fall asleep in the snow and die.

At some point the null quit working. Hopefully it would keep pursuers off our trail long enough for us to get completely away.

The sun was well up when we reached our exit. We had to crawl out through a two-by-two-foot hole that was about twenty feet up the side of a steep ridge. To get me out, Price settled me onto my back and pushed my arms up over my head. I watched him. His sapphire eyes met mine, and then other hands grabbed my wrists and pulled me through. Gravel dug into my back and a few bits got shoved down into my waistband.

Price was swift to crawl through after that. I couldn't see much. The sun was just coming up. I tried to stand up, but my body ignored me. Instead, Price hoisted me again and carried me down to where the two vehicles waited and set me on my feet.

"We're clear," Jamie announced.

"I wish we could be sure," Taylor said. "Riley? Can you tell if anyone's out there?"

"No!" Price shouted, gripping my right hand. "She's given too much already. God—"

He broke off with an animal sound, his hand tightening on mine so that it hurt. I didn't mind. Neither did I let it stop me. What I had to give was his and theirs. My family.

I let myself drift into trace sight. It was easy enough. Coming out would be harder. I was closer to that world right now than the real world; closer to dying than living.

"No one," I said, and slumped, resting my head on Price's chest. The trace dimension didn't let go of me. I floated in the cold dark full of spun ribbons.

"Riley?" Price said and shook me.

"Mmm?"

"Are you okay?"

"Mmm." Eloquent I was not. Neither was I okay. But I was in my element. In the trace. Surely that couldn't be all that bad.

He shook me again, and ran a hand over my forehead and face. "She's freezing." Though the words were quiet, they were edged in panic. "Her lips are blue. So are her hands."

"Give me a minute," Leo said, and I heard the crunch of footsteps in the snow. A minute later, he returned. He and Price juggled me, wrapping me in a blanket. Then one of them held a bottle of water to my lips.

"Drink," Price commanded.

Obediently, I swallowed the trickle. Suddenly my thirst became overwhelming. I gripped the spout with my teeth and sucked on it like a baby. I gulped, and Price pulled it away.

"Easy now," he said, then offered it to me again.

I finished it, and then I heard the crackle of paper.

"Open your mouth," Taylor ordered.

I did, and a piece of chocolate settled onto my tongue. Sweetness burst in my mouth, and I moaned, even as my stomach growled. As it did, reality tugged me and I pulled away from the trace dimension. That's when I realized I hadn't just opened myself up to the sight. I'd slipped inside it. Just over the edge, not far, but far enough to risk my life.

The water and chocolate gave me enough strength to steady my legs, though it didn't make me feel any warmer. Neither did the blanket. I made myself stand on my own, though Price kept his arm around my waist.

We loaded into the two vehicles. One was a blue Expedition. Leo and Jamie folded down the rear seats and set Mel's body inside, covering her with another blanket. Then Leo, Taylor, and Dalton climbed into the front seat together, which was a whole lot of awkward with the bucket seats.

Taylor ended up sitting half on Dalton's lap and half on the console.

Jamie got behind the wheel of the Avalanche, with Arnow up front beside him. Price laid me on the backseat and got in with me, putting my head in his lap. For the moment, I felt safe.

I should have known better than that.

Chapter 18

AS WE DROVE slowly out over the rocky and rutted road, Price continued to feed me chocolate. He ate a protein bar, offering me bits. Eventually I was able to eat on my own. I struggled upright and drank another bottle of water, all the while snugged up against his side. Jamie had the heat on high. Even so, I felt like a Popsicle. Even Price didn't heat me up, and given his anger, I should have been on fire.

I wasn't quite sure what I'd done to piss him off this time. Neither did I ask. I didn't need to be the floor show, with Jamie and Arnow the audience, and anyhow, I didn't regret anything. Except Mel.

"I'm sorry about your stepmother," he said suddenly, as if reading my mind.

"I'm sorry about your mom."

His lips twitched and twisted, then settled back into a flat line. He wasn't ready to talk about her. Fine by me. I didn't have much to say that didn't involve a lot of four-letter words. But then he surprised me.

"Better she'd died than yours."

I couldn't disagree with that, so I said nothing.

We'd only gone a little over a mile when Jamie stopped. Leo jumped out of the Expedition and came back to talk to us.

"Thinking of heading southeast into Durango for now. They're going to have Diamond City blockaded pretty good." He peered over Jamie's shoulder at me. "You doing okay?"

"Never better."

Price made a growling sound in his throat. "Liar," he said.

"I'm not dead yet, anyhow."

"Too close."

"I'll give you that," I said, seeing that I was only stirring his anger hotter. I really didn't want to be arguing with him. I held his hand through my blanket, more to disguise the fact that my hands were made of ice than anything else.

"What's in Durango?" Arnow asked.

Jamie and Leo flicked a look at her and then exchanged a meaningful look. Jamie nodded. "Let's go."

As Leo returned to his vehicle and Jamie rolled up the window, Arnow repeated her question.

"What's in Durango?"

"A safe house."

"How safe?"

"Very."

Considering I didn't even know about it, I figured it had to be. Anyway, it was somewhere that the feds probably didn't know about, and until Dalton got there, neither would Vernon.

Despite the fact that we were still in danger, that at any moment someone could swoop in on us, I fell asleep.

I couldn't have been out long. I came awake when the Avalanche jerked to an abrupt stop.

"What's wrong?" I asked groggily, knuckling my eyes. My brain felt slow as cold molasses.

"Company," Price answered tersely.

He helped push me upright. Through the windshield, I could see that we were on pavement. The road was narrow, and trees grew close along the sides. Leo's Expedition had stopped ahead of us, blocked by a gray Hummer. I glanced behind us as another rumbled up to close off our escape.

"Riley, get the guns," Jamie said quietly.

I leaned down and reached for one of the drawers at the bottom of the seat. There were two, side-by-side, each full of a variety of weapons. Price moved his legs to let me access the one beneath us. Inside were four .45 autos with a dozen full magazines as well as boxes of bullets. There was also an assortment of explosives.

I passed two guns to the front seat, even as Price fished one out for himself. I took one out, checking it. Like the others, it was loaded. I handed out spare magazines.

"Give me a couple of grenades," Jamie said.

I did as requested. Price was rifling through the drawer and taking whatever struck his fancy. I wasn't going to bother with anything but the gun. At this point, I wasn't sure I had the wherewithal to actually shoot straight, much less lob a bomb. Everything I was trying to protect would probably end up in the blast zone.

The doors on the Hummer behind us opened and several black-clad goons got out, followed by—

"Vernon," I said, my lip curling, just as Jamie started swearing.

"Isn't that your father?" Price asked. "I thought his name was Sam."

"It was. Now it's not," I said, and I grabbed the door handle, jumping out before anybody could stop me.

Strengthened by fury, I stormed around the rear of the vehicle, my hand white-knuckled on the grip of my gun. I'd forgotten I was holding it.

"What the fuck are you doing here?" I demanded, aiming it at him.

Two of his goons jumped in front of him and another lunged forward and knocked my arm up with all the force of a sledgehammer breaking concrete. I let out a squeal of pain. He grabbed my forearm, holding it over my head as he twisted the gun out of my grip with his other hand.

At that point, someone—Price—plowed into him, knocking him down. The goon didn't let go of me until I was falling too. I landed on my stomach and caught a boot to the jaw. My head snapped, and I yelped and rolled away. Stars and splotches whirled through my brain. I lay still, trying to get my bearings.

Hands hooked under my arms and lifted me.

"Riley? Are you all right?"

I blinked at my father's question. All right? I wanted to tell him I hadn't been all right since my mother died, but I let the words die before I spit them at him. I hung between two of his soldiers, one a man, the other a woman. I'd have shaken them off if I could, but my knees were made of rubber and the ground kept shifting up and down in rolling waves.

"Riley?" Vernon repeated. He pinched my chin gently and turned it to get a look at the damage to my face. "That looks ugly. You may have broken your jaw."

"Right. *I* broke it," I croaked, and as much as it hurt to talk, he probably was right. "You had nothing to do with it. Or my fingers." I held up the hand that had been holding the gun. Two of my fingers were swollen to twice their size. I thought the goon must've popped them out of joint.

"You were pointing a gun at me. My people are paid to protect me."

I cut to the chase. "What do you want? Why are you here?"

Before he could answer, more hands gripped me from behind, and I was pulled away from his two minions. I stifled a moan as my head jostled and spikes of pain jolted through my jaw and up through my eye sockets.

"Keep your filthy hands off her," Leo snapped.

At that point, I was willing everybody to keep their hands off me. I was getting to feel like a prize in a game of keep-away. I pulled myself away to stand on my own.

My vision was finally clearing. Price and Vernon's goon had separated and stood panting and having a staring contest. Vernon was flanked by the two black-clad minions who'd picked me up off the ground. Another six circled around, surrounding us. *Us* included Dalton, which surprised me. He stood just behind Taylor, a little on the outside, but definitely not joining Vernon's crew. On the other side of Taylor was Arnow and then Price. Jamie and Leo stood on either side of me, both looking ready to commit murder.

For a long moment, nobody spoke. Vernon scrutinized us. He exchanged a look with Dalton that I couldn't read at all.

"What do you want?" I repeated finally, when no one else spoke.

"I came to offer my help. None of you can go home. You just went to the top of the FBI's most-wanted list, plus a couple dozen other agencies'. Not to mention becoming a valuable commodity to every underworld organization in existence. I can protect you."

"Use us," I corrected. "Don't act like this is some gesture of kindness and goodwill. You want us in your pocket."

Vernon gave a little shrug. "It certainly benefits me if you aren't in the power of others. Should you choose to work for me, I would definitely make it mutually beneficial. But more importantly, I would not like to see you come to harm."

I snorted. "If that were true, you'd have been in there trying to help us."

"Mel's dead," Jamie announced at the same time.

At that, Vernon went still as stone. He hadn't known. That was strange. I'd assumed Dalton was telegraphing our whole mission to him somehow. Maybe Vernon only had Dalton lojacked and had to debrief him for the rest.

"I am sorry," Vernon said, looking away into the trees. Emotion flickered over his features, almost like grief. But then he faced us again, his face blank as paper. "I hope that she did not suffer. Who was responsible?"

We met the question with silence.

"I killed her," Price said finally.

"It wasn't your fault." Leo spoke the words before I could even open my mouth.

"Like hell it wasn't," Price ground out. "If not for me, she wouldn't have been there. If not for me, she wouldn't have end up crushed to death."

"If not for *me*," I corrected. "I'm the reason she was there."

"She was there because she chose to be," Taylor said.

"Because we're family and we have each other's backs," Jamie added with finality. "No matter what." He gave Vernon a pointed look. "But you wouldn't know anything about that kind of loyalty, would you?"

"I'm here to help you," Vernon responded.

"Because we could be useful to you," Leo said. "No thanks. We can take care of ourselves."

"No, you can't," Vernon said. "You're powerful and resourceful, but you have no idea what you're up against." He looked at Price. "I can get your brother back for you. You won't have to risk yourself or anybody else." He flicked a glance at me.

"See? That's the difference between us and you," Taylor said bitterly. "We're going to help him because he needs it and because he's our family now. You couldn't give a shit if your kids are in trouble. You'll only give a hand if there's something in it for you. Far as I'm concerned, that makes you number one on my most disgusting fathers list."

She spit on the ground to punctuate her repulsion, something I'd never seen her do before. Taylor did not spit. Ever. Fashion divas did not spit.

"No," Price protested. "You can't help me, especially after what I did to—"

I was about to jump on him when all three of my siblings rounded furiously on him.

"When we want your opinion, we'll give it to you," Jamie snapped.

"Shut your pie hole." Taylor prodded a finger into his chest.

"We'll help if we goddamn want to," Leo said.

"And you can learn to like it," I whispered, my lips and jaw having swollen so much that making words was more effort than it was worth. I wanted to smile. And cry. Dear Lord, how I loved them.

Price looked dumbstruck. For that matter, so did Vernon. As much as he could, anyhow. As far as I could tell, he hid his feelings behind a face frozen by massive doses of Botox. All the same, his eyes widened, and something flickered in their depths. Maybe disappointment, maybe surprise. Maybe it was indigestion. At that point, I was past caring.

"We need to go," I said. The words slurred. I winced as I realized that two of my teeth were loose. I probably had a waffle-stomper pattern on my face.

Vernon looked around us and finally took a long breath and let it out. "Jackson Tyrell is a name you should get to know," he said finally, totally out of left field.

"Who the hell is he?" Jamie demanded, scowling. His arms were crossed, and he still held his gun. That surprised me. I thought Vernon's minions would have disarmed everyone.

"Look it up. But when you watch the news later, know that he was behind it," he said cryptically.

"Behind what?" I asked.

He looked at me. "You've still got the key? Remember, I'll come if you call."

With that, he nodded to his goon squad, and they all headed back to the Hummers.

"Shouldn't you go with them?" Taylor asked Dalton.

Vernon paused as he started to get into the vehicle. The two men exchanged another look. Dalton looked away, scanning each of us, ending at Taylor. Something flashed between them. A secret of some kind.

"You need me."

I wasn't sure if he was telling her that or asking. I also wasn't sure if he meant all of us or her in particular.

"I don't need to worry that the guy who has my back might also stab me there," Taylor said. "None of us do. Anyway, you belong to him, right? You owe him a debt you can't repay, or something, so you should go get busy on that."

He jerked as if slapped, red spots burning in his cheeks. "I have done nothing to betray you. Any of you."

"But you will, first time dear old dad asks you to," Taylor said. "We can't afford to trust you. We're up to our armpits in trouble already. So go."

Dalton stared, his mouth moving like he wanted to say something. Then he shook his head and shoved past her. He dug in his pocket and held something out to me. "Here. Maybe you should get a few of your own."

I reflexively held my hand out. He dropped yet another heal-all pendant and chain in it before crossing to Vernon's Hummer and squeezing into the front seat. The doors slammed, and a minute later, they disappeared up the road and we were left alone in the wilderness.

None of us said anything for a long moment, then Jamie looked at Leo. "We've got trackers somewhere."

"How did they bypass the nulls?" Leo looked at me, gaze settling on my swollen jaw. "Are you up to looking things over?"

"I'm really up to not getting followed anymore," I mumbled and then headed for the Avalanche. I just wanted to get somewhere safe where I could shower, sleep, and eat, not necessarily in that order.

I opened myself up to the trace, reaching out my senses to see what active magic was around. Neither vehicle bore any signs of a tracker. I shook my head. "Must've been Dalton."

"Good riddance to him then," Taylor said. "Let's get on the road." She started to walk away, then came back to me. Taking the pendant from my hand, she hung it around my neck and activated it. "No point wasting it. You look like hell."

"Trying to set a new fashion trend," I said with a failed attempt at a smile. "Are you okay?"

"Why wouldn't I be?"

"Dad. Dalton. What's going on with the two of you?"

She gave a little shake of her head. "Later. Let's get out of here." She pulled me into a gentle hug, and then pushed me toward the Avalanche before retreating to the Expedition.

I climbed inside, ignoring the wormy feeling of being healed yet again. This time I didn't scoot over to Price. I stared out the window, thinking of Vernon, thinking of how wrecked all our lives were now. A few days ago, my worst enemies were the Diamond City Tyet lords. Now I was up against every law enforcement officer on the planet, the Tyets, and a villainous stranger. Jackson Tyrell, if Vernon was to be believed. Vernon—there was another one. I had enemies everywhere. I should probably start checking under the bed and in the couch cushions. They could be breeding anywhere.

And I was a Kensington.

I leaned my head against the window. Price reached over and tucked the blanket around me. After awhile, the heal-all finished its job and shut down.

"What the fuck?" Jamie jammed on the brakes, skidding on the snow and ice. We kissed the Expedition's bumper. It too had stopped.

"Where did he come from?" Arnow asked.

Dalton stood outside the front passenger door of the Expedition. He rattled the handle and banged on the glass. Inside I could see the shadow that was Taylor shake her head. The Expedition rolled forward. But Dalton wasn't going to be left behind. He put a hand against the back door and vanished. A split second later, he reappeared inside.

The brakes flashed again as Leo stopped. Jamie shoved the Avalanche into park and grabbed his door handle. The rest of us followed suit. By the time I came around the front, Taylor had flung herself out of the vehicle and had yanked open Dalton's door.

"What in the hell do you think you're doing?"

He was sitting awkwardly on the lowered seat. I didn't want to think about the bundle lying next to him. He swung his legs down and stood. "I've decided to accompany you."

"Not in this lifetime. You're my father's dog. Go lick his boots and let us get on with our business."

Dalton's face went livid, those red spots returning to his cheeks. I have to admit I was enjoying watching his discomfort. He'd put me through the grinder. He deserved a little in return. I suppressed the urge to cheer Taylor on.

"I am joining you," he said loftily.

That had all of us staring.

"You're what now?" Leo asked.

"You will need help against your enemies and I am quite competent."

"And if we say no?" I asked. "Then what?"

He looked at me. "It will make helping you harder, but I will not back down."

"Why?" Taylor folded her arms, her jaw jutting. "How do we know you're not going to be passing information to Vernon? Hell, he used you to track us."

"I expect Riley can unwind the tracking magic," he said. He leveled a burning look at Taylor. "You know as well as I do why I'm joining you."

I frowned and exchanged a confused look with my brothers. What did that mean?

"So you've become a white hat all of a sudden? Captain America running in to save the day?" Taylor rolled her eyes. "You can whitewash over your spots all you want, but that doesn't change that the fact that you have them."

"I am no better than I have ever been, and if I wanted to do the Captain America act, I'd be off doing it. I may not be the most virtuous person in the world, but neither am I so corrupt that I am willing to give that kind of evil a pass without making an effort to stop it. You can't stop it alone. None of you can."

"Did I miss something?" Price asked. "What the hell are you talking about? I know this can't be about rescuing my brother."

"The rest of us want to know as well," Leo said.

Taylor licked her lips. Finally she spoke. "There was more going on in the facility." She glanced at me. "We checked into level nine like Vernon suggested. It was—" She broke off, pressing her fingers against her lips. She shook her head. "There just aren't words, and this isn't the place." She sighed and then shrugged. "I guess we let him come with us. I'll—*we'll*—explain when we get somewhere safe. Riley? Can you take the tracker off him?"

I raised my brows to ask, *Are you sure?* She gave a slight nod.

The spell was easy enough to find. There's a flavor to that sort of magic. It hurt, as minor as the effort was. Worse, it reminded me just how cold I was. The burn of it pulsed inside my bones.

We loaded up again.

The Expedition rolled forward. Jamie watched it, unmoving. "I don't like this," he said. "I don't like this a whole lot."

I didn't either. I didn't say it. I felt like my father was pulling our strings to make us dance. It was beginning to feel like everything we did fit his plan, even when he said it didn't. I clenched my hands in my lap. Just what the hell had we gotten ourselves into? Taylor had said we were armpit deep in trouble. I had a bad feeling she'd underestimated by quite a bit. We were so far in a hole we were halfway to China.

Chapter 19

THE SAFE HOUSE was a large cabin north of Durango in the middle of nowhere and three-quarters of the way up a mountain. We parked the cars in a dugout garage totally hidden in the hillside. An underground car like the one between Mel's house and mine carried us up.

Mel. Who would never be there to open the door and pull me in. I wanted to cry for her, for all of us. My grief ate at my insides like acid.

We lifted her out of the Expedition and set the stretcher in a little storage space off to the side. Leo covered her with a blanket, and then he and Jamie fashioned a metal coffin around her. To keep the vermin out until we could bury her.

The thought of rats or snakes getting at her twisted my stomach violently. I turned and threw up in the corner. Taylor came and put her arms around me, and then Leo and Jamie did the same. We stood there together for a long minute, sharing our loss and love for Mel, then Taylor pushed us apart, swiping at the tears running down her cheeks.

"We'd better get going before we freeze to death. Riley's an iceberg."

Leo and Jamie nodded and wiped their own tears away. I was the only one who hadn't cried. I couldn't. Part of me didn't think I deserved it. Or maybe I didn't think Mel deserved to have me slobbering over her when I was the reason she was dead. Or maybe I was just too damned cold.

Price watched all this from ten feet away. He didn't try to hug me, didn't try to speak to me. That made it worse. Like he knew I was to blame, too. Except that he thought he'd killed her. But no one could fault him for his talent exploding on him. He'd protected all of us from the worst of it. He'd done all he could to rescue everybody before he ran dry of power.

The cabin had four bedrooms, a loft, a big kitchen, a huge fireplace and lounge, and three full bathrooms. Jamie guided Price and me to the master suite before he showed the others to their rooms.

"We're completely off the grid here," he said. "Nobody even knows this place exists. It can't be spotted from the air and there are no roads in. We're as safe as we can be. Get cleaned up. I'll get some food going and coffee. There's not much that's fresh, but we'll make do until we can fetch something."

Awkward silence fell between me and Price once we were alone. He prowled around while I stood by the foot of the bed, watching him. I was pretty sure what he was thinking. That he was too dangerous for me, that he should walk away. Very noble. Never going to happen, but very noble.

"Bullshit," I said, sitting on the edge of the bed.

"What?"

"It's bullshit. Whatever idiocy is spinning around inside your skull. I'm guessing the biggie is that being with you is all kinds of dangerous and blah blah blah, so you've decided you should abandon me. That about cover it?"

He blinked at me, then looked up at the ceiling. "You can laugh, but it's true, Riley."

"It's also true that I'm in trouble whether I'm with you or not. Imagine that. Me wandering around out there fighting my battles alone without you. How does that sound?"

"Never," he growled.

"Never what?"

"That's never going to happen. I'm not letting anyone hurt you again."

I didn't bother to tell him that that was a promise he couldn't keep. I was winning this argument, and mentioning that would send us off the rails again.

"Does this mean you've decided not to walk out on me?"

He came to stand in front of me. He stared down at me, his eyes turbulent. "I should, but I'm not that noble."

"Then it's settled. Now promise me you won't try. Unless you don't want me anymore. Only then." My voice shook a little with the last.

He pulled me up against him, pressing his forehead to mine. "Not want you?" he asked raggedly, then shook his head. "That's not even possible. I love you, heart and soul. Look what I did to you. I came so close to killing you with my own hands." His voice dropped and turned agonized at the memory.

"Not your fault."

He gave a harsh bark of humorless laughter. "I should have known you. I should have protected you. Instead I hit you. I had my hands around your neck. This talent turns me into a monster. How can you possibly still want me in your life after all I have done to you? After all you've suffered because of me?"

"Every relationship has issues."

That made him smile despite himself. "I'm serious."

"So am I. Nothing that happened was your fault. I love you. What more do you want me to say?"

His hands cupped my face, and his thumbs pushed my chin up until I met his gaze. It bored through me. His kiss turned my bones to liquid gold. His tongue delved inside my mouth, tasting and branding. Where he touched, heat blossomed and the flames crackled through me. I leaned into him, wrapping my arms around his neck and pulling him tight. The kiss was an affirmation of all I felt. We'd been together—I'd been inside him—and had shared ourselves on a level beyond words, beyond the physical. But I needed the physical. I needed to touch and hold and be held. I needed to hear the way his breath turned ragged, to feel the way his hands ran over my back and clutched at me. I needed his heat and his smell.

Too soon he lifted his head. His sapphire eyes had a skim of white over the top—like pearly frost. A tremor ran through him. A wind swirled around us and picked at the curtains and bedspread. Price pushed at me, his eyes closing, his face pulling into a mask. I held him, my hands fisting into knots on his torn coveralls.

"Pull it back in," I said. "You can do it."

He shook his head, his mouth rimming white.

"I—It won't." He shoved harder. He opened his eyes, and the white was more pronounced. "I've got to get out of here before I hurt someone."

He thrust me back, breaking my grip. I leaped forward, wedging myself between him and the door and planting my hands flat on his chest.

"Stop," I said. "You can handle this. You know how. Just do what I taught you." A weird electricity sparked on my arms and in my hair like static on steroids.

His mouth twisted and his forehead furrowed with concentration. "I can't—"

"You can. Relax. Just calm down and release your pull on the magic."

His attention turned inward. Though the wind in the room didn't increase, neither did it disappear. Price gave a hard shake of his head as if to clear it.

"Just feel the flow," I said. "Look for that place where it feels like it's coming from and close the door on it. Visualize."

Sweat dampened his skin. His mouth pulled down. His entire body shook with the effort of what he was doing. I held my breath. I couldn't let him lose control. I also couldn't stop him. He had to stop himself. I was too depleted to get inside him again.

I slid my hands up to press against his cheeks. "Relax. Don't fight who you are. Let your instincts guide you."

I wished I could be more useful. Like tell him to turn this dial, flip that switch, press that pedal. But it wasn't that easy. Magic was personal. You learned by trial and error and depended on an instinctive knowledge that came with being what you were. Price's talent had been suppressed so long, and he was so afraid of it, of losing control, that he was fighting against his magic, rather than embracing it. The result could get more than ugly.

"You controlled it enough to create cocoons, to close your bullet wound, and to create barriers to keep yourself contained. All without knowing a damned thing about what you were doing. Remember that. Remember what I showed you when I was inside you."

All of a sudden the wind died. The room still felt tight with pressure, as if it were holding its breath, and the hairs on my arms still twitched and prickled with magic energy.

"Good," I crooned. "You're doing it. Just a little bit more."

Another minute passed. Then the pressure lightened, and the magic in the room dissolved. Price staggered back, bending and catching his hands on his knees, panting hard. Before I could move or say anything, he straightened up. His eyes were once again back to normal.

"I have to get out of here. I have to get away from you and anybody else until I can get this thing under control," he said without preamble.

"No." I lifted my chin. "We're in this together. I've helped you twice now. I can do it again."

"And if you can't? I'm a fucking walking disaster. I'm not safe. Hell, kissing you set me off. What happens if I get pissed or hell, if I have a nightmare? We don't know what I might do. It's too damned risky."

"I'm willing to take my chances."

"I'm not."

"Too bad. You can never hide from me. I can find you anywhere, dead or alive. So if you try to go running off, I'll be right behind you." I grinned. I wasn't losing this argument. I had all the weapons. "Think about it. How much trouble could I get into doing that? I mean, I'd be on my own. Think of all the chances I'd probably be taking. All the seedy places I might go. All the dark alleys I'd wander down. I'd probably get careless and who knows what could happen then?"

He rubbed his hands over his face. "Christ. You would, wouldn't you? Just to drive me insane?"

"Yep. See, here's the thing. I'm really not willing to do without you. No matter what. So is it settled? Can I safely shower without having to worry about you scurrying off somewhere?"

He nodded.

"Good. Because I'm really tired, really hungry, and—" I didn't finish. We still needed to bury Mel. To grieve. Bleak loss sucked at me, and I hardened myself. I couldn't fall into that now. Later. Now I had to be strong. We all had to be strong.

AFTER I'D SHOWERED and Price had disappeared into the bathroom, I checked the closet and found a selection of men's and women's clothing, all of it with the tags still on. Nothing fancy. Jeans and tee shirts and sweaters, mostly, plus underwear. The last was all basic cotton, but in a variety of styles and sizes. Jamie and Leo had been prepared for a wide range of visitors. I found an outfit that fit, and got dressed. The pants were a little long, but I turned them up. I pulled a sweater over a tee shirt and donned a pair of thick wool socks before returning to the bedroom.

I lay down to wait for Price, but almost instantly stood up again. I felt fidgety. I paced restlessly, looking out the window to see a world of white, and then paced again. All that had happened in the last forty-eight or so hours tumbled through my head.

I heard the water shut off, and a few minutes later, Price came out, a towel wrapped around his hips.

"Clothes are in the closet," I said. "There should be something that fits."

He disappeared inside and returned, wearing a similar outfit to mine. "Ready?"

Thunderous blows to the door interrupted before I could answer.

"Come on, you two! Come see the news!"

I ran to the door and flung it open, but Taylor had already fled back up the hallway and toward the stairs. I followed, with Price hard on my heels.

The scent of garlic and tomato sauce wafted up to us from the kitchen. It should have tantalized my hunger, but foreboding knotted my stomach tight. We found everybody else in the living room, watching the big-screen TV above the fire crackling in the brick fireplace.

On the screen was an image of violent destruction. Fires burned up mountain ridges in the background, and in the foreground, right behind the blond reporter, was a smoking black hole in the ground. It looked like a meteor had hit. The hole must have been the size of a football field. The ground around it was melted into slag. Black smoke billowed through the air. Emergency vehicles from every agency under the sun parked around the perimeter, lights flashing like a patriotic disco. It might have been a scene straight out of an end-of-the-world horror flick.

"Is that—?" I broke off.

"Think so," Jamie said, never looking away from the screen. A wooden spoon in his hand dripped tomato sauce onto the wood floor. It looked like blood.

"Sh!" Taylor said. "Listen."

". . . targeted attack. We have no word yet on casualties, though we have learned that at least one hundred and twenty people are unaccounted for at this time," the reporter said. "Again, for those of you just tuning in, this morning at around nine thirty a.m., a massive explosion and fire destroyed the Marchont Research Center, fifteen miles southeast of Diamond City. Sources have determined that the event was magical in nature and incinerated everything down to bare stone. Searchers have not yet located any survivors."

"Who would do this?" Taylor asked. "There were people trapped in there."

"Better question is who could do it," Dalton said. "And why."

Something in his voice caught my attention. I looked at him. "You already know."

He met my gaze, his unworldly silver eyes ringed with blue. "So do you."

"Jackson Tyrell." When you watch the news later, know that he was behind it. Those had been Vernon's words. I wasn't the only one who remembered.

"Who is he? Why would he destroy the place?" Arnow asked.

She gone pale and her hands trembled. She must've known more than a few people inside.

"I don't know," Dalton said. "What I do know is that there are now no witnesses to what happened there. It is also likely the FBI will blame all of you for the destruction."

"If they even know we escaped," Price pointed out.

"If they do," Dalton agreed.

"What are the odds that nobody does?" I asked.

No one answered.

"Hell," Leo said, thrusting his hands through his hair. "I need a drink."

"Price's mother said her lunatic people were on their way, too. Maybe it was them," Jamie suggested.

"They thought Price was some sort of demon because of his magic. It seems unlikely they'd use the magic they claimed to hate to do their dirty work," I pointed out. I frowned. "There were maybe seventy-five people in that building. Where's this hundred and twenty number coming from?"

But then my brain caught up to my mouth.

"Crap." I'd seen the gray trace on the ridges, overwhelmed by the other force moving down. Those bodies had likely been torched along with the remnants of the building.

"Crap?" Price asked.

I explained. Then we all exchanged looks.

"I'm not sure it had anything to do with us or Price," Taylor said suddenly, she stared at the TV, her eyes shadowed. She'd not looked away from the coverage since Price and I had come downstairs.

"What do you mean?" asked Leo.

She shook her head once, slowly, her arms crossed, her hands gripping her elbows. "Level nine."

I crouched beside her. "What about it? What was down there?"

She closed her eyes. Her face looked haunted.

I glanced up at Dalton. "What was down there?" I asked again, this time to him, impatience making my voice sharp.

Dalton scraped his bottom lip with his teeth, leaving behind white stripes. Finally he answered. "It seemed to be a research facility."

"What kind of research?" Price asked.

Taylor opened her eyes. "Evil." She shook her head. "There was hardly anything there. No computers, no papers. Like they'd been expecting us and cleared everything out before we got there. All but the burn room."

"Burn room?" I prompted when she fell silent.

"It smelled," Taylor said. "Like . . . meat." She clamped her teeth together.

I recognized that look. Like she was holding back a scream and if she opened her mouth, it would come flying out.

"One of the rooms was an incinerator," Dalton explained. He reached out to put a hand on Taylor's shoulder, but pulled back before he touched her. He jammed his hands into his pockets. "The burn process had begun, but wasn't so far along we couldn't see inside."

"People," Taylor said. "Bodies stacked up like the Nazi concentration camp pictures. But they'd been mutilated and . . . modified."

"Modified? What do you mean?" I didn't want to ask. I didn't want to know. Price pulled me back against his chest. His warmth barely permeated through the sudden cold freezing my veins.

Taylor shuddered, and this time Dalton did lay a hand on her shoulder, almost like he couldn't help himself. My eyes about bugged out. Was he showing feelings? Of a human nature? Was that even possible?

As for Taylor, she ignored him. "From what we could see, some had missing bits. Others were Frankensteined together with parts that obviously came from someone else. Some looked mutated, like their mothers had been guzzling a thalidomide and nuclear-waste cocktail. That wasn't the worst."

I waited for her to say what the worst was, my body tensed like someone was about to punch me. The silence stretched.

Finally it was Dalton who spoke. "There were children among the dead."

Leo and Jamie swore, and Arnow's expression went blank. Her eyes held a world of emotion I couldn't read.

Taylor glanced around at each of us. Her eyes glittered with fierce, cold rage. Her voice was conversational. "They'll have to be stopped."

All of us nodded, even Dalton.

"We have to stop them," she clarified.

"Of course," I said. "We will."

Because it had to be done, and nobody else would do it. Mel knew that. That's why she'd gone into the compound with us. Why we all had. It was the right thing and necessary. It's why Touray risked himself to help the people in the accident. Why he was determined to clean up Diamond City. His monkeys, his circus.

I looked at my companions. My family, the man I loved, and two people I'd never thought I'd ever be able to trust. Only somehow I did, at least for this. They weren't going to let something this awful stand without trying to stop it, either. We were a team.

I felt a wild laugh bubbling up inside me. I clamped my teeth to keep it from escaping. My save-the-world to-do list kept getting longer: Rescue Touray, rescue Arnow's friends, and stop whoever was doing Frankenstein experiments on people. Oh, and help Touray clean up the city.

I had to wonder, just when in the hell did we become the lone rangers of the scary Wild West?

Acknowledgments

I have had a great deal of support and aid in the writing of this book—both professionally and personally—for which I'm very grateful. I want to thank everyone for being there for me, for cheering me on, letting me bitch and moan, telling me when I veered from the road or when I crashed, and for providing all the extra bits that go on behind the scenes of creating a book. I especially want to thank my editor, Debra Dixon, everyone at Bell Bridge Books, Brittany Dowdle, Lucienne Diver, Christy Keyes, Barbara Cass, Sue Bolich, Devon Monk, SFNovelists, Clay Cooper, Markus Harris, and Justin Barba. I cannot give enough thanks to my family, especially as I struggled through the tough times of the last couple of years. To those who I should have named but didn't, know that I am grateful for your support, knowledge, and expertise. And finally, you, the readers, thank you for reading, for liking my books, for telling your friends, for spreading the word. You are the best readers ever.

About the Author

Diana Pharaoh Francis is the acclaimed author of over a dozen novels of fantasy and urban fantasy. Her books have been nominated for the Mary Roberts Rinehart Award and *RT Magazine*'s Best Urban Fantasy. Find out more about her at www.dianapfrancis.com.

Printed in Great Britain
by Amazon

77955486R00125